Invitation to Sin

'I must not do what I know to be wrong,' said Justine, her words denying the desire her body was feeling for Armand. 'My body blazes and hungers for you in a way I've never known, and if I willingly make love with you then it is a sin and we shall be damned for it.'

'You may not do what you know to be wrong,' replied the gypsy, 'but I must do what I know to be right and if I force you, Justine, if I take you here and now, then you will commit no sin. Let me take the sin for you for I do not believe in such nonsense.'

Invitation to Sin

CHARLOTTE ROYAL

BLACK
lace

Black Lace novels are sexual fantasies.
In real life, make sure you practise safe sex.

First published in 1997 by
Black Lace
332 Ladbroke Grove
London W10 5AH

Typeset by SetSystems Ltd, Saffron Walden, Essex
Printed and bound by Mackays of Chatham PLC

ISBN 0 352 33217 4

Chapter One

Justine gave the fiftieth black habit she had washed that morning a final thump. She tried not to think about the two hundred and fifty habits that still waited to be laundered. Instead she thought about the break she had promised herself at this point. She dried her bright red hands on the skirt of her dress. They were so cold she could hardly feel them. It was a fine autumn day, but the snowmelt that watered the old stone fountain in the middle of the courtyard came straight down from the high mountain tops. It was sparkling crystal clear, but so cold it froze you to the elbows.

A gust of warm air blew over the high convent wall from the direction of the orchard. It smelt deliciously of apples, and Justine wished she had been sent to pick fruit. She loved working in the orchard with its bent old trees and plaited-straw beehives, but she had drawn washing that day, and she knew better than to argue.

She had smuggled a hard, rye bread roll out from breakfast, and now she took it out of her pocket and began to crumble it into little round pellets. 'Coop, coop! Where's my pretty darlings?' she called, making her voice sound low and engaging. Her pink lips screwed up into an inviting pout as she spoke. The autumn sun was warm on her face as she waited for a response to her coaxing. 'Come

1

on, chickies, come see what Justine has for you.' She scattered a few hard pellets of bread on the ground a little distance from the fountain.

Water gurgled as it gushed out of the hands of the smiling stone cherub in the middle of the round basin, and splashed into the pool below it. The constant inflow of fresh water was washing away the soap suds Justine had created by her vigorous pounding and scrubbing. The last few bubbles glinted in the sun as they floated down the overflow channel that ran through the middle of the cobbled courtyard. Justine turned her back on the ominous black piles of washing next to the fountain and called out once more. 'Coop, coop, coop! Come and get it sillies! Ah, at last! Where have you been, you pretty things?' Wings fluttered all around her as the first greedy doves arrived.

The convent kept white fantails, and Justine had made a special pet of one friendly bird. It was easy to recognise her pet because it was so much bigger than the others and it came to her at once. It gripped the slender arm she held out to it with pink scratchy claws, tilting its head on one side to peep up at her with iridescent eyes. 'I saved a special titbit for you, darling,' she murmured, slipping the biggest piece of roll between her lips.

Sharp as a whip, a voice behind her snapped: 'Justine! Stop that at once!'

Startled, Justine let the pellet of bread fall from her mouth. All around her, wings fluttered and smacked as the white doves rose in a protesting cloud. Her eyes followed the birds with unconscious longing as the flock rose, wheeled, and settled on the grey slate roof of the infirmary. The doves would not fly any further away, not while they could see food waiting for them on the grey cobbles of the courtyard, but they would not come any closer to the scarecrow in the black flapping robes who was glaring at Justine. Instead they paced the lichen-starred roof cooing to themselves.

'Sister Agnes!' cried Justine. 'You scared them all away.'

'Away is where they should be,' snorted the nun. Her face was screwed up in disgust and the balmy sunshine was cruel to her lined face. Her eyebrows were like two caterpillars crawling over her forehead, and a third furry line wriggled across the top of her lip. Justine felt sorry for the old woman, but she had to look away, down to one side. She did not want to look at the nun's thin lips opening and closing under the bristling moustache as the lecture continued: 'Revolting creatures. How you can let them touch you is beyond me. You should be working, not messing about with vermin. And pull up your blouse, child. You are showing an indecent amount of skin.'

'Sorry, Sister,' said Justine, tugging at the offending garment. 'It's far too big for me. It keeps slipping.'

'Couldn't you find anything more suitable?' asked the old nun, eyeing Justine's outfit with disfavour. Justine's over-large muslin blouse slid provocatively over her smooth young shoulders. The filmy white fabric was sheer from much washing and wearing, but it had been of fine quality once and still felt good against Justine's skin. Her chocolate-brown bodice had also been a beautiful garment in its time, only it was too small and clinched in her tiny waist in a way that emphasised her curving breasts. Her faded brown skirt had pretty stripes, but it was too short by several inches, and her trim little ankles flashed indecorously at the world. At least her clogs were the right size, but they were heavy and ugly. Justine had never had a new dress in the whole of her life, nor did she expect ever to have one, although sometimes at night she imagined how it would be; the delicious smell and texture of new fabric against her luxury-starved skin.

'Well?' barked Sister Agnes. Her moustache quivered over the thin lips. 'I'm still waiting for an answer.'

'Sorry, Sister,' said Justine again. She sometimes thought she spent her whole life saying, 'Sorry, Sister'. There were so many rules in the convent. So many ways to transgress. Sister Agnes was still frowning so Justine added, 'There were no other clothes in the poor box.'

'If there was anything better you wouldn't deserve it. Not until you learn to look after what you have. Look at the water stains all down your front. Time and time again you commit the sins of waste and bad housekeeping. I despair of ever making anything of you. No decent house would have such a sloppy maid. Well, never mind that now. Father Gabriel is here to see you. He is waiting in the interview room.'

'Father Gabriel! How lovely. I'll go at once.'

'You certainly will go at once. As if you would dare to keep the good father waiting. He shows you an uncommon amount of attention as it is. Taking you away from your work. Nonsense over books and learning and suchlike. Far more than a wicked orphan child deserves . . .'

But Justine was speeding across the courtyard, leaving the grumbling nun to the piles of clammy washing. As soon as she ducked into the stone arched corridor that led from the courtyard into the main convent buildings, the air struck chill on her arms. Even on a sunny day after a long summer, the massive stone buildings never got warm. Running was forbidden anywhere within the confines of Our Lady of Perpetual Sorrows, but Justine pattered as fast as she could down the crumbling stone corridors that led to the interview room. She had not been expecting a session with Father Gabriel and she had not had time to prepare her lesson – if it was a lesson he wanted her for today.

Her heart was beating hard as she reached the heavy wooden door. With a shaking hand, she smoothed the many chestnut locks that had escaped from her thick plait to tumble around her face and pulled her skirt straight. Then she knocked on the dark panel.

'Come!' said the well-known voice. She pushed at the creaking door eagerly and made her way into the room where he waited. Father Gabriel was standing motionless, as if looking out of the stained-glass rose window that dominated the room. One whole wall of the interview room was a miracle of light, pattern and colour. Light from the massive round window cast jewelled patches over the magnificent carved desk Father Gabriel was leaning on. The room was quiet, peaceful and timeless. It smelt of beeswax and smoke, and the harsh yellow soap it was scrubbed out with daily. Soft shadows draped the ceiling, veiling both the statues that wept under it and the stone angels that prayed in the corners. The live yellow hearts of many candles flickered under the gaze of the painted saints on the walls.

The dark figure by the window made no move and Justine hesitated, not sure what he wanted her to do. When he still gave her no sign, she knelt on the scrubbed stone flags to await his pleasure. Although her body was moulded into an attitude of prayer, Justine's mind was on earthly matters. The folds of a long dark robe hid the figure of the man who stood before her; but she could see the nape of his neck rising from the softly draped cowl of his robe, and above that the smooth lines of his shaven head. He was pale, white like marble. Justine thought him beautiful, as perfect as a statue – nothing like his flock of wrinkled work-worn nuns. But Father Gabriel was a young man, and noble too. He was the youngest son of the Waldgraf family. A family more powerful than the queen in this area.

They owned all the land within two days' march, right up to the borders of neighbouring Transylvania. The sunny fertile valleys that the peasants cultivated; the heavy secret forests where woodcutters felled rich timber and wolves roamed by night; the tumbling salmon-filled rivers; even the wild mountain tops where the convent perched, so high up that the nuns struggled to raise any decent produce in the thin soil. All this land belonged to the Waldgraf family, and they lived like feudal lords on the profits of it.

Justine's thoughts were broken as the man by the window stirred, sighing a little as he breathed her name, 'Justine.'

'Yes, Father.' She was aware of her young blood racing around her veins as she spoke, making little of the cold of the flagged floor. A tiny pulse beat in her temples and another beat softly between her legs, thrilling her, sending little nibbles of delight down the length of her labial folds. As she felt the blood surging to this most intimate of areas – the sweet secrecy of her woman's place – Justine imagined

5

her delicate vulval folds unfurling. She could feel them flushing a rosy pink at the heart. She could even imagine how her sex looked as it engorged; for all the world like the sweet-scented orchid she had found in the woods last summer.

The pink-veined petals of that orchid had held a tiny whorled bead that trembled in the depths of its scented tunnel. Justine could feel the heart of her pleasure vibrating gently in a way that reminded her of the inner secrets of that flower. Although it was still wrapped in cowled folds of protective flesh, her clitoris was reacting to the presence of Father Gabriel, blooming gently like a flower in the sun.

Lozenges of coloured light fell on Justine's kneeling form as the dark shadow moved away from the window. She closed her eyes and began to shiver with anticipation as cloth whispered nearby; he was coming to her. She held her breath as she felt the air move behind her. Light caressing fingers began to play with the tendrils of hair that had escaped her plait. So light was the touch that she might almost have imagined it, save that the ghostly fingers were undoing her plait, had loosened the black velvet band that held back her hair. She heard a sharp intake of breath as the heavy chestnut mass tumbled free over her shoulders. The long curls began tickling her skin, stimulating her nerve endings with an unaccustomed feeling of freedom.

She deliberately kept her eyes closed, savouring the anticipation, stretching her other senses as far as she could, heightening the feelings that were rising within her. She could smell the damp stone of the convent all around her. This familiar scent usually only registered on her senses if she concentrated on it. Now she took a deep breath and inhaled the cold, cobwebby, mushroom perfume that was the base note of the convent. Then she inhaled the top notes that dreamt within it: the hot smell of candle wax; the warm smell of beeswax; and the sacred blue smell of incense.

There was her own smell too. A faint breath of herbs came from her softly waving hair, and from her skin, warmed as it had been by the autumn sun outside, rose the perfume of life: the scent of a woman who was warm and alive, excited and sensual.

There was another sensual human being in the room too. Even in the dark behind her eyelids Justine had no trouble identifying Father Gabriel's musky tang. Her nostrils quivered as she inhaled his much loved male scent. His light searching fingers continued to run through her hair as she knelt, eyes closed, savouring his nearness. Justine tipped her head back with a delicious shudder as the fingers circled, massaged, circled again. It was like being shampooed by fairies. Divine sensations rippled through her; how good she felt.

Father Gabriel began lifting great masses of her hair, lifting them high, then letting go and allowing the tresses to float down. 'Your hair has all the colours of a rainbow in it,' he said softly. Justine allowed her lids to slide open and peeped through her lashes. Light from the stained glass was falling over her body, glittering in her hair.

'I like my new blouse,' she said dreamily, looking down at the rosy pink glow that coloured the frail muslin of her ragged top. 'I get so bored with plain things.'

Hands massaged her neck with light tapping movements, then they slid over her shoulders and under the filmy fabric of her blouse. The lightest of touches caused it to fall free, slipping over her shoulders to lie in folds over her tight-laced bodice. The tops of her breasts swelled in curving mounds from the softly draped muslin, and Justine felt pleasurable weight in her nipples as Father Gabriel trailed his hands lightly over the curves of her bosom.

At the same time, he bit and nipped softly at her neck; along the nape, under her ears. His breath was warm and soft, thrilling her with its gentle caress. His hands were circling, stroking; he seemed to be glorying in the beautiful curves that spilled over the top of Justine's bodice. Flickers of pleasure spiralled softly, deep within her, and she leant into his embrace, pushing her breasts hard into his hands.

Then he slid his hands under the firm grip of the bodice, taking each nipple between his fingers as he did so. Justine began to pant gently as he rolled the rosy buds slowly between his fingers. The bodice held her tight, not allowing her to breathe as freely as she wished. For the first time she moved her hands, bringing them up to tug at the laces that bound her so tightly.

'Allow me,' purred the voice behind her. Father Gabriel took his hands away from her fast-hardening nipples so that he could move around to kneel in front of her. 'My dear Justine,' continued the purr. 'How beautiful, how very beautiful these ripe, swelling orbs of yours are.' His hands slowly, languorously, unthreaded the black leather thongs that held her bodice laced tightly. He paused frequently as he unbound her, raining little kisses on each centimetre of breast that he uncovered.

When all but the last two holes were undone, and Justine's breasts hung free, poking deliciously over the foam of muslin that had slid down around her waist, Father Gabriel stopped, neatly folded the bodice over so that it acted as a wide belt and strapped it into place with the long black bodice laces. Justine accepted this passively. Sometimes she thought it would be nice to get naked – to be completely free to feel the kiss of skin upon skin, but Father Gabriel did not like it that way. Always he preferred to see her partially dressed. He liked to see her the way he was arranging her now, with her clothing acting as a provocative foil for her semi-naked beauty.

His fingers fumbled with the cloth around her waist and trailed across her belly. They animated a blaze in her nerve endings, those gentle touches. A deep conflagration began to flicker between her legs and she shifted her position slightly, squeezing her thighs tightly together to increase the luscious feelings that were centring there. Little pricks of rapture bolted through her as she did so, and she bucked with pleasure and squeezed her muscles again in order to increase the sensation.

'You really do love it, don't you? You are like a shame-less angel the way you wallow in the pit of sensuality. Only a strumpet would flaunt herself as you do. Only a houri from the fevered nightmares of the very depths of a

man's depraved imagination could haunt me as you do.'
There was pain in his deep husky voice. He almost groaned
as he cried sharply, 'The last time! Ah, it hurts me to think
of it, Justine. This is the last time we shall praise God in
our private fashion. The last time I shall have thee naked
before me.'

Justine felt passionate hands grip the sides of her breasts
tightly and warmth as he buried his face in the canyon his
hands had created. Lips, hot and wet, sucked at her. A
tongue, long and quivering, licked at her. Fresh rapture
coursed her veins and pulsed with her blood. How sweet
his kisses were. What glory it was to praise God together.
How could this be the last time?

'The last time? Why? Did I displease you? Oh, Father
Gabriel, what have I done?'

'It is none of your doing, child. Do not worry about that.
You have not sinned. Indeed, you have a chance to show
how well you can do and to repay the generosity of the
convent that has raised you. You know that I have been
training you to be a governess? Well, the time has come. I
have found a position for you. You are to go to my
brother's house.'

Because his voice was muffled by the kisses he was
bestowing on her breasts, his words took a little time to
reach Justine. When their meaning sank in, she leant
forward. 'Your brother? The count himself? At his castle?
Dear God! I am not worthy! The nuns said that no decent
family would allow an orphan – one who may be of gipsy
descent, or even the child of murderers – near their
children.'

'Trust me, Justine. Would I have spent so much time
teaching you if I had not thought you were suitable? True,
your eyes are dark, but your skin is fair and your figure
aristocratic. I'll warrant you are the by-blow of a noble
family. There is good blood in you or you would not have
been so teachable.'

'I've tried my best to please you, Father. But Reverend
Mother . . .'

'I'll speak to her before I leave. Oh, I know she has

decided you are to be a kitchen maid. She's a pious woman, as befits her station, but she lacks imagination. You were meant for better things, Justine, and I have shaped you for them.'

Justine trembled all over. The convent was the only life she had known, and she had never left its protective walls. It would have been hard to leave even for a modest position. The thought of entering the house of the highest family in the land and being entrusted with the learning of their children was making her shake all over.

'What is it? Do you wish to enter the cloisters?'

'Oh no, Father Gabriel. No matter how I pray, God sends me no vocation. All are agreed that I should leave. I try to work willingly at whatever I may be set, but, oh, Father, I do love books so much. It is more than I have ever dreamt of, to be in a position where I may read and perhaps learn a little. I am shaking because I am afraid. I am afraid of letting you down. Of being found wanting.'

'The low opinion the nuns have of you girls is justly bestowed in the case of most of the orphan clods they raise. But not you, Justine. You have the figure of a lady and the face of an angel; but over and above the physical, there is a rare and delicate sensibility about you. I perceived it when I first took the decision to teach you, and your quickness confirmed the rightness of my choice. And, again, when I selected you for my special attention. No, Justine, I am determined on this course. You will not let me down – I have moulded you so that you will succeed.'

'I will pray to God for the strength to serve you well.'

In her agitation Justine had risen somewhat from her knees and Father Gabriel straightened himself and snapped, 'Be still! You do not move unless I say so.'

Justine sank back to her kneeling position. In her excitement she had forgotten the rules. Father Gabriel made the rules and she kept them. He told her what to do and she did it. Now she was afraid that she had angered him. He was pacing the stone flags just in front of where she knelt. His brows were drawn together so that it was hard to read his expression. His black robe swirled as he paced. 'You

10

will do very well. You know Latin, Greek, Maths, all that is necessary.' He looked down on Justine and said impatiently, 'Don't quiver so, Justine. My brother has written to request a governess from the convent. Inconveniently, the last one died suddenly. You are the only suitable candidate just now, so you must go.' Then he added, almost to himself, 'I should have told you after our session. I suppose it is a great matter to you and there are things I must tell you. I must warn you . . .'

'Yes, Father?' Now her initial terror was fading, a great cloudburst of joy was breaking inside Justine. Her dear Father had arranged to send her to his own family home. Perhaps he wanted her to be near him. They all knew at the convent that it was only a matter of time before he was called to run the great cathedral in the fabled city of Valea. And Waldgraf Castle was less than a day's ride from the city. How good he was to her. How much he must love her. Perhaps they could meet again. Happiness danced in her mind as she waited eagerly to hear what he would say. He seemed to be hunting for words. That was not like him. Father Gabriel was so fluent, so knowledgeable. Was he trying to say goodbye after all? Justine raised sorrowful eyes to meet his imperious gaze.

'Justine, the things that we do together, the physical things . . .'

'We do them to praise God, Father,' recited Justine glibly.

'That is so. But now I must caution you. You already know that they are secret things; things between you and me only?'

'Of course, Father. I have never spoken of them with anyone.'

'Good girl. But now I must tell you that, until you are married, you must never do them with anyone else. Do you understand? You must remain chaste until you are united with the body of your husband by God.'

'Of course, Father,' said Justine. What was another rule in a world bounded by so many? 'Anything you say, Father.'

11

Satisfied by her promise, Father Gabriel moved round to the front of the desk and pulled out the heavy carved chair that belonged to it. He dragged the chair around to the side of the desk and placed it where could he sit in it and see Justine's kneeling form. As his burning gaze raked her naked breasts and creamy shoulders, Justine was caught up in the excitement that began humming in the air between them. He seemed to feel it too. His eyes were fixed on her breasts. 'Touch them,' he commanded. 'Run your hands over your breasts. Titillate them, and let me see all your pleasure. Hold nothing of your naughty sensuality from me. Do not attempt to hide your sluttish joy in those magnificent nipples; for I know it already.'

As he spoke, he settled himself deeper into the wooden chair and stretched out his hands and forearms along the backs of the carved dragons that formed the arms of the great chair. He blocked much of the light from the window and Justine shivered as his dark outline loomed above her. She shook back her heavy hair and brought trembling hands to her breasts. She was very aware of the Father's brooding gaze as she began gently to stroke herself. The stroking felt good, but she longed for his touch. She wanted to feel his hands on her breasts. She wished it was the Father who was fondling her. But at least she knew she was pleasing him. The gaze of the dark shadowed figure was growing intent. She could see lust clouding his eyes like the bloom on a dark grape. His tongue came out to lick his lips as he began to instruct her.

'Squeeze your breasts together. Yes, I like to see that. Now put a hand under each nipple. Flick the very tips of your nipples with your fingers. That's good. Put a hand into your wicked sex. Rub it in the love juice that I know must be flowing there.'

Justine obediently slid her hand between her legs, feeling the pubic curls brush her fingers as she gently slid her fingers inside the opening to her sex. She was wet; love dew was seeping slowly from the walls of her aching vagina. The muscles of her woman's place bore down hard on her questing fingers. There was a deep unsatisfied ache

12

within her, but there was pleasure in not satisfying it too, or at least not satisfying it yet.

'Rub that hand into your nipples. I want to see the halo of your teats glisten and shine pink as you touch them.'

Justine withdrew her hand, crinkling her nostrils as the sweet smell of sex perfumed the air. Then she rubbed the shiny fluid into each nipple, into the areola. The darker tips of her breasts were fully engorged – heavy, swollen, much bigger and redder than usual, and, oh, so sensitive. Her skin had rapidly absorbed the liquid that had come from deep inside her, and Father Gabriel was not satisfied.

'It's not shiny enough. I can't see it gleam. Spit on your fingers. Rub it in well, roll your sinful teats between your fingers. Now you just pinch those angelic breasts of yours. I want to see that creamy skin blush rosy red under your taunting fingers.' Justine fondled her breasts, following his directions precisely, spitting into her hands and sliding the glistening saliva wetly over her aching nipples. Pleasure burned in the tip of each breast like the autumn bonfires that glowed in the orchards outside.

Justine gloried in her lowly position. Kneeling at the foot of her Father, exposing her breasts for his pleasure. The loose sleeves of her white muslin blouse whispered up and down her arms as she fondled herself, but she made no move to slip them out of the way. Father Gabriel liked to see her clothing move, teasing him, taunting him.

'Be wanton!' he commanded. 'Pout! Crease up those delicious sinful lips at me. Seduce me with your flickering, snakelike tongue. Shake your hips as a whore in the marketplace. Show me how madly the desire for sex runs within you.'

Still kneeling before him, Justine did all that he asked her. It was a wicked pleasure to arouse him. It gave her a deep and shivery thrill to wriggle her bottom like a shameless bitch in heat. It was a guilty delight to press out her lips, to run her tongue over them in sinful invitation. Great shivers of sensation scorched her breasts as she continued to pinch them lightly. Father Gabriel's intent gaze was falling now on her mouth, now on her naked

13

breasts, now on her gradually reddening skin, her swollen inviting nipples, her lips. It wouldn't be long . . .

'Ah, temptress,' he groaned. His pale white hands trembled along the carved arms of the chair. 'Approach me now. Be as a harlot and seduce me with your movements.'

As she began to inch towards him, moving as sexily as she could, thrusting her breasts at his hungry eyes, very aware of the curve of her buttocks wriggling succulently as she crawled, Justine was suddenly gripped by an intense feeling of sadness. The last time! The tableau she was playing in seemed to glow with significance. She was kneeling at his feet now. His white marble feet with their well-shaped nails. He was wearing fine leather sandals and the black robe that flowed over them was made of thick sensuous silk. Justine couldn't imagine Father Gabriel groping in the communal wardrobe for a homespun robe as the nuns did. His robes were cut in the monastic fashion, but they were made from fine fabrics, and a luscious ruby ring gleamed on the hand that was now lifting the robe over his well-shaped legs.

As Justine moved closer and kissed the smooth pale skin, she inhaled his deep musky smell and listened intently to his light, racing breathing. She tried to imprint every detail on her memory. The shape of his legs with their scattering of light hairs; the way his thighs swelled gently; the jewels of his manhood that lay waiting for her. All these things were precious to her as never before. She must remember them, she thought frantically. She must emblazon them upon her brain so that she might have the memory of him to console her for the time to come, when they could meet no more.

Holding the robe high, Father Gabriel motioned her closer. She caught a glimpse of his erect penis before he dropped his robe again. The robe went over her head, whispered around her ears and dropped to the floor with a soft puff of air, imprisoning her in the tiny dark world it created. She sighed deeply and stretched her senses once more, feeling the sweet ache of her nipples, the pleasant heaviness of her breasts. Her woman's place was warm and wet in response to her sexual arousal. She was full of sensual delight as she rubbed her head against the hardness of one marble-hard thigh.

Her pleasure increased as she tilted herself slightly to kiss along the length of Father Gabriel's smooth tapering penis. It was made of white marble like its master. Long, thin, elegant and smooth, the slender shaft jutted out above the neat little balls that nestled in a wisp of curling pubic hair. Justine kissed her way to the base of Father Gabriel's cock, then she very gently took one ball into her mouth, rolling it lightly between her lips, feeling his testicle move within its purse of dimpled skin. Then she turned to the other testicle, mouthing gently at the fragile orb. She felt a ripple run through his body and then a soft touch from his erect penis which was by her face. His cock seemed to kiss the skin of her cheek as it jerked and twitched in response to her attention.

Heat was rising in her pleasure centre. Her clitoris throbbed and pulsed in time with his gently moving cock. His pleasure was her pleasure. His arousal was her arousal. And as she softly sucked and licked at his balls, then flicked her tongue along the intimate ridge that led from his balls to his anal opening, she inhaled of his fragrance deeply and gloried in the effect she was having on him.

She could not reach as far as his rose-coloured anus. The way he was positioned on the wooden chair prevented her from licking along the full length of the crevice that led to it. Father Gabriel liked her to pay full attention to this part of his body, but today she wriggled herself back to a position where she could attend to his glorious manhood instead.

It was too dark to see much, enfolded in the black silk tent he had created around her, but she could smell the musky perfume that his skin was giving off as it heated in the glow of sexual arousal. Its smell flowed along her senses as she licked like a little cat along the delicate soft skin of his shaft, eagerly lapping up the salty bead of fluid that she found sliding from the tip, rolling it around her lips, savouring it on her tongue.

Father Gabriel's whole body was trembling now in a deep thrilling rhythm. She changed her position again, moving back a little so that she could draw the tip, and then the whole of his penis into her mouth. As she sucked him into the warm wet cavern between her lips, she placed her hands on the base of his shaft so that she could hold him tightly.

She loved to hold him like this so that while she sucked his penis she could caress his balls and run her fingers into his intimate places; the delicious folds and creases under his testicles and the private path that led to his anus. Justine sucked him deep into her throat, and trailed light, loving fingers around his male glories. It was too sad. It was breaking her heart to think this was the last time she would fellate him so.

The last time. The words beat in her head in time with her racing pulse. She sucked harder, kissed and sucked and licked with greater intensity. Could he not feel her passion and sadness? Something of her feelings must have got through; Father Gabriel groaned as if in agony and gripped her head tightly between his knees.

His knees now held her so that she could not pull away even if she wished to. The pulse beat even louder in her ears. Her whole world had narrowed inside the dark silk cave he had created. All she had now was the world of sensation. Intense, thrilling, sexual sensation. All she could feel was the pulse and beat of her sexuality. Her breasts and vulva burned, sending fervent messages to the mouth that was so eagerly enfolding his manhood. The sensitive inside of her mouth registered only joy at the feel of a man's hard penis.

Father Gabriel's cock was so hard that the skin was stretched tight. With the tip of her sensitive tongue she could stimulate the blue tracery of veins that twisted and throbbed on the surface. She gave a little satisfied sound as she licked and very softly nibbled at the tiny raised worms of the veins. The knees pressed so tightly to her ears muffled her hearing, but she felt the priest's body vibrate and was aware of his deep voice as he muttered above her.

16

Father Gabriel had been still up to this point, allowing her to suck and lick as she pleased. But now, with more inaudible words, his stillness broke and he began to thrust frantically, fucking her mouth, gripping her tightly with his legs. As his cock thrust in and out of her mouth, his hands gripped her head tightly through the black silk that covered her, so that she was a sweet prisoner of his desires. For a split second, Justine was afraid of the passion she had conjured up, but his excitement was contagious: a giddy blackness swept her limbs and she was drawn up into his spinning vortex of desire.

She moved now in his rhythm, swallowing his length easily. She revelled in the feeling of her lips sliding over his saliva-wet cock. She burrowed into him like a little animal, stretching her mouth open wide to accommodate his plundering penis. It was so easy to do, this sucking swallowing pattern of movement that mimicked the orgasm that was now gathering and swelling within him, causing the heart of his body to harden and coil, ready to explode into her mouth.

So close did she feel to him that a sympathetic orgasm snapped around her body as he came with a series of gasping cries and jerking explosions. She felt his hands grip and then slip on the silk over her head. His knees opened and closed as his body thrashed in an orgasmic frenzy. Thick hot sperm appeared at the back of her mouth and her throat opened and closed in an automatic gesture that swallowed his offering before she was consciously aware of it. She gulped eagerly at his first precious gift, aware of its coppery taste and then the slickness of a second gout which splattered on her lips as Father Gabriel's penis moved back and then spasmed like a wild thing in the entrance to her mouth. A third and then a fourth fountain of sperm creamed around her open lips before his penis stopped jerking and he slowly juddered to a halt.

His hands tightened and relaxed on her head before sliding over the black silk and away. His powerful thighs closed around her ears one last time before lolling open to release her. A little reluctant to end the intimacy, Justine gently spat out his softening penis and turned her head to kiss his knee lightly.

The black silk tent around her was lifted and, with a whoosh of cool air, the world was hers once more. Justine licked at the salty taste that coated her lips and moved back a little so that Father Gabriel could rearrange his robe more comfortably. Her heart beat hard and her clitoris fluttered as she knelt before him waiting to see what he would do. Sometimes, often, he sent her away at this point to quench the passion he had roused in her as best she might. But today, if today were to be the last time they would ever come together, surely he would continue with those pleasures that made her his willing slave.

Chapter Two

Please God, don't make him send me away, prayed Justine. The silence began to stretch out. She was afraid he would leave her. She couldn't stand it. 'Father Gabriel,' she burst out, 'oh, Father Gabriel, stay with me a little longer.' Her hands were clasped as if in prayer as she gazed up at him fervently. He seemed very remote, high above her in the great chair, a dark silhouette against the glorious colours of the rose window. It was difficult to meet his godlike gaze, so she fell on his smooth white feet and began to kiss them passionately.

'You want me to stay so much?' came his mocking voice. 'But not for my benefit, I fear. I think you want me to please you, is that not so?' Despite the mockery, Justine relaxed at the note she heard pulsing under his words. Interest, warmth, sexuality – whatever it was, that note meant that Father Gabriel still wanted her. Sexual thrills rippled over her and a sharp tingling between her thighs caused her to press her legs together in ecstasy, prolonging the sensation, heightening her giddy anticipation.

'I think,' said the languid voice above her, 'that you had better tell me just what hellish pleasures you have in mind. What perversions would satisfy your lust?'

Justine shuddered all over. She to ask him for what she wanted? She would not dare. She kissed his feet harder,

19

but her brain would not begin to frame even the beginnings of a request.

'There is nothing you want? Then you had best leave me and be about your duties.' He pulled his feet away.

'No, don't go!' Justine cried. 'Whatever the Father pleases. Whatever the Father wishes me to do is my pleasure.'

'What the Father pleases today is to hear you speak. To hear from your own wanton lips what forms of wickedness haunt your dreams and stir your body to desire.'

Shyness still crippled Justine. The priest shrugged and said, 'If you have no desires to tell me, if your mortal body craves me not, I shall leave.' He got to his feet and pulled his sandals free of Justine's clutching hands. 'Ask and ye shall receive,' he said dryly as he moved away from her.

'Wait, Father. There is something. I often dream of it. I hardly dare tell you; surely a pleasure so sweet must be sinful.'

As the priest turned back to Justine, his lips curved in a thin smile. 'Ah, you blush. How pretty a sight. Your cheeks are tinged with a glorious patina, and the blush continues down your curving marble breasts and turns them rosy. Why do I find red skin on a woman's breasts so appealing? It kindles the ultimate in carnal cravings; it ignites my passion more swiftly than a vision from paradise. But then, you are a vision of loveliness, and surely you came from paradise.' He bent over her and stroked her face with gentle fingers before allowing his hands to drift to her flushed breasts. Then he bent his knees and crouched low enough to plant a row of kisses over her fluttering flamingo-pink orbs.

The touch of his hard lips over her skin roused Justine's ardour further and she breathed deeply as he kissed her. She was aware of her folded bodice clinching in her belly, aware of the soft shivering touch of the muslin blouse sliding down her shoulders and around her waist, but most of all she was aware of those lips – those burning, scalding lips that sent sumptuous feelings shuddering over her breasts like the blessings of the saints.

When he stopped his delectable kissing and nuzzling, she felt cold, so bereft that she dared to moan a protest, pulling him back to her longing breasts. Father Gabriel responded by bending his head and sucking the whole tip of each breast into his warm wet mouth, first one, then the other, and biting each nipple once, sharply.

Justine cried out as the pain stung through her body. Tears prickled briefly at her eyes as she stared in horror at the deep, almost blue ring of indented tooth marks that now circled each nipple. 'Dear God! What do you do to me? What mood are you in?'

'Do you question me? Must I whip you again to teach you the rules? Have I not told you that you are an instrument for my pleasure? My mood has not changed. You do as I bid you, and today I bid you tell me of the sexual desires that tempt you into the wicked ways that entice me so. This is an order, Justine. Obey it now.'

'But what must I tell you?'

'In the night, in the depths of the dark, velvety night, I think that the devil visits you, Justine. And I think he whispers to you of sin, black carnal sin. And as he whispers of lust and animal cravings, I think you touch your secret place and dream of the things we do together. I think that physical lust dews your body and you twist and turn, racked with the longing to have your dreams come true. Now they will do so. Tell me what sensual desires haunt your dreams and they will come true.'

Father Gabriel took one breast tip in each hand and began to massage gently. His strong, cool fingers ran lightly over the painful bites and, magically, the pain melted and dissolved. The cruel electric throbbing became transmuted. Sensation still burned and pulsed, but now it was an exquisite melting fervent sensation. Thrills as delicious as any Justine had ever felt radiated from each nipple, pulsed through the areola, and shimmered over her breasts like a velvet cloak of sensual gossamer. The feelings rocketed down every shivering muscle; the feelings overwhelmed the swelling heat burning in her clitoris; the feelings brought a touch of heaven dancing around her vulva.

Father Gabriel brought his head so close to her that she could see every pore in his skin. His eyes, his dark, intense eyes filled her world and took away her modesty. 'What will you tell me, Justine,' he demanded. 'I would learn of your secret desires.'

She could not disobey such a direct command, but the words she wanted to say were so shameful, so embarrassing, that they gathered in a huge knot in her mouth and Justine could hear her high voice shaking like a little girl's as she struggled to say, 'It, it pleases me when you put your lips to my woman's place.'

'Your what? What did I tell you it was called?'

Now she felt a wave of crimson sting her body and the low, husky tones of a stranger vibrated in her ears as she replied: 'My, my cunt. You told me it was my cunt.'

'And so?' demanded the merciless voice of her tormenting lover.

'And so, it would please me if, if you were to put your lips to my cunt.'

'Only put my lips there? Is there nothing more you would have me do?'

'If you kiss me, if you kiss me there ... if you kiss my woman's place ... my cunt, the feelings overwhelm me. Once, ah, once, you licked me and sucked me and nibbled me there and I swear to God I felt the pleasure in me for a week after you had gone. Forgive me, Father, but I have sometimes dreamt of this experience and wished that it could happen again.'

His dark gaze stabbed her. She felt like a trout impaled on a cruel and gleaming gaff. The intensity of that look stabbed her to the heart, exposed the dreadfulness of her lustful cravings. Then the heat of his eyes fell on her breasts. They poked above the clouds of muslin at her waist and trembled like a double sunset. Father Gabriel stared at them for a long, tense moment, then he moved abruptly. His knees clicked as he stood up, and for a swooping second Justine thought he was leaving her.

But he didn't leave. Instead he bent his knees, almost like a monkey, stooped down and picked her up, straightening his back with a little grunt as he cradled her in his arms. Justine leant into his strong hard chest and stroked the silk of his robe. She could feel his heart beating hard and she linked both arms behind his neck to draw him closer to her, to increase the intimacy. He carried her the few steps to the big wooden desk that stood before the window. Pools of coloured light lay across it like the pieces of a broken rainbow. The desk was so long that as Father Gabriel laid Justine down, she was able to stretch to her full length along the polished wooden top. The wood was smooth, lustrous. Deep golden lights gleamed in its well-waxed depth.

Justine slipped a little on its lavender-scented surface as Father Gabriel was settling her and she felt something bump against her head. The hard shape moved and then disappeared off the edge of the desk. She twisted and grabbed after it in a panic. It was the big silver inkstand made in the shape of a sacred heart. She knew it was filled daily with freshly ground ink. But her trembling hands missed it. Her own heart beat hard and she cried: 'The ink will spill.'

As she heard it thud on to the flagstones, Justine guiltily imagined a flood of sin-black ink staining the floor of the interview room, bearing witness to her crimes. But Father Gabriel bent low over it and said: 'Hush. Lie back. There is no harm done. The top stayed fast in the neck of the bottle.'

Justine lay back obediently. She could hear little clinks as Father Gabriel prudently cleared the desk of its other items: a heavy leather blotter, a quill pen in a silver stand, a silver cross. His feet made soft padding sounds as he walked across the room away from her. Where was he going? Justine turned her head to watch him, feeling the smooth wood cool her cheek.

He was standing under the carved and painted statue of Our Lady that stood gently smiling over the interview room. He looked into the plain wooden box that stood under her feet. He took a beeswax candle from it, then, after a short pause, another one. To Justine's surprise, he did not light the candles and place them with the others that flickered under the benign gaze of Christ's mother. Instead he came back over to the desk and held both candles in his hand as he looked down at her.

Shudders chilled the nape of her neck and travelled from there down the length of her back. What could he be planning to do? Arousal throbbed sharply between her legs and her bitten nipples simmered as if he were still touching them. Her knees felt odd and weightless. Justine hoped he would not ask her to stand. She didn't think she could, so violently was she trembling.

'Slide down towards me. I want you to bend your knees. Let your legs fall over the end of the desk and lie there so I can reach the intimacy of your woman's place. Yes. Just like that. Now, pull up your skirt.'

Justine reached too slowly for her faded brown skirt. She felt a breath of cold air on her legs as the cloth was flipped up for her. Then she heard a deep chuckle. 'Are you so shy with me? Well, never mind. I will expose your vice to the world for you. No! Do not pull the fabric over you so. You must not cover yourself. I want to see your body. You must not cover your nakedness.' Her belly quivered as he wrapped the voluminous folds of her skirt around her waist. She could feel his fingers, sure and knowing, as they brushed across her stomach. He folded the skirt, then her white blouse, so that a roll of white muslin lay above her bodice and a thicker roll of brown fabric lay below it. The rest of her body was naked, open and trembling to his gaze.

The wood of the desk was cool under her back. Firm hands parted her knees and cool air kissed the purse that held her sex. She felt wild and wicked. At the same time she felt woefully embarrassed. The secret place between her legs was open to the world. Anyone could see her naked sex. Father Gabriel could clearly see the secret folds of her womanhood that surely had never been exposed so wantonly before. The same firm hands now slid down her legs, they tickled her ankles before returning to stroke her

24

inner thighs. Justine shut her eyes tight. In spite of her shame, or perhaps because of her shame, she could feel fluid gathering at the entrance to her vagina, where Father Gabriel could not help but see it; so he must be aware of the lust that was sweeping over her.

Justine shrank from her imaginings. What was Father Gabriel looking at as his firm cool fingers flicked lightly at the folds of her outer labia? His voice was warm as he whispered, 'What passions burn through you, you shameless witch. Look here! Oozing proof of your desire. As I touch you I see you stiffen! Your sex is hardening even as a man's penis does. I touch you and you writhe. Oh, yes, you like that, I can tell. How about if I stroke this pretty little wrinkle here? Ah, how delicious. You get harder and sexier as I speak. Justine, I do believe that the devil sent you to tempt me. You were made to drive a man wild.'

As the cool hard fingers teased her, Justine could feel hot blood thumping in her ears. The red blood stung as it raced around her trembling body. She could feel it pumping directly from her heart to pulse and throb in the second heart of her body: her clitoris. Her vulva was stiff, engorged with the hot blood that flowed so violently around her nearly nude body. All the normally soft folds and wrinkles of her labia felt stiff and large, as if the light of the day had caused them to grow and ripen like an orchard fruit. Justine pressed her legs together, trapping Father Gabriel's tormenting fingers; then she let her legs fall apart and felt her hips snake as she pushed up to meet the man who was pleasuring her.

Restraint and embarrassment were leaving her as her arousal mounted. Justine's breath came faster between her softly parted lips. They too felt swollen, and she began to bite them gently, pulling and worrying at the lower lip with her teeth. The man who was watching her laughed softly. His searching fingers now lifted the protective folds that lay around her clitoris and squeezed them gently, exposing the little pip directly to the cool air.

In response, Justine's hips lifted off the table and twisted up towards him. She had made no conscious decision to

25

thrust her vulnerable sex at the Father so blatantly, but her body was now moving with a sex-driven will of its own. Something cold and hard flicked at her clitoris and Justine threw out her legs as wide as they would go. The cold, hard, alien thing then slid away from her clitoris and tickled a delicious path all the way to the entrance to her vagina. 'The portal to heaven is wet and ready,' gloated Father Gabriel. 'I think that a seductress such as you will be able to enjoy fully the immorality of what I am about to do to you.'

The cold, hard penis-shaped object nuzzled briefly at the entrance to her sex before pushing up hard into the opening that led to her womb. It filled the gaping need that was screaming inside her. She bore down hard with her pelvic floor muscles, gripping the object, somehow expecting to meet soft skin and human hardness. Then the messages from her woman's place exploded into her brain and she realised with stunning, horrified impact that the object inside her was not part of a human body, but an inanimate object; a candle. The big, beeswax candle she had seen Father Gabriel take from under the statue of the Virgin.

'Dear God! This is sacrilege. I will burn in hell for this.'

'Have I not told you and told you that I am allowed, nay sanctioned by God to do with you as I wish? Justine, you are a woman and made for man's pleasure. How can this be wrong?'

Father Gabriel could never be wrong about anything. Justine had trusted him from the day after the pain of her initiation into what God wanted from a woman had faded. Indoctrinated as she had been by the nuns, he had needed to whip sense into her when she first realised what he wanted, but now she knew better. She was made for men's pleasure, that she understood. But this! This was surely for her pleasure and Justine shivered uneasily under the torrent of sensation caused by the snakelike hardness of the object inside her. How could this be right?

Another cold hard object tickled her clitoris. It was the other candle. Perversely, a wild, shivering excitement flooded her being. She was melting, collapsing into another dimension. She cried out loud as the slick wax of the candle flickered over and gently circled the dissolving bud of her clitoris. His hands were inexorable. She could not resist them or stop them as they guided the candle around every secret nerve ending in her labia. It was too good. Too meltingly, achingly good. Fresh chills swept over her as she felt the candle move in a different way. It slid back, mercilessly back, to its ultimate destination: the most private of her places.

'Sweet heaven have mercy upon me,' cried Justine. 'This monstrous act must not take place.' But even as she uttered the words, her traitorous body was lifting itself once more and straining up towards the man who must be possessed by God. What mortal being could ignite such a passionate fire? The feelings that blessed her body were never kindled by a human hand alone.

The candle slid back and circled the entrance to her vagina, pressing around the tip of the other candle, the one that was already buried in her sweet chasm of delight. Justine tensed, expecting to feel herself stretched as the second candle joined the first one deep in her vagina, and she arched her back, opening herself for the expected invasion. But it did not come. The candle left her shivering quim and slid back to rest at the entrance to her anus.

He will not allow this monstrous abomination! The polished wood slid under Justine's back as she squirmed and writhed upon the top of the big desk. Why would her body do nothing to save her? She could not stop him. She could do nothing but register a melting delight that surely could not be terror. Her breath caught wildly in her throat and her heart fluttered like a swallow trapped in a barn as she felt the insistent nudging at the opening to her virgin anal passage.

'Sweet heaven. My God, what do you do?' She was panting, babbling, unaware of the exact nature of her words. Aware only of the wicked, savage rapture that swept her and the floating extent of her passion.

The dark figure that was bending over her chuckled. 'I do only what you ask me to do. You dreamt of forbidden pleasures and now you are about to be violated. The Virgin's candle will be sliding up your arse. And you'll like it, Justine, I promise you that. You will enjoy every, shameful second.'

The candle twisted and nudged at her anus and entered just a little. It rotated slickly and opened the muscles, sending entirely new sensations racing around her body.

'This is all wrong!' said Justine. 'This is so bad and so terrible that I'll surely go to hell.'

For an instant the bottomless pit opened up below her and she could smell brimstone. Then Father Gabriel dragged her back. Drops of sweat from his hot face dripped on her as he hissed through his contorted mouth: 'The only sin is doubt. The only sin is to hold back. I demand that you give in to the true feelings that are ravishing your body now. This is an experience that you have longed for. This is an experience you will masturbate to for years to come; hold nothing back, Justine. Let your body take you to heaven. Your body and the things I will do to it.'

Justine opened her mouth to tell him that he was all wrong. But the words that forced their way up from the depths of her being shocked her with their lasciviousness. 'Put it in me,' she panted, 'put it in me now.' The candle in her anus nudged, twitched, thrust a little further into her passage and, at the same time, Father Gabriel began to move the other candle, the one that was inside her vagina, sliding it in and out of her sex, mimicking the actions of a male member with both candles at once. Justine lost all reason, all control over her actions. She was possessed by a demon she had never met before, never known existed. 'Fuck me with it!' she howled. 'Violate me. Stick it up inside me.' Her surging passions choked the words in her throat. The animal lusts gripping her mangled her utterances and she could no longer form sentences. Verbal communication failed her and she clutched at the sensuous silk robe of the priest with savage hands. She was all sensual feeling. All erotic sensation. When Father Gabriel placed a hand over her mouth she bit it.

'Enough!' he panted. Lust was black in his eyes but he

had enough control to continue, 'Do you want the Reverend Mother to hear you? To find us like this?'

The taste of his skin in her mouth shocked her back into common sense, and she spoke more softly although her body twisted like a mad thing under his grip. 'I'm sorry. I'll be quiet. But sweet heaven, what feelings you give me. The sensations inside me are almost too much to be borne. I dance on the edge of madness, on the edge of desire. Give me the satisfaction I crave or I will surely lose my reason.'

'Are we beasts to copulate in seconds? I choose to keep you hovering on the edge of the abyss. I want you always to remember this intercourse. I want you always to remember the heights that I took you to.'

Both hands had returned to hold the candles that pillaged her intimate parts, and Justine caught her breath in a sobbing gasp as he pushed on the one that was just about an inch inside her anus. The smallest of movements was magnified. It feels like a tree trunk from the forest, she thought. It feels so big and so hard that it will split me, I know it will.

'Be careful,' he warned as a second, louder gasp escaped her. 'If you dare to cry out again I will walk away. You will burn for the rest of your life, waiting for satisfaction that will not come. Speak to me softly lest I leave thee thus – naked and trembling on the edge of a desire that no other man can fill.'

The candle in her anus slid a little higher, and now Justine could feel it rubbing against the other candle, the one in her vagina. The sensation was deadly. Although the Father had once, on a never to be forgotten occasion, buggered her with one long, slim, aristocratic finger, she had no other experience of any kind of invasion of her back passage. It hurt and it stretched her, and it felt all wrong, and it felt all right. As the candle slid in to its full extent, she could not help but squeeze her muscles to increase the alien, but shiveringly good feelings that the two hard objects were producing. Lips burned into her lower belly as Father Gabriel bent his shaven head to kiss her naked stomach. Justine opened her eyes to look at him, to imprint a picture of his face on her heart, but it was hard, so hard to concentrate on anything but the trail of those burning lips as they moved closer and closer to her quivering open sex.

Father Gabriel stopped stimulating her with the candles, although he left them both thrust deep inside her, the candle in her anus pressing on the candle in her vagina, so that she could not forget them, or ignore the wild feelings they aroused as she waited, shaking, to see what he would do next. He took both hands to her vulva. Breath hissed between her teeth as he took the lips of her labia in competent, knowing hands. He spread and lifted the sensitive folds so that the skin was stretched tight, causing the bud of her clitoris to pop up like a smooth round pea out of its protective pod.

Justine's bare heels beat against the wood of the end of the desk and her hands came away from her sides to slide over the smooth blue shadow of his head. She was aware of little prickles under her fingers; his rough thick hair was growing afresh, defying the priestly tonsure. His head twitched under her fingers. He did not like to be held, and Justine's hands fell back to her side once more even before he lifted his head to say, 'Take your hands away.' Her hands clenched and unclenched as the very tip of a hot, pointed tongue licked at the core of the volcanic miracle that was erupting in her pleasure centre. Almost at once, orgasm began to rise in her. The delicious feeling of his hands pulling the skin tight was almost enough to send her over the edge. Now the flicking, hot, wet, licking tongue was lifting her, pushing her towards an explosion that promised release.

Father Gabriel seemed to know that she was too close to the point of no return to prolong matters. With a sudden, shocking movement he swallowed the whole of her clitoris, sucking it hard, drawing as much of the tiny nub and its surrounding flesh into his mouth as he could. He was giving her a love bite! The swallowing sucking movement pulled the whole of Justine's consciousness into awareness of the great good feelings that gathered and spiralled inside her. Only the black surge of passion was real. Only the sweeping convulsions that came out of nowhere and completely took her over were important.

Her orgasm massaged her gaping hungry need. Its ghastly spasms carried with it a deep feeling of rightness. Pulled by the tidal force that was sweeping her, Justine's back arched high up off the desk, her sweaty palms pushed down hard on the polished wooden top as her body surged up and down, shaken by the terrible, delectable, fearful, wonderful, twists and turns of an orgasm that took her singing through the stars of the galaxy to the very gates of paradise.

Father Gabriel stayed with her, his dark-robed figure bent over her thrashing body like a storm cloud. His hands held her labia and his lips were like branding irons and most of all – most of all – his tongue flickered over her clitoris and his mouth kept sucking and pulling so that sensation overwhelmed her again and again and, incredibly, once more.

Three times Justine crested razor-sharp peaks on her way down from her original celestial high. As she finally shuddered to a halt, as her hips began to drift, all cotton candy sweetness and melted marshmallow now, back to earth and on to the desk, Justine felt his mouth releasing her.

She was given no time to bask in her languorous feelings. Immediately Father Gabriel released his grip on her pleasure bud, he pulled her towards him. She slid over the shiny wood of the desk top and landed with her feet on the stone flags. Justine nearly fell. Her trembling legs would not hold her. She shivered and shook as if it were ague and not the secondary ripples of sex that swept around her body.

Firm hands caught her under the armpits and she was twisted around and bent over the wooden desk with her buttocks spread wide to the air. The hard edge of the desk bit cruelly into her belly so Justine went up on tiptoe so that she could balance herself comfortably, with the roll of

31

cloth around her waist protecting her from the hard edge.
The movement tipped her bottom up saucily.

'Oh, but you know how to drive a man wild with desire.
When you wave your arse at me like that, I swear, I would
brave the very demons of hell themselves in order to take
you.' As he spoke, Justine felt Father Gabriel's trembling
hand fumbling at the candle in her vagina. It came out
easily. She was wet, running with love dew. It flowed from
her entrance like sweet honey, and for a fleeting second
she felt hot lips eating her there, as Father Gabriel sucked
of her manna.

Then, something warm and solid nudged at her lips and
forced itself between her teeth. Justine tasted wax. Without thinking, she opened her mouth to protest, so then
Father Gabriel was able to push the whole candle fully into
her mouth. She bit down on wax that tasted of her love
juices.

Two strong hands parted her buttocks and a searing
length of cock slid home as Father Gabriel plunged deep
up inside her like a saint entering heaven. Justine's grunt
of satisfaction was muffled by the candle and she realised
that Father Gabriel had effectively stopped her from crying
out loud again. He had gagged her so that her cries could
not bring the Reverend Mother, or any passing, curious
nun on to the scene.

And she wanted to cry out again! The feelings that
overtook her now, as Father Gabriel thrust and rammed
inside her, were more savage than those of the copulating
wild timber wolves that Justine had once seen, high up in
the pine forests in the mountains behind the convent. Now
she too wanted to howl at the skies and bite and scratch at
her partner. Her mind yowled with animal passion as
Father Gabriel paused in his headlong movements to stand
panting with just the tip of his penis inside her.

His hot breath rasped on the nape of her neck and he
began slowly, hotly, sinfully, to slide his marble cock down
the thin walls of her vagina. His penis pressed unbearably
on the dark object that was filling the passage on the other
side of her soft and shivering velvet walls. Justine vibrated

gently under him, as equally slowly he pulled out, and then pushed in, and then slowly, languorously pulled out again. He was pushing her over the edges of reason! Her head swung from side to side and she breathed hard over the muffling candle in a series of great gasps that kept time with his movements as they became more urgent. Hah! Hah! Hah! went her breath in her ears. The soft wax filled her mouth with the taste of honey and her own juices. The sweat that dewed her skin began to form drops, then to gather and run in shining streams over the hot skin of her body. She saw it run over her breasts and drop from the tips of her nipples to splash on to the wooden surface she was bending over.

She was fire. She was ice. She was nothing but nerve endings and a receptacle for the ram, ram, ram, of the organ that was making her die. Making her melt. Making her fly once more off the edge of the path of mortality and flinging her up to feel at one with the stars in the firmament. Her orgasm took her and shook her and finally dropped her back into the room. Father Gabriel was still moving, still fucking. He had not come yet and the amazing sweet savagery of his penis made her spit out the candle and sent her gasping for mercy. 'You are too much. You begin to hurt me now. Take that thing out of my passage at least, give me some relief.'

Hot breath hissed in her ears and she could feel the sweat that slicked his body mingling with the sweat on her buttocks as he continued to plunge madly inside her. His voice was choked with passion as he panted, 'Be still. I revel in the feeling. Ah, the abomination in your arse slides over my manhood and grips me with guilty delight. I love the wickedness. I love to fuck you with that thing right up inside you. It makes me . . . ah, it makes me shudder . . . it pleases me, it dominates my senses.'

His hands left her buttocks and moved around in front of her so that he could grip her sore breasts. He was pinching and rubbing her bitten breasts so that they flared and throbbed within his caressing hands. But why did it inflame her so? Why were her hips beginning to rotate and shudder? A heavy sexy feeling tugged at her lower belly. It was urgent, compelling, and she surrendered to it just as the Father whispered urgently, 'Can you tell me truthfully that you wish me to cease and desist at this moment?'

'No, Father. The feeling has past. Now, ah, now, I want you once more.'

He stopped. She was cruelly balanced, tipped over the desk edge. She felt as if it was only the hardness of the cock inside her and the way he was holding one breast in each hand that kept her upright. 'Want me?' he hissed.

'Yes,' she murmured, knowing it was true. Her earlier discomfort had passed off. Now she shuddered blissfully under the onslaught of his changed strokes. His orgasm was imminent. She could sense it in the shortening of his breath, the fierceness of his thrusting, and in the quickening urgency that gripped his every movement. The feeling caught her up and as he began to pant and thrust wildly, caught up in the spasm of his own orgasm, Justine came once more in a savage deep clutching that was so hard that she felt a muscle or two might tear deep inside her from the sweet, incredible joy that was wrenching her so.

The long, blissful moments of carnal joy culminated at the same time for them both. For a long, hot, sticky moment they stood locked together. Justine felt one, feather-light kiss on her shoulder blade, a sweetness to treasure like a sacred relic, then he had pulled away from her and the air felt cold on her lonely back. He was standing behind her, holding his robe up. 'Clean me,' he ordered. Justine moved away from the table and fell on her knees. She wriggled into a position where she could begin licking affectionately at the now kitten-like penis. She cleaned every spot, revelling in the salt tang of the sweat drops that clung to his sparse pubic curls, the heavier smoothness of his semen, the distinct perfume of her own juices.

Then she began to dress herself. Her nipples flared under the tight bodice, sweet bruising throbbed in her intimate passages, her clitoris felt large and dry between her legs. They were all good feelings. She rejoiced in the physical proof of her Father's devotion. She would be sad as they faded away, because they would never come again. 'Let me attend to your hair,' said Father Gabriel. He had pulled the heavy chair back into position. The room was in order once more. There was only time for this last, sweet intimacy. Justine shivered under the touch of his fingers as he smoothed her hair as efficiently as any mother might. 'There. I must leave you now. But I will see Reverend Mother before I leave.'

She said softly, 'Thank you, Father.'

'Teach my brother's children well, Justine.'

'Shall I never see you again, Father?' she paused trembling, waiting for his answer. She couldn't bear the silence that drew out between them.

'I think not. I may visit the castle on occasion, but my advice to you is to stay strictly within the nursery and to have nothing to do with the great house. You are too beautiful. It might not be wise to draw my brother's attention to you.'

'Wise?' said Justine's lips. Beautiful! sang her mind. He called me beautiful. It was a memory to treasure, to lean on, to ease the pain of this parting.

'Keep strictly to your duties and all will be well,' said Father Gabriel, rising to his feet.

'Wait, Father. Tell me more,' begged Justine.

'You know all that you need to. Do not seek to delay me.' Justine felt his hands brush the top of her head for the last time. 'God bless you, my child,' he said. Ignoring her soft cry, he strode to the door. Justine's body tensed all over as the door shut with a muffled heavy thump that severed their connections for ever.

The coloured lozenges of light from the stained glass window crept right around the room as Justine knelt before the statue of the Virgin. 'Dear Lady, bless him and keep him safe,' she prayed. 'Lord keep him and grant all his desires.' The two candles she had lit were gutted stumps and the sweet sound of voices at Evensong had been a background to her muttered prayers for the best part of an hour before someone came to find her. One of the oldest orphans stuck her matted head around the door.

'Oy! Mush!' she said coarsely. 'Reverend Mother do want you – and it's not to give you nothing you'll want, neither. She ain't half in a bait.'

Chapter Three

*J*ustine felt sick to the pit of her stomach when she saw the fury in the ice-blue eyes of the Reverend Mother. She curtsied as low as she could, as if the extra politeness would ward off the storm, but as she stood trembling with her head politely bowed and her hands clasped behind her back, the tension that coiled and surged in the room told her that nothing, but nothing, was going to ward off this tempest. All she could do was try to ride it out.

Reverend Mother had said nothing so far, but her hands were white-knuckled as they gripped the edge of the black desk. The desk and the chair that she sat in were the only items of furniture in the room. The Reverend Mother kept her space as cold, as bare and as empty as her heart. The walls were plain white. The floor was plain wood. Only the ceiling gave any relief. It was painted a deep celestial blue and it soared over the stone pillars and arches in a softening blessing that made the room beautiful in spite of its sparseness. The rolled parchments that held all the business of the convent filled the deep shelves that were cut into the stone under each arched window. Justine looked at them now, trying to pick out words in the spidery black writing that ran across the yellowing scrolls, trying to ignore the silent fury that was blasting her across the table.

She could not do it. She had to look up. The eyes that met hers cut into Justine's heart like lasers. She flinched, and shivered all over. The words, 'I'm sorry, Reverend Mother,' rose to her lips automatically, but the rote apology had no power to save her now.

Reverend Mother still did not speak. One clenched hand slipped into a desk drawer and reappeared briefly, before blurring into a vicious strike. A snakelike strap bit into the table with a crack that sent zigzags of fear hissing along Justine's nerves. Reverend Mother's headdress flapped out behind her as she slammed the belt so violently into the table top that marks appeared in the polish.

Justine cowered back as the frenzy continued. A vision of her little truckle bed rose up before her. It was hard, it had no sheets and no pillow, but how she wished she were safely in it, with her head under the one thin grey blanket that each orphan was allowed. It took more than a dozen heavy blows, before Reverend Mother was spent enough to raise her head and lean panting on the desk. Her breath was loud in the still room. Her eyes bit into Justine. 'You were to be a maid. I trained you as a maid.' Her voice was rough with emotion as she spoke.

Justine was mortally wounded to be the cause of such passion. She let the vision of her precious books fade away. 'I'm sorry, Reverend Mother. I'll be a maid, Reverend Mother.'

The strap crashed down on the table and another bruise appeared on its gleaming surface. 'You will do as Father Gabriel commands.'

'But Reverend Mother – '

The belt whistled down and Justine jumped back. The black figure darted around the side of the desk in a ratlike scurry and towered menacingly in front of her. Justine fell back, but the black figure followed, one step at a time, sandalled feet hitting the stone floor with a horrible flapping sound. She pushed her face close to Justine's: 'Don't you "But Reverend Mother" me. You will do as Father Gabriel says. Just as I will do as Father Gabriel says. Just as this whole place does as Father Gabriel says. And if

Father Gabriel says you are to be a governess then I will have to send a witless orphan to occupy a position she could never be fit for. And if your tainted blood gets the better of you, and you disgrace me and this convent, then I swear to you, Justine, whether I am dead or alive, I will pursue you to the ends of the earth and make you pay for it.'

Justine's back was now against the wooden door of the room. She fumbled behind her for the door handle as the strap cracked into the door frame above her head. The Reverend Mother was pressing so closely up against her that Justine could feel the disgusting intimacy of the woman's breasts nudging her through the fabric of the heavy robes. She had bad breath, perhaps fury had turned her stomach. Gusts of rotten meat came from the spittle-wet mouth as she continued to rave. A soft unbalanced gleam tempered the rage that blasted out of her cold eyes. Justine was trapped. She was pressed too tightly against the door to open the heavy latch, nor could she push the Reverend Mother away. Her years of training held her prisoner as firmly as her physical position.

The strap slammed again and Justine felt the wind of its passing on her face. 'He takes over the running of my convent without so much as a by-your-leave,' screamed Reverend Mother. Justine felt a strange and unaccustomed feeling moving deep within her. It took her a moment to place it, this rare emotion, but then she realised what she was feeling – anger!

'Don't you treat me like this,' she cried. 'I said I would do your bidding and be a maid. If it's so important to you, why don't you go and tell Father Gabriel what you want me to do. But do not use me this way.'

The Reverend Mother fell back aghast. It was a rare child who dared even a rebellious look after any length of time spent at Our Lady of Perpetual Sorrows. To be answered back was such a new experience that it checked her anger momentarily. She looked almost perplexed.

Justine felt the woman's power over her slipping. Adrenaline rushed through her veins and made her heart pound.

She pushed home her advantage. 'It is wrong of you to punish me for his ruling.'

The Reverend Mother's breathing was loud in the room. She drew herself up and said, 'It is not wrong of me to punish you for the sins I perceive in you: pride, disobedience, insolence. The bad blood in you will lead to your ruin. Your very birth was a sin, Justine. Your whole life should have been spent in sorrowful labour to atone for it. The sin of pride led you to aspire to be what you are not, and that has led you into the sins of insolence and disobedience. There is no hope for you. You are damned.'

She stood quite still, glaring at Justine with those cruel, remote, Arctic-blue eyes. Anger still warmed Justine. They stood in silence. She's waiting for me to crack, thought Justine, and she straightened her spine and put her chin up.

A mouse-scratching on the panel of the wooden door at her back broke the spell. Glad to escape the evil glare that was attacking her, Justine moved away and opened the door. Sister Bertha's anxious face peeped in.

'I found a suitable gown, Reverend Mother,' she squeaked.

She was followed into the room by Sister Agnes and Sister Theresa. They all cast curious looks at the black leather belt in Reverend Mother's hand and at Justine. If Justine's face were mirroring even a quarter of the feelings that were boiling within her, then she could understand why the nuns looked at her so strangely. The Reverend Mother looked strange too. Crimson blotches flared high on each cheek and her hands were trembling. Yet after she had coiled the strap, crossed the room and stowed it into the desk drawer she said, 'Bring the travel garments in, Sister,' and her voice was steady.

When she saw the pile of rich fabric over Sister Bertha's arm, Justine was temporarily distracted. A skirt of striped black and grey satin that rustled and gleamed dully with richness. A bodice of soft mouse-grey velvet, the pile deeper than the richest animal pelt in the wild. Crisp frothy white lace petticoats and a long hooded cloak.

In response to a nod from Reverend Mother, Sister Bertha thrust the garments at Justine. The nuns moved away from her and modestly turned their backs. As Justine stripped off her old clothes, adrenaline still hummed in her nerves. The highly charged emotions of the day sang in her blood. What colour there was in the plain room shone brightly and the flickering candle shadows seemed to be charged with significance.

Defiantly, she dropped her old things into an untidy heap on the floor. The undergarments and lace petticoats she picked up first were a marvel of newness. Sharp intakes of breath made her look over to the huddled backs of the nuns. Reverend Mother's voice was a muttering goblin chant. Ice crystals formed in Justine's stomach as she picked up the rustling taffeta dress. All her life she had wanted to wear a beautiful dress like this one, had tried to imagine how it would feel to pull a garment that smelt new over her head – but never had she dreamt it would come to pass in such a nightmare situation!

By the time she was fully dressed, Justine was trembling again. Whatever Reverend Mother had told the nuns had put shocked and disgusted looks on the faces they now turned to her. Sister Agnes shook a red and swollen finger at Justine, 'Wicked child,' she said. 'Leaving me with all that washing. I always told you that you would end up in hell.'

'Is Castle Waldgraf hell?' asked Justine. 'Is Father Gabriel the devil to send me there?'

The nuns sucked in their breath at such defiance. The Reverend Mother's face was cool and remote as she said, 'All roads lead to hell for one such as you. I am glad that the sisters have witnessed your depravity, because I want them to understand why I take the step I do now. I order you to leave this moment, Justine. I consider you too dangerous to mix with the other orphans for even one night longer. Furthermore, although, of course, the arrangement about your wages being paid directly to us still stands, I will cancel it after the eighteen years I consider you owe us have passed, because, from this

41

moment, you may consider yourself excommunicated from Our Lady of Perpetual Sorrows.'

Justine shuddered like a tree under the blow of an axe. Then confidence flowed into her as she touched her warm new clothes. Her head tilted proudly. She picked up the warm cloak and its weight gave her the strength to ignore the fact that it was now dark outside the protective walls of the convent. There was a small basket under the cloak. It contained a tiny purse and six hard bread rolls. Her heart leapt at such riches. 'I am ready to leave,' she said proudly. 'I am looking forward to taking up my new position.'

The last coin in the tiny purse had gone by the time she reached the nearest village to Castle Waldgraf. The castle was only a short walk from the village, but it was already midnight and Justine did not want to arrive late and bedraggled so she stopped outside the inn to think things over. Icy stars twinkled in a cold and remote sky. It would freeze hard tonight. Justine crept around the side of the white-washed building and into the stable yard. A regiment of soldiers was obviously quartered there. She waited until there was no one around, then she slipped into the building nearest her.

The ammonia tang of horses stung her nostrils. Cobwebs draped the rough stone walls. Leather harness hung from hooks in the rugged beams. A brush was propped up next to the big stone water trough and a bucket stood next to it, but it didn't look as if anyone ever used them. The occasional scrape of a hoof and much steady chewing told Justine that the horses were at the back of the stable. This end seemed to be used for storage, including piles and piles of hay. Justine took off her new clothes and hung them carefully from a nail in one of the rough beams. Then she burrowed into the sweet-smelling hay and slept.

A mouse scurrying across her face woke her from a drugged and nightmarish sleep. Moving like a swimmer under water, Justine rose shakily to her feet. Her head was so heavy that she nearly lay down and went back to sleep again. But the thought of her verminous sleeping companion forced her awake. Ominous blue smoke hung thick in the air, confusing her. Then she realised that the little mouse had saved her life: by fleeing across her face as it escaped from the fire that was attacking the back of the stable, it had roused her from her smoke-induced daze.

Justine took a deep breath in an effort to calm the panic she could feel rising inside her, but she drew in a lungful of acrid smoke that made her cough. Water started from her smarting eyes. She coughed again and rubbed her eyelids. Dear God. She was wasting time. What should she do?

She took a shaky step towards her precious new clothes. They still hung from the nail in the rafters. Justine didn't want to leave them. Flame licked out from under one of the rough beams and dripped down the front of her new dress. She put out her hands as if to save it, but the dress had caught fire. It burnt quickly. The heat made Justine fall back. The dress twisted horribly as it burnt, almost as if someone were writhing in agony inside it.

Justine abandoned any hope of saving her clothes and turned for the door. But she had left it too late. Part of the roof fell in with a crash. Sparks blew up into the suddenly open night sky. Justine took a few useless steps towards the door. She had to get out. But burning debris blocked the entrance. It was almost as though the fallen roof beams had been put across the door by malevolent demons, so perfectly did they bar the way.

Justine looked around her and a sob rose to her lips. She couldn't get out. She looked towards the back of the stable. Smoke coiled all around in a greasy muddling haze, and she could not see much. But she could hear the horses, the poor horses, as they screamed out their final pain, and she knew there was no getting out that way. Her skin felt hot. She held out one trembling arm, as if for guidance, and the small hairs on it began to crisp. Her tongue felt huge in her trembling mouth as she tried to pray to Our Lady.

The greedy roar of the fire was louder. Justine ran a few

steps, halted, ran a few steps the other way, halted again. The fire was blazing towards her from every direction. Like a small trapped animal, Justine looked around for a corner to hide in. She circled once more, feeling her heart beat in a frenzy. Then she saw the big stone trough. Water! Her body took over and carried her across the stable and into the water trough before another conscious thought had entered her brain. Cool water flowed over her. It was a big trough, and it was more than three-quarters full, but would it be deep enough to save her?

Justine crouched in the milk-warm water shivering violently. A sharp pain bit into her head. Instinctively she put up her hands to it and she screamed when the pain bit them too. It was another moment before she realised that embers were caught in her hair, burning and tormenting her. She ducked her head under the water to douse the embers. In her panic, she inhaled water, and had to come up for air, coughing and spluttering.

'By the cringe,' said a deep, slow, lazily amused voice above her. 'A maiden in distress if ever I did see one.'

He looked like the devil himself to Justine. Flames swirled behind the tall, swarthy man who was standing over the trough regarding her with such amusement in his eyes. Firelight gleamed on strong teeth and danced along the gold rings in his ears. He was larger, more vital and alive than any human being could possibly be, and the burning hell around them seemed to be adding to his enjoyment of life.

Without hurrying, he shifted the weight of the large black cloak he was carrying, and, with a polite, 'Excuse me,' to Justine, dunked it in the water trough. Dark face intent, he lifted and dropped the cloak in the water, hefting it with the familiar motions of a housewife at her wash. When he was satisfied, the dark man swung the dripping garment over his head. Water streamed from its sodden folds. 'I know where there is a window,' he said, briefly meeting her eyes. 'I'm going to make a dash for it. Care to come under my cloak?'

Justine acted without thought once more. This time she

hopped out of the trough and scuttled under the sheltering folds of his wet cloak like a duckling burrowing into its mother's wing. 'Hold tight!' he roared into her ear as he guided them forward into the dark. She followed him blindly, trusting him. He halted and she bumped into him. He had stopped in front of a stone wall. From the movements of his body, Justine guessed he was feeling along the stone, hunting for a window. Steam was forming under the cloak and it was getting hotter and hotter. 'It's here somewhere. I didn't escape the soldiers to be taken by the fire. I know it's here . . . ah!'

He lifted the cloak high and Justine felt a rush of cold air on her skin. There was a meagre window slit before them, but it was small, so small. Justine turned round and began to say 'I can't – ' but he lifted her in his great arms and she found her head in the embrasure and her bare arms scraping frantically along the stone of the narrow opening. Her muscles trembled as she heaved with all her strength, feeling his hard hands pushing at her legs and feet. She thought she was jammed and would never get free, but with a final wrench that pulled out a great chunk of hair and took all the skin off her arms she shot out of the opening like a cork out of a fermenting wine barrel and plopped in a heap into the deep, malodorous mud of the stable yard below.

Justine lay on her back looking at the blessed stars in the blue-black sky and breathing in great gulps of clean icy night air. Beside her the stable burned in a hellish orange blaze. A dark bundle flew out of the window and dropped next to her. Clothes scattered from it. A soft voice said in her ear: 'Don't just lie there gawping. Help me pick them up.'

She turned to him quickly. The man was naked! Embarrassed, she looked away from his body and up into his merry eyes. 'You're safe! How did you get out so quickly?'

'I'll tell you all my secrets another time. But for now, I need to get out of here.' He retrieved his clothes then smiled into her eyes as he took her hand to pull her away from the inferno. Firelight gleamed on his naked limbs, outlining the muscles that worked so steadily beneath his sweating skin as they crossed the yard. The sky was a deep blue against the red of the fire. A few horses ran loose, galloping aimlessly in their panic. People ran about like chickens with a fox in the poultry house. A man cannoned hard into Justine and ran off swearing. A fine grey horse, wearing a bridle, and loaded saddle bags that had slipped to one side, loomed up out of the confusion. It swerved to avoid them, but Justine's dark hero leapt up and caught a trailing rein. Holding the maddened horse firmly he fixed the saddle straps with one hand and stuffed his clothes untidily into one of the saddlebags. He then swung himself up on to the horse's back. He met Justine's eyes and gave her a neat little salute. 'Farewell. Always a pleasure to rescue a naked maiden.'

As he uttered the word 'naked' he looked at Justine's slender body as if for the first time. His fine dark eyes lingered over her swelling breasts. She jumped forward and caught at his stirrup. 'Don't leave me here,' she implored.

He turned his dark eyes on Justine. 'Can you ride a horse?'

'Of course I can,' she lied. Red flames danced in his black eyes as he stared down at her. Justine gave the stirrup a frustrated shake. 'I don't want to stay here,' she said staring into his eyes urgently. 'I can't take any more of this insanity. I can't stand to hear the horses die.'

He looked at her for a moment longer, the expression in his eyes unreadable, and then shrugged. 'Jump up then. But be sharp about it: the soldiers are looking for me, and I'm stealing this horse.'

Stealing! That's a mortal sin, thought Justine. But even as the automatic response flicked through the surface of her mind, she was stepping up on to the strong bony foot that the stranger held out for her, and she brushed the troublesome stricture away completely as she settled on to the back of the horse.

He hardly waited for Justine to wrap her bare arms around his naked waist before urging the horse on. She could feel his muscles working hard down the length of his back because her breasts were pressed close into his naked flesh. She held tighter as beneath her she felt the horse's unaccustomed movement. She felt stiff hairs tickling the unprotected skin of her legs. Her delicate woman's place, stretched open across the creaking leather saddle, quivered with the vibrations from the horse's galloping hooves as they thundered over the hard track that led to the forest.

Opening up before them were the dark scented pine trees, and the cool autumn night studded with stars. Life burned in Justine's veins. She was deeply thankful to be alive. She said a quick prayer for the poor horses and any souls who might have perished in the inferno. Then she abandoned herself to the immediacy of the wild movements of the horse beneath her as they rode through the living night.

Chapter Four

*T*he smell of smoke woke Justine and for one wild
moment she felt sick. Then her other senses kicked in
and she became aware of scented pine needles under her
cheek and cool green moss before her eyes. Somewhere
behind her a mountain stream roared, and the wind was
sighing in the tops of the forest trees. She sat up quickly
and then groaned out loud.

'Stiff?' inquired a deep amused voice. Justine looked up
into laughing male eyes. She suddenly remembered that
she was naked – and so was he. He seemed to be completely unaware of his nudity, but hot blood stung her
cheeks and she turned away from his gaze shyly. Then she
couldn't resist peeping at his naked body from under her
lashes. He was tall and well muscled. His skin was as
tanned as a peasant's, as if he often went bare under the
sky, or worked out in the fields with his brown muscular
arms. He was as swarthy as a gipsy with his flashing dark
eyes and fine-bridged nose, yet there was nothing of the
sly poacher about him. His long dark hair fell over a
straight back that might have been a soldier's. He
reminded Justine of a scholar or a priest, or even the doctor
who sometimes came to the infirmary to carry out oper-
ations. She couldn't work him out.

Her rescuer turned away to bend over a neat campfire.

Small clear flames crackled neatly within a ring of stones. A thin plume of smoke spiralled into an autumn sky that was the pale blue of a robin's egg. Two limp rabbits lay on the ground and, as Justine watched, he took out a thin blade and began to whet it. 'Stiff?' he asked again, without looking up from his task.

'Stiff?' she replied. 'Dear God! I never felt such pain in my limbs.'

'That's because you never rode a horse before.'

Justine looked at him guiltily. He had caught her out. 'I'm sorry,' she said.

He laughed out loud, and his eyes sparkled at her. 'Don't be. You did exactly the right thing, for if you had told me the truth I would have left you. And as it is, here we are, together and alive in this fine place with breakfast not far away.'

Justine got painfully to her feet, catching her breath as she did so. Her hair fell forward as she moved, and she crinkled her nose in disgust as the smell of smoke rose from it. 'I smell as bad as I feel,' she exclaimed. 'And I'm soot and dirt all over.'

'The river is just behind you. I'll be there myself as soon as I've dealt with these coneys. There were some clothes in the saddle bags. See, I've hung them over that branch to air. I stole a farmer's nag by the looks of things. Good, because he carried snares and cooking gear, but bad, because I doubt he was over particular about his linen.'

'Was there any soap?'

'Afraid not, pretty maid. You'll have to stay in a good long while: the river will wash you clean.'

'My name is Justine. I am to go to Castle Waldgraf, to be a governess there. Will, you, I mean could you – ?'

He picked up a rabbit and began to skin it expertly. 'Escort you there? I expect so, Justine. If you will accept the protection of Armand the gipsy.'

He was a gipsy then. 'I would be glad to travel with you, sir,' said Justine. She watched him for a few minutes longer, but he didn't look up, or say any more about himself, so slowly, a little reluctantly, she turned away and followed the noise of running water until she came to the river, and the waterfall. Justine could feel the cold mist flung up by the waterfall on her skin. She scrambled further down the river bank, towards the deep pool that lay under the fall. Rainbows gleamed in the spray and there was energy in both the sound of the water and the touch of the cool air. She sat on one of the smooth round boulders that lay scattered along the river's edge and began to comb her thick mane with her fingers. Great lumps of burned and evil smelling hair fell out.

Just as she finished combing her hair, she became aware of eyes watching her, friendly eyes that appreciated her nakedness. Mischievously, she tipped her head back and shook out her rippling chestnut hair. It waved down her back, gently caressing her skin. Its great mass was a warm living weight tickling her shoulders and just brushing the hollow above her waist. She put out first one long slender leg, and then the other one, stretching and examining them in the pale sunshine. Justine got to her feet slowly and, still aware of the appreciative eyes, she placed her hands in the small of her back and stretched her whole body, arching her breasts up towards the pine forest, knowing that Armand was watching her, wanting him to like her.

She turned slowly and took the few steps to the edge of the water. Clean mud oozed between her toes as she paddled out into the stream. The gurgling water was so cold that it snatched her breath away. She pulled her hair to one side and over her shoulder, so that the full length of her naked back was bare. She hoped that her skin was creamy and unblemished, and that the curves of her naked buttocks were pleasing. For some reason, she wanted Armand to admire her. She wanted that very much.

She splashed across the shallow part of the stream towards the deep green pool. Foam creamed and bubbled at the far end where the cataract landed, but on this side of the pool, the water was smooth and delicious. Justine plunged forward, throwing her whole body into the deep emerald depths in a dive that was clumsy but took her deep. Water drummed in her ears and she felt the suck of the waterfall. She kicked for the surface. As soon as her head was out in the open, she let out a screech. The serpent bite of the icy water was all pain to begin with, but as she continued to yodel and splash vigorously, a sweet wild exultation began to pulse in her veins.

There was a great splash and a naked body swam past her, moving fast through the clear green water. Then a sleek black head broke the surface like an otter. As Armand shook his upper body, droplets of water sprayed out, sparkling in the sun like diamonds. 'By the cringe! That's bracing,' he shouted, as he met her eyes.

'I love it!' cried Justine, smiling back. She threw herself backward into the water, deliberately creating fountains of spray to catch Armand, kicking her legs as hard as she could, before rolling over like a dolphin and swimming towards the cataract. She approached it carefully, for she was not a strong swimmer, but there were plenty of boulders in the shallows to the side of the waterfall. She scrambled up on to one laughing, allowing the weight of the water pouring over her head and shoulders to wash away the smell and the memory of the fire.

Armand scrambled up beside her and she felt his wet cold body slide against hers like a slippery rainbow trout. His mouth opened and closed as he said something to her, but she couldn't hear a word for the roaring, tumbling water that crashed over her head and her ears. She looked up into the dark face that hovered so near hers. Clear water ran over his brown skin and muscled body. Drops glinted in the gold rings that swung from his ears. He was laughing, energy sparked in his black eyes. A honey-sweet wildness woke in Justine as she responded to his bare wet presence.

Armand swayed towards her, his eyes intent, but teasingly she moved back. She was not to be won so easily. His dark eyes approved of her move, and he laughed again and blew a pleading kiss towards her. Justine blew a kiss back, but as he reached out to take her in his arms, she leant away, moving deeper into the plume of water, feeling its increased power beating down on her head. The pressure was too strong, and she moved to the edge of the waterfall. The water still pounded down, but it was manageable here, invigorating and refreshing.

She closed her eyes to the running crystal sprays and tipped her head back to allow the stream of water to wash her clean. She knew Armand was looking at her; she could feel the warmth of his attention. She felt his body touch hers as he moved closer. His body now sheltered hers from the water that tumbled all about them. She felt safe and protected with his hard muscular body shielding her from the force of the water. When she felt cold hard lips pressed fervently to her throat, she did not move away, but relaxed into the caress, enjoying it; laughing as he blew bubbles in the water that cascaded over her neck and shoulders, sighing as his kisses turned more serious. Armand took his time, kissing the smooth curve of her throat inch by feathery inch; lightly kissing the long elegant centre line of her neck; softly tonguing the gentle hollows that lay under her ears.

Justine opened her eyes. He was staring at her as if he wanted to devour her. The sight of his dark intent face made her shiver. There were deep shadows under his high cheekbones and water drops gleamed in the bandit growth of dark stubble that covered his cheeks. Armand tilted his head and looked at her even more closely. He appeared wild, elemental, like an Indian chief as he sat there on the boulder, water cascading over his dark skin and foaming over his hard muscles. The streams of clear water ran through his wild black hair which lay long on his shoulders. His whole body was a monument to male power and force, but in the tender curve of his lips there was softness, and in his eyes a deep and loving wonder.

He put out one wet brown hand and touched Justine's cheek gently. She could see that his eyes were not a true black; they had glowing hearts, like topaz imprisoned in coal. 'You are by far the most beautiful woman I ever rescued,' he said softly.

Justine ducked her head, embarrassed to meet his gaze. 'How can that be? I am just an orphan, and I have no fine clothes like a lady – indeed, I have no clothes at all.' Hot tears stung her eyes at the thought of the mouse grey velvet and her lip quivered. She turned away, ashamed of her vulnerability.

A strong hand took hold of her chin and Armand forced her to face him. There was no mockery in his dark eyes. Indeed, he seemed to understand for he said gently: 'Don't fret about your losses, Justine, although I can see that you feel them. The farmer's clothes will not be stylish perhaps, but once you reach Waldgraf, I have no doubt that your employers will care for you.'

'I'm not vain,' said Justine in a small voice. 'There were years of good wear in those clothes.'

'Think no more of it,' advised Armand, his eyes tender.

Justine shivered. She was afraid to be so close to him. 'I am getting chilled,' she said, knowing it was an excuse. 'I need to swim once more.' It was cold in the shadow of the waterfall. Her flesh was covered in fine goose bumps and her nipples were crinkled up tightly against the freezing water. Armand touched first one nipple and then the other with light fingers, watching the water splash over her breasts and around his hands. His voice whispered like a soft summer breeze, 'Clothes could not make you more beautiful than nature made you.' And his smile said that he meant every word. 'You are perfect like this – naked, free, as natural as a water sprite.'

Justine bit her lip and looked away from his eyes, at her toes, fish white in the bubbling water. 'Let's swim,' she said shakily. Life in the convent had not taught her how to accept compliments, she reflected ruefully. Then she screamed in surprise as Armand swept her up in his cold wet arms, laughter in his eyes. He plunged back under the full force of the booming waterfall and the sound of her protests were swept away with the foaming water. When they came out into the pool, Justine beat her tiny hands against his immobile back. 'Let me go! Let me go!'

'With pleasure! You're harder to hold than a wriggling eel.' He kissed her before letting go. Justine saw drops of water sparkling on his thick black lashes. Then she screamed out once more as the world spun about her in a glorious arc as she crashed into the pool. The sun danced and sparkled on the green surface and she floated on her back, looking up at the sky. Armand dived in next to her. 'Are you sure you are human?' he asked, his eyes teasing as he emerged. 'With your hair floating all about you and your long pale limbs, you remind me of a water nymph.'

'No nymph, sir, but a mortal maid, and a cold one too. I must return to land.'

Laughing straight into her eyes, Armand caught her hand. 'Here, I'll help you. Scramble up over this boulder.'

The smooth round boulder felt warm from the sun. Justine saw tiny jewel-like ferns growing in the cracks and crevices of the tumbled boulders as she scrambled her way to the top of the bank. She was aware that as she opened her legs, bent her knees and pushed herself upward, Armand could see the dark purse of her sex. The curves of her buttocks quivered as she imagined his gaze, and warmth started to tickle her clitoris in tiny sweet waves. When she got to the top, she looked down. Armand had made no effort to climb. He was laughing up at her, admiration in his eyes. 'I was waiting in case you fell,' he cried. Justine blushed deeply, knowing that he lied, knowing that she was responding to him. More warmth was flowing around her body than could be accounted for by the caress of the autumn sun.

With a sudden quick scramble, he was beside her, smiling intimately into her eyes. 'The rabbits will not be cooked yet. Let's dry off in the sun on that patch of turf there.' Without waiting for an answer, he walked over to the grass. Justine watched his back view. His legs were brown, somewhat browner than his back, and his buttocks were lighter still, although they were still tanned, proving that he often went naked under the sun. Strong muscles corded his legs and back. Justine's eyes were drawn to his buttocks: smooth, taut, tight, firmly muscled, each cheek moved confidently as he walked. A few drops of water clung to his naked body, winking as the sun caught them. He looked like a fine wild animal, all male, all grace, all power. He reached the patch of grass and flung himself full length. 'Come on,' he called, looking over towards her.

Shaking her head as if to clear it, Justine took a few quick steps and sat herself on the short turf next to him. It smelt sweet in the sunshine, and little herbs grew among the green blades of grass. She felt too shy to meet the tender eyes that shone down on her, so she drew her knees up to her chin and rested her head upon them. Her hair fell around her, almost covering her body. Below them the river bubbled and raced. Above them hawks soared in the blue sky, and she could hear wood pigeons cooing gently in the edge of the forest.

A soft hand stroked the top of her head, lifting and playing with the strands of chestnut hair that were beginning to dry in the sun. 'Are you warmer now, Justine?' came his soft voice.

His touch made her shiver, and she had to swallow before she could reply, 'Yes, indeed. The sun feels very warm, although it is early yet.'

'Very early,' came the soft reply. 'I see no reason to hurry along with our journey, do you?'

She heard him stir next to her on the grass, and then the light touch was joined by another as his second hand joined the first. Armand moved behind her and began to massage her shoulders lightly, gently, evenly, and yet he reached so deep that he touched nerves that no one else had fathomed. Justine sighed and arched her back like a little cat. It was nice, so very nice to be petted in this way, to be touched and caressed by this dark muscled man who seemed to understand her body so well.

Justine hugged her knees a little tighter, but then the good feelings seduced her and she let them go, sitting up straighter so that Armand could continue his gentle work. 'There is no hurry,' she agreed idly. 'It's very pleasant to sit here so.' The knowing competent hands moved down her back, circling, kneading, massaging.

'Lie on your front in the grass,' murmured Armand. Willingly, Justine complied. The grass fronds tickled the tips of her breasts. Her skin was warm, roused, responding to the touch of the man who was pleasuring her so. Armand stood astride her, then leant down and picked up her hands and tucked them under her, so that one lay under each breast. Justine pressed her body into her hands. Her breasts fitted just nicely into the hollow of her curved fingers and she wriggled and sighed as she began to touch herself gently; just lightly touching the delicate skin of her breasts, just slightly adding to her pleasure.

Armand swept up her hair and placed it over her left shoulder, pausing to kiss and nibble the back of her neck in a way that sent ripples of delight down to the very base of her spine. Justine felt tension gathering there, at the place where her back dimpled on either side of her back-bone and knew that desire for this male was rising within her.

But he was in no hurry. Now that he had her lying in front of him, spread out in the position that he wanted her, he crouched down over her and resumed his leisurely massage. Each time he walked his thumbs up the side of her spine Justine arched her back and sighed with delight. Each time he moved the palms of his hands in gentle sweeping movements over the skin of her buttocks, the sexual tension that coiled in the base of her spine grew greater.

He moved down to her feet next, kneading and caressing them with strong agile fingers, even rubbing between each tiny toe. Then his hands moved up first one leg to her knee, then the other leg to her other knee. Justine drew in her breath sharply as his fingers touched her inner thigh, and he lightened his touch at once, so that her saddle-sore muscles melted and responded to his gentle doctoring.

When he found the big muscle that curved around her buttock she couldn't help gasping aloud. Sexy shivery sensations radiated out from it and tickled her belly, quivered inside her woman's place, hastened the unfolding of her desire. She moved as if to roll over and face him, but a hard hand pushed her back, making her keep her position, face down in the grass below him. Justine lay still and shivered beneath Armand's touch. Feeling her heart beating quickly, quickly, quickly, until it beat nearly as fast as the horse's hooves had galloped last night. So fast that it made it difficult to breathe as she lay there. Her quickened breath came and went between lips that felt larger than usual. She had moved her arms so that they lay folded under her chin, and she could feel her hot breath blowing on the fine hairs of her forearm as Armand began his deadly stimulation of the other cheek of her buttocks.

He seemed to be able to find the exact line that her shuddering desire was following, pinching and kneading the big muscle as if he were a baker making soft bread dough out of Justine's firm flesh. Then he stopped for a moment, and she lay shivering below him, feeling the sun warm on her back, hearing the river roar down below, but most of all, feeling a soft melting that was taking place deep in the slit between her legs.

She felt Armand part her legs gently, just a few inches wider, and she shivered all over as she realised that he must be looking at the folds of her sex as they dangled between her legs. His hands returned to her buttocks, and she relaxed as they slid over her curves, but then the stroking motions curved round over the sides of her legs, paused briefly to caress her inner thighs, and then explored gently the folds and crevices of her dark woman's place.

At his touch in that most intimate and secret of places Justine felt a series of fine quiverings begin in the pit of her belly and heat flush all the pores of her skin. Blood raced around her body and pumped faster through her pounding heart to fill and stiffen the folds of her labia. Her vulva felt heavy, as if it were engorged and enlarged, and she shuddered all over once more as Armand slipped two commanding fingers into the entrance of her vagina.

Inside her woman's place was deep and silky. Armand's fingers slid over a surface as smooth as ice with feathery snow over it; but the ice was hot with Justine's deep wet yearning. She heard Armand give an appreciative sound of satisfaction, so she was surprised when after a few seconds touching he removed his fingers. Then she heard him inhale, and she knew that he was enjoying the scent of her juices. And she heard his lips smack as he tasted the fragrance that must be lingering on his fingers. She felt accepted and admired, judged and found attractive. His gentle attentions made her feel as carefree as a blissful baby, loved and petted, rocked and cared for. She was a dreaming passive receptacle for his pleasuring, until his next movements shocked her body rigid.

Armand bent his head over her buttocks and held one trembling cheek open wide in each strong hand. Justine writhed and sighed as the strength of his hands held her secret places open for his inspection. She was all melting pleasure. She arched her back and thrust out her bottom towards him, thinking that perhaps he was going to mount her from behind in a wild and tempestuous manner. But he didn't. He continued to hold her open and the moment grew longer. Justine waited shuddering. Then she let out a gasp that was almost a shriek as a hot and pointed tongue tip flicked wetly into the rosebud rim of her anal opening. She clenched her buttocks in surprise and embarrassment and jerked her body away. She felt Armand's tongue slip away from her anus. She tensed, waiting for his reaction: it was not anger, but a deep and loving chuckle which relaxed her, even though she felt his arms come out to push her down to the ground again. 'Lie still, and you will enjoy my attentions,' he ordered.

'No! I cannot let you.'

'Why not? I want to. I want to make love to every secret crevice of your body. There is no part of you that is not perfect.'

Justine lay trembling, unsure how to answer. It seemed all wrong that he should lick her there, and yet, and yet, his sudden assault had sent wild and glorious passion racing and tumbling around her. She was surfing the crest of a high wave of pleasure, and she was honest enough to admit to herself that she had enjoyed it.

Armand was stroking her buttocks with gentle soothing hands, almost the way one would soothe a frightened horse. Unconsciously, Justine relaxed under his long gentle strokes and her quivering body began to drift softly closer to the position that Armand wanted it to take. 'Tell me, Justine,' he said softly, 'has no man breached you there?'

A memory of Father Gabriel sliding the long slim candle into her back passage floated across Justine's mind and was gone. 'No man,' she said in a trembling voice. 'Although once, someone put, put a thing, up there inside me.'

'Did it hurt you? Because if so, I will not touch you there, I promise.'

'No, it did not hurt.'

By now Justine was soft and compliant, her buttocks were once more spread wide open, and she felt Armand take her in a strong fresh grip and begin to nibble the smooth curves of her bottom. The rough caress of the stubble on his chin felt so shiveringly good that her legs opened themselves wider, even wider, and her belly just tilted into the ground in a manner that enabled Armand to reach her back passage once more. He kissed his way slowly and inexorably towards Justine's anus and she waited with bated breath. Afraid of the next touch, and yet longing for it too. She felt like a giant jellyfish, boneless and pliant, drifting helpless on the currents of passion generated by the dark desires of the man who held her so masterfully.

'Justine,' breathed Armand, stopping between every word to plant a kiss around the rim of her anus. 'Justine, I'm so glad that I am to be the first with you. I want you to remember me always, and a woman will remember the man who takes one of her virginities; who introduces her to the first pleasures of her body.' And the hot and pointed tongue tip slipped wetly into her anus once more.

Justine stiffened again. She couldn't help it. Her body just reacted like that. But then she relaxed, and the strange compelling feelings that Armand's kisses were creating began to take over. His hard wet tongue flicked and licked. It darted deep inside her and then pulled out to plant feathery, tickly, exhaustingly good licks around the crinkled rim of the opening of her anal passage. Justine melted and then froze, burned and then softened as sharp shocks of pleasure were followed by marshmallow-soft ones.

As if someone else owned and operated them, her hands circled her breasts and pulled at her own nipples, adding to the pleasure that hummed through her body. Her back arched and her legs opened, encouraging Armand in his shameless pillaging of her anal opening, his shameless exploration of a region that no man should ever know.

Justine drew herself up on to her knees and leant forward. Now she was spread openly in front of him, supporting her own weight and offering access to her secret places willingly. Armand let go his tight grip on her buttocks and reached forward to tickle the hairy folds of her labia as they swung so invitingly before him. Justine cried out as he touched her. His mouth sucked and his tongue continued to probe her intimate places. The sensation in that area of skin just around the anus grew greater with every passing minute of his attention. And now his gentle fingers were unerringly spreading open the delicate folds of her labia and finding the button of her clitoris. As soon as his long strong forefinger landed on the sensitive heart of her pleasure, an orgasm began to gather at the base of Justine's spine. She threw her head down and bit into her forearm, abandoning herself to the pleasure she thought was coming – but Armand withdrew both his mouth from her anus and his hands from her sex.

Shaking like a birch tree in a gale, Justine rolled over from her belly on to her back and tried to throw her arms around his strong brown neck and draw him down towards her – to tempt his penis into her vagina, to satisfy the leaping pleasure he had created and which now demanded to be filled. But laughing down at her with confident dark eyes, Armand refused to be drawn. He was as immovable as an oak in the forest. Justine could not bend him to her will. Indeed, he pulled out of her grip and stood up, still laughing at her. 'Patience, you little wildcat. You shameless queen in your shameless heat! Lie on your belly once more and wait for me. Have faith that I will allow you the completion you crave – in my own good time!'

Hot and shaking, Justine did as she was bid, rolling her tender and responsive body back on to her belly, taking her breasts in her hands once more, lying on the sweet turf to await Armand's pleasure. She heard his faint steps going away into the forest. High above, a hawk gave a wild and lonely scream, nearby the river bubbled. Justine inhaled the sweet smell of herbs and waited for Armand to return.

Every sense was alert, every pore in her skin was alive, every faint breath of the wind over her naked body was significant. Each second of time that ticked by lasted for eternity as Justine experienced the sensuality of her body, the depth of her arousal, as she lay waiting, waiting, for Armand to return. Her breasts felt hot, sweet and heavy as she touched them. She lifted her hands, touching and teasing her own nipples so gently and yet so effectively. Her belly felt round and feminine. Her lips were soft and open, engorged with gentle sensations as her warm breath tickled them with every exhalation. The tension at the base of her spine had grown. It dug into her with savage claws that had steel talons, and yet it was sweet too, that terrible deep need. It was satisfaction to know that as she lay there shaking in the thrall of primitive desire, the man who would release her from it was nearby.

Justine pressed her legs together and let go. Pressed once more and let go. Her clitoris was hot and fully engorged. Large, stiff, hard, it throbbed and pulsed in a wholly pleasurable beat, sending out radiations of delight that suffused the folds and soft wrinkles of her woman's place. Every crinkle and wrinkle of her vulva was aware, alive, trembling with pleasure. Deep inside her dark tunnel, dews were collecting, beading her soft and clenching vaginal walls, slithering down the dark muscled folds and pooling at the entrance of her legs. From there the ethereal liquid slid down the tender tops of her inner thighs in a frosted dew that glistened in the sunlight.

Justine, lying pressed into the ground, felt the vibrations of Armand's returning footsteps. A dizzy shock of sexual arousal swept over her and she melted and pressed herself deeper into the protecting earth, and then lifted her buttocks and opened her legs in blatant invitation to him. She trembled and shook with the strength of her feelings. She wanted him to end the frustration that held her on the edge of exploding into an orgasm, but she wanted this moment to last for ever – her lying there helpless with sweet passion and deep lustful pleasure. Him walking towards her with his firm determined tread, bringing who knew what for her sexual temptation and pleasure.

'Lie still, little sweetheart,' said the deep voice above her, and once more she felt Armand's knowing hands on her buttocks. But this time they felt strange. They were coated with a thick, greasy, slippery substance that slid in an oily slick across her shaking cheeks. Justine felt liquid trickling down into the crack that lay expectantly between her legs. She inhaled deeply as she felt his hands slide into the slit between her buttocks and dribble fresh liquid in there. She recognised the fruity, oily smell of fine olives, and she knew what he was doing. The knowledge sent guilty frissons racing around her body and as the oil oozed gently into the crevices and folds of her sex, she entered another, higher plane of sexual arousal.

Armand's hands felt even softer now, as they slid and slipped and lubricated gently. The fruity scent grew stronger as it warmed between his hands, and Justine lay shivering with delight as he massaged the soft liquid substance into the tops of her thighs. But all the time his hands anointed her flesh so gently, she was waiting for him to return his attentions to the clandestine area that shivered between her buttocks. Slippy greasy hands pulled the folds of her labia open and anointed them thoroughly. Her dark curling pubic hair coiled into wet curls as the sweet liquid wet them. She felt Armand's fingers twining deeply into them as he touched her mound of Venus with soft and authoritative movements.

His questing fingers touched her clitoris. A mighty orgasm threatened to take her as his oily fingers brushed over it. But he withdrew the touch she yearned for, leaving her quaking like a boat with no moorings in the storm of desire that was shaking her. 'Armand,' she breathed. She thought that if only her shame would leave her she could tell him not to stop. She longed to beg him to continue with the movements that were taking her reason, but shyness held her silent.

She heard his soft chuckle. 'My sweet impatient darling! You must not be in such a hurry. I have many, many delights planned for you. I want to take you to the heights that can be reached by the application of a little, just a little refinement.' As he spoke, a slick oiled fingertip was nudging the entrance of Justine's anus. It stretched her open and she gasped and forgot what she had been thinking of. The strange sensations were so compelling that they filled her universe.

She heard the glug, glug, glug of liquid leaving the neck of a bottle and then stiffened with surprise and pleasure as two very wet hands snaked underneath her and took hold of her breasts in a tight grip. Her skin welcomed the touch of the liquid. Armand's hands slid over her breasts in a gentle stroking movement, lubricating them well. Her feelings of pleasure grew until it seemed that each one of her nipples had magically sprouted the same kind of nerve endings as her clitoris, because the sensations that gathered there now were as good and as powerful as those that brought her to orgasm when she felt them in her pleasure place.

Just as she felt it inevitable that she would crest those intense feelings of pleasure and shudder to a climax, Armand's hands left his teasing soft exploration of her nipples and swept down her belly in a motion that stirred fresh delights there. Then he removed his hands from her body and she heard him move away and stand up. She heard him walk around her where she lay kneeling and trembling on the ground and she looked up to meet his eyes as he knelt down on the ground, facing her. Staring at her intently, he took her face in his strong oily hands and she smelt the sweetness of olives once more. His eyes got closer and closer and then vanished as he kissed her. He looked so strong and dangerous, with his dark hair and muscled body, but his kisses were as gentle as spider webs as they softly wrapped her face in a blizzard of loving caresses.

His lips were firm and demanding, but there was a wild-honey sweetness below the passion that Justine responded to with all the ardour of a starving child as he planted soft butterfly kisses on her eyelids and nose. He placed the flask of olive oil in her hands. 'Anoint me, Justine, so that I may enter you,' he said softly, gazing deeply into her eyes as if he would enter her body with them.

Trembling she sat back on her knees and looked down at the tiny flagon. It was made of glazed brown clay and etched with a fine pattern in red. She poured a little of the clear yellow oil into her hands, watching it pool between her fingers. Armand took the flask from her and corked it, so she had both hands free to touch him. He watched her intently as she reached for him.

His cock was erect before her, springing eagerly from a tangle of vigorous black curls. His manhood was brown like the rest of his body. A layer of purplish veins grew over his penis, like ivy over the trunk of a tree. As she smoothed one lubricated hand after the other down his fine shaft, she felt the warm hard mass pulse in her hands. Armand's smooth brown cock was a warm and delicious thing to get acquainted with. It was friendly and whole-some, and his balls lay in their nest of dark curls like two brown eggs.

Justine's hands slid to the base of his cock and burrowed into the hair at the bottom of it. Sunlight gleamed on her hands as the oil darkened his pubic hair. She gently cupped his balls and worked the oil around them, then slid her hands back to brush the opening of his anus. He drew in his breath sharply and caught both her hands in his. His eyes were savage with lust. 'Come away from there, temptress.'

She looked at him teasingly, 'But I like to caress you so.'

His eyes grew larger and blacker, 'And I like you to do it. But this lovemaking session is for your pleasure,

Justine.' His hands slid over her oiled breast and belly as he spoke and came to rest in the dark 'v' of her mons. She felt as if she could fall into the infinite regard of his black eyes and drown. His soft voice continued, 'This time I want to be special for you, Justine. I want you to lie back and relax and allow me to pleasure you.' Strong oily fingers parted the folds of her labia and Justine tipped her head back and sighed deeply in ecstasy as she looked up at him. She longed for him to continue, to touch her just in the heart of her pleasure and bring her to the climax that she felt was so close.

Instead, his eyes stern, Armand pinched her clitoris in a hard oily grip between two fingers. The first pinch hurt and she shuddered all over and cried out. Then she felt those strong merciless fingers pinch her again, and this time the feelings were good. Her whole body drew itself up and her legs parted expectantly. She knelt in front of him, gazing into his slitted eyes, trembling and longing for a third hard pinch on her clitoris, the one that would take her to heaven.

But Armand, wicked, knowing, teasing, looked at her steadily as he took his hands away and laughed his deep chuckle once more. She arched her back and tried to push closer to him, trying to get their bodies to touch as closely as their eyes were meeting. 'Minx!' he said laughing, still holding her gaze. 'Back down on all fours then, and I'll see about satisfying you – but in the way that I yearn to have you.'

Obediently, Justine fell forward again. She rested her weight on her elbows and shuddered all over as Armand went behind her. He spread her knees open with a hand that might have come straight out of a furnace so hot did its touch burn. She was kneeling with her bottom pointing up into the air and her legs spread open in a blatant invitation that felt wicked and shameless even while it felt good. She could feel the weight of the sunshine on the dark hairy purse of her sex that was so unused to such exposure. Her vagina opened and shut deep within her. But with a trembling sick fear she knew that it would not feel the satisfaction of a male member inside it, not yet anyway; this time Armand had different ideas.

The tip of his penis was nudging now at the pink oyster of her anal opening. She was not resisting him, but still her back passage was tight and closed to him. A fresh splash of oil hit her sensitive skin, and she felt Armand take time to massage it into her aching and longing labia before returning to lubricate her tightly muscled anus. With so much more oil sliding over her bottom, he was now able to slide his glans inside her. Justine felt broached, invaded, and she cried out loud, although she hardly knew what she wanted to say. Armand stopped pushing at once and reached his hands around to her front, tangling them in her pubic curls, tickling at her clitoris. He stimulated her until she shuddered all over and bowed before him in total surrender. Then, the hard, inexorable tip of his penis nudged at her anus once more – and this time his iron hard length slipped over the oil and deep up inside her.

The good feelings fled. Justine tensed and shivered all over. Armand held still until she relaxed, then moved the oiled slippery perfection of his cock gently in her anal passage. As Justine slowly became used to the feel of his hard cock thrusting deep into the portal of her soul, pleasure returned. His fingers beat lightly over her clitoris, and pleasure deepened within her. Different pleasure. A deeper, richer more significant pleasure took hold of her now. Justine's body relaxed and decided to allow Armand to invade her in this perverse manner. She groaned and moved softly against him, encouraging him to fuck her as he would.

He had been waiting for this moment and he moved deeper at once. His cock was now fully immersed inside her anal passage and yet she wanted more. His fingers were touching her still, spreading the folds of her labia and brushing lightly, rhythmically against the pink shivering pip of her clitoris. That deeper stranger pleasure was gathering like a storm cloud and Justine felt her body melting and flowing into individual atoms within her.

As she melted, Armand pushed his manhood deeper

inside her. then he took his fingers away from her clitoris and drew out his cock. Justine shuddered and protested. She didn't want him to stop. But he was only rubbing fresh oil over the iron-hard length of his penis. And he was soon ready to re-enter her. When she felt the tip of his cock nudging at her anus, Justine, shyness gone, cried out to him to hurry, hurry, and put it inside her once more.

As she felt the alien, hard, pushing, stretching invading length of his cock inching its way up inside her anus, Justine felt tears come into her eyes because of the celestial significance of this moment. Armand had been right: losing her anal virginity was special. Armand's dear hands went unerringly to the spot that craved for him and her clitoris exploded under his onslaught. Justine began to gyrate her hips to increase the pleasure that was now taking over. His cock plunged inexorably home while two fingers darted into her vagina and the other hand stimulated her clitoris.

She couldn't stop now! She would kill anyone who tried to stop her now. Armand's massive cock filled her back passage with a glorious invasion that was tipping her over the edge of reason and into sublime insanity. His touch was sweet as it stimulated the more accustomed pleasures of her vagina. And his fingers, his strong commanding fingers, held her clitoris tightly now, increasing the pressure as her pleasure grew.

He rammed into her. His thighs slapped into her buttocks. She wanted him to do it harder. She wanted him to continue sinking his prick into the strange unexplored depths of her anus – because she had never felt such raging, sweating, sweet-breasted passion as in the orgasm that struck her now. It swept her over the brink just a few seconds before Armand reached his own climax, so that they surfed the swells and breakers of euphoria together. Their melting bodies strained together in a long, sweaty, celestial series of orgasmic spasms. Then a deep and wrenching twist somewhere in the very centre of Justine's being let her off the hook of carnal desire. She felt glorious sweet release as her sexual tension discharged. Her body opened and exploded, bursting wide open like a dandelion clock, drifting in a sweet feathery cloud of timeless white bliss before slowing down once more and returning to everyday reality.

Justine inhaled sweet turf and heard the lulling babble of the river. Armand's heavy body lay across her back, stuck to her body with oil and sweat. She wriggled slightly in protest and he took his weight on his arms to relieve her. Justine shivered and cried out as his penis shrank inside her. 'Are you hurt?' asked Armand at once.

'No, indeed not. But it feels so strange inside me there.'

'Let me hold you so, and I will come out of you gently.' Armand guided his softening, but still large, penis out of her anus and Justine shivered all over as he left her. Armand smiled into her eyes as he gathered her up in his arms, wrapping her up in a sweet protective embrace. Justine met his eyes then snuggled into his chest. She could feel his heart beating fast below her and sweat gleamed on his skin. He stroked her face with a gentle and loving touch, over and over. Her body was limp and relaxed. She lay purring in the sun, considering the strange new feelings that softened and tingled inside her newly broached anus. Armand continued to stroke her lovingly, until the running babbling noise of the river, and his gentle soothing, just lifted her over the borders of consciousness, into the sweetness of a daytime sleep.

Chapter Five

Nearly a week later, a scratching noise woke Justine in the middle of the night. She sat up in bed and looked around her. The room was well lit by the fire that crackled in the stone fireplace. The big stone tower room was quiet. The other three beds were empty. Justine guessed that the maids were still dallying with their young men. She didn't hear the noise again. It must have been a mouse; there were many of them in this rambling sloppy castle.

She snuggled back under the pink feather counterpane, thinking to sleep once more. But she was wide awake, so she sat up and thumped the hard white pillow before lying back in the brass-railed four-poster. The bed she had been given was typical of Castle Waldgraf: it was warm and comfortable, but it sagged badly under the frowsty feather mattress and each of its brass rails was out of kilter. And she was still waiting for the new bedding she had been promised.

The housekeeper was not delaying from meanness, but from indolence. A careless generosity ran through the domestic arrangements at the castle that was a perpetual wonder to Justine, used as she was to the convent's spare austerity. Take the fire for example: so long as the girls carried the fuel up themselves, no one seemed to object to four lowly maids keeping a fire burning non-stop. And how nice the warmth was. Justine stared into the fire sleepily, enjoying the light from the dancing flames as much as the warmth, which was rather swallowed up by the vast stone room. Generations of maids had sneaked in layers of tattered velvet curtains and purloined dusty rugs to warm and decorate the room, but it was still a forbidding apartment.

No one seemed to care much what one did. Justine had slept alone in the room since she arrived. Her roommates darted in, thrown off their starched aprons and then darted out again like gaudy dragonflies, all in their finery to impress the men with. It was very strange, and Justine felt almost, but not quite, homesick for the chilly order of the convent.

She heard the scratching noise again. Not a mouse, but something at the window. An owl, perhaps, or a bat? The tower, one of the many that loomed out of the castle's walled enclosure, was a soaring spike-topped edifice that offered a smooth and faceless exterior to the world. Nothing human could be out there. Justine picked up a tattered red velvet shawl and wrapped it around her shoulders before jumping out of bed and pattering across the floor on bare feet. Perhaps some poor creature was battering at the window, attracted by the gleam from the fire.

The window was high above her head, so she dragged a black wooden chair beneath it and stood on it to reach the window. A dark demon's face grimaced at her through the blurred diamond panes of the window. She gave a little shriek and stepped back, but a voice hissed above her, 'Justine! It is I – Armand. Let me in!'

'Armand?' A heavy iron latch closed the window tight. She had to exert all her strength to open it. She heard scratching noises on the stone, then Armand's face reappeared around the thick green glass, his eyes full of mischief as they met hers. He swung himself in through the opening and knelt on the broad windowsill.

'At least this window is bigger than the last one you and I negotiated together.' He fumbled around his waist area and Justine saw that he was unwinding a rope that had been knotted into a harness.

'How did you get in here?' she asked, thinking of the terrible drop and the vicious rocks beneath. 'No one could climb up these sheer walls. I do not believe even you could do so.'

His eyes sparkled again. 'Indeed I could not. No, I merely let myself down from the top of the tower by means of this rope.'

'But the guards! They would kill you!'

His smile only grew wider. 'They have to spot me first and, let's face it, Justine, discipline is not of the highest in this place. It is lucky that I am not the enemy, for I think I could have sneaked six elephants in with me, had I a mind to.'

'Armand! You risked your life – or the mines, which are worse. Dear God, they have been telling me such stories of that wretched place – oh! How can you laugh so!'

'If I smile it is because I am so happy to see you again. Dear Justine. You are even more beautiful than I remembered. I like you in that flowing nightgown thing; and your hair becomes you vastly in that braid.'

'Come by the fire,' said Justine awkwardly, shrinking from his admiring look. A breath of cold fresh air came in with him as Armand jumped down from the window ledge and followed her over to the fire. The best of the rugs lay before it. Justine and Armand sat down on it facing each other. His eyes never left her face, and she looked down and smoothed the rug's silky surface with her hand. 'Is it not beautiful?' she inquired. 'It is such a deep green and the roses so lifelike.'

Armand was smiling at her, but his eyes were kind. 'If you like it then I like it. You shall have ten in our home if you wish it. That is, if you will come with me, Justine.' Her mouth fell open as she stared at him with astonished pure eyes.

'Would you be so sorry to leave the castle?' he asked.

'Why no ... only I had no thought of such a thing. Indeed, it is very strange here and I do not think I like it at

71

all ... but I had never dreamt ... I thought this was to be my life now ...' She trailed off in bewilderment. Her heart was beating hard and her knees shook. Armand! Armand wanted her! She had not stopped thinking about him since the moment he had deposited her at the entrance to the great castle and ridden off down the rutted track that led back to the village. She had felt cold and bereft as she watched him go, and she felt warm and fulfilled now that he was back with her – had risked death to be with her for, indolent as the guards were, in this time of war they would shoot first and ask questions later, of that there was no doubt.

'I have quite taken you by surprise,' said Armand easily, smiling at her. 'Tell me, are we likely to be disturbed here?'

'I think not, and even if anyone comes back, it makes no matter. They think me very strange for choosing to take no lover and will probably encourage me now that I have one.'

'Choosing to take no lover. I am very pleased to hear that. But why, Justine? You are a beautiful healthy woman. Why do you not wish to take a lover?' His eyes told her that he really wanted an answer.

Justine felt hot blood in her cheeks and hers was almost the voice of a child as she whispered. 'I went to confession after I arrived here, and the priest said that what you and I did was very wrong, and that I must never make love again, except with my husband.' Then she paused. She owed him the deeper truth, the truth that lay in her heart and meant even more than the priest's strictures. 'I did not think to ever see you again, but your memory was so sweet that I could not bear to let another man touch me where you had touched me. There was no one I wanted. No one but you.'

Armand looked at her with dizzying tenderness in his dark eyes. He was different tonight. His bandit stubble was gone, revealing a strong jaw with a cleft in the chin. She felt the silk of his white shirt slide over her cheek as he pulled her to him, and the throb of his heart beating under his leather jerkin. 'Dear Justine,' he said softly. 'It makes

72

me so happy to hear that. Perhaps, then, you will not mind leaving your books and the great libraries of Castle Wald-graf to throw in your lot with a poor gipsy. I was almost afraid to try my luck, your eyes shone so excitedly when you told me what was to be your future.'

'I have not so much as seen a book yet,' said Justine sadly. 'The library is run by a mad friar, who guards the books as if they were his, and he thinks that women who read are an abomination against the Lord. Perhaps in time I might win him over, but there is no weight on my side. The children think books are the devil and so does their tutor.'

'Tutor? I thought you were to have the teaching of them.'

'So did I. But I was sent for only to chaperone the girls, and they wish to learn nothing. Both they and the boys run wild, and their parents encourage it.'

'So you will not be too sad to leave?'

Justine turned to him eagerly, tilting her head to look at his strong handsome face in the firelight. 'Oh, Armand. I was trying to make the best of it, since it was to be, but I cannot tell you how happy I am that you came.'

He tipped his head down and touched her face with gentle fingers. His eyes were loving. He gave her soft butterfly kisses with his eyelashes. Then he drew back and waited an interminable time, looking at her as if he were memorising every pore on her face, before leaning slowly towards her, whispering the words in a soft voice, 'So you'll come with me?'

'Indeed I will.'

Their lips met in a long, sweet passion. Justine felt the rightness and charm of their kiss. He was her natural partner. It had been written in the stars so. She was content with her fate, more than content. He broke the contact of their lips, but only to look at her tenderly and say, 'Come then, there will be plenty of time for kissing later. Let us quit this place before someone discovers us. Have you any belongings to pack?'

'No. I have been given some clothes, but only one outfit. I will change into it now.' Justine leant forward, unable to

73

resist giving Armand another kiss on his sweet curving mouth. 'It's a pity I will have no fine clothes to meet the priest in, but I will not mind that, for I am marrying you.'

She felt Armand stiffen beneath her lips, and a cold premonition gripped her belly. How could she have thought his lips sweet or his eyes soft? A hard and vicious stranger turned cruel eyes upon her. 'Priest, Justine? I mentioned no priest.'

'But you asked me to come with you. Surely you meant . . .'

His eyes were burning straight into her soul. 'I am a gipsy, I told you that. What have I to do with Popish cant? The church is nothing to me, Justine. Nothing to me or my kind. If it pleases you, we shall wed in the manner of my own people. You shall have a fine gipsy wedding and I will take you publicly to be my bride. But you must be satisfied with that. Is that not enough for you?'

'But our immortal souls . . .' said Justine slowly, looking at him in agony. 'We shall burn in the flames of hell for all time if we commit such a sin.'

'Dear God, how they have brainwashed you. Justine, it is all a fairy tale to keep the peasants good. You will not see the fine lords and ladies abiding by the rules of the church, no, nor free-thinking gipsies, neither.'

Armand removed his protective arms and Justine sat cold and shuddering by the fire. Torn by her feelings. She loathed the castle. As soon as Armand had offered her an escape route her whole being had cried out to take it. She wanted to be free of its lazy corruption. But her interview with the travelling priest was still strong in her mind. Only yesterday he had offered to hear the confession of any who wished it. Most people refused, preferring to take their peccadilloes to the mumbling priest of the castle, who had long ago succumbed to the pervasive decline of Waldgraf. But Justine had liked the traveller's strong honest face, and so she had gone to him. She had not mentioned Father Gabriel, nor the fact that Armand had taken her most unnatural virginity from her. Still, she had told him enough

74

to make him frown and spend a long time lecturing her. He had been persuasive, and his voice was still in her ears.

But she loved Armand. Justine wrapped her arms around her knees and bent her head on them. She began to rock backward and forward unconsciously as she sat there, a huddled pool of misery on the moss-green carpet with its fine pink roses. She could not see Armand's face above her, so she did not know that it softened greatly as he looked down on her, nor could she know that he planned to bind her to him with the strength of his passion. She could only hear the hard note in his voice. 'Justine, I did not risk my life for nothing. I wish to make love to you again before I go, whether you will or no.'

'Armand, I may not,' said Justine in a low voice. 'My act of contrition would mean nothing if I were to again commit the same carnal sins with you.'

His eyes were tender, but determined. 'Then let us find new erotic sins to enjoy – I can think of one that would take you to heaven.'

She stretched trembling hands out to him, her delicate gestures pleading with him to understand. Tears stung her eyes. 'Tease me not,' she begged. 'It is not that I do not desire you for I do, believe me, Armand. My body blazes and hungers for you in a way that is entirely new to me. But if I wilfully and knowingly make love to you then it will be a sin and we shall be damned for it.' She finished on a choking sob.

'You shall be damned for it, not I, for I do not believe in such nonsense,' said Armand, his eyes fierce. The fire crackled as a lump of coal fell and they both jumped. Justine fumbled for the coal tongs through a blaze of tears, but a strong hand took them from her and mended the fire. Iron claws caught at her throat. He was so strong and yet so considerate. She loved him so dearly, yet her whole life had trained her to put what was right above her own wishes. It was the hardest test she had ever faced.

'I must not do what I know to be wrong,' she said, voicing her thoughts. Armand looked hard at her face, and there was respect in his eyes: respect for her integrity, and sadness because she was rejecting him. He turned away slowly and Justine knew he had accepted her decision. Fresh tears shook her. The sad droop to his shoulders as he walked towards the window darted to her heart and pierced it like an arrow. She put both hands up to her mouth and bit her knuckles fiercely. She wanted to make him happy, but he was suffering because of her. It was a heavy load to bear.

Then Armand spun on his heel and turned to her with a wicked grin springing to his lips. His eyes raked her body. 'You may not do what you know to be wrong,' he said thoughtfully, 'but I may do what I know to be right, and if I force you ... Ah, Justine. If I take you against your will, then you will commit no sin. I will do it all. Let me take the sin for you.'

'I cannot allow you to do that,' said Justine sadly.

Armand's smile grew broader and his face more determined. 'I don't think you heard what I said. I will commit the sin for you. You have no say in the matter.'

Justine backed away from him, holding her hands out. The red velvet shawl fell to the ground as she did so. 'Please, Armand. You must leave now, I command it.'

He took a few paces closer, and the size and bulk and power of his masculinity impinged on Justine as if for the first time. His eyes met hers with a physical force. She was breathless suddenly. Her chest felt tight and it was hard to breathe. She fell back one step, and then another. Implacably, he followed. Her knees shook and trembled beneath her in the most traitorous way. She fell back two more steps and she was pressed against the rough stone wall of the tower room. Armand stooped and picked up the shawl. Something about the dark expression in his eyes warned her, and she turned and fled just as he lunged for her, holding the shawl like a fishing net he would entangle her in.

Justine's bare feet touched first the softness of a rug, then the coldness of the stone floor, then the tickling pile of another rug as she scurried around the room trying to escape her tall dark hunter. Her breath came in sobs and

76

seemed to catch in her throat before passing over her lips. Adrenaline hummed through her nerves as her body geared itself up for flight, flight from the deadly menace that pursued her so closely.

She felt the wind of his passing several times, but she twisted and darted around the room so fast that he could never quite catch her. She leapt over the battered dark wood furniture and trampled on the four-poster beds as she fled. But he was always behind her. Always a few steps away. She knew she could not outrun him, so she tried to break for the door.

But he was there before her, and Justine felt the soft folds of the red velvet shawl float down over her head and engulf her. Armand held her tight. She could hear him panting and feel his heart beating hard. She was panting too, and a fine sweat dewed her skin. For a few moments they stood so together, then, still with the shawl over her head, muffling her hearing and cutting off her vision, Armand pulled her across the room.

'I think this is your bed,' he said, in a low intimate voice, 'because no trinkets adorn it and no clothes hang from the rails; except for one very ugly grey dress which must be for the governess, and, much better than that, a supply of black stockings. They are also very ugly and very thick, not at all the type of garment that should deface a body as lovely as yours, Justine, but they are perfect for what I have in mind.'

He threw her on to the bed. Justine lay winded for a second, but then as she realised that his strong hands no longer gripped her, she wriggled over on to her knees and tried to crawl off the bed and untangle the shawl all at the same time. She had just got out from under the smothering folds when Armand's lazy hand gripped her tiny ankle and his familiar deep chuckle rang out. 'Nice try, angel, but you're no match for me.'

Her mouth was free of the muffling shawl now, so Justine cried out angrily, 'Leave me! Get out or I'll scream and the guards will come and they'll shoot you and I'll be glad – do you hear me? I'll be glad if they shoot you.' She was pulling with all her strength at the solid brown hand that held her ankle so tightly and trying her best to kick herself free, but she could not. He was so strong. It was as if she were trying to break a hole in the castle walls with her soft bare hands. She could make no impression on him.

He chuckled again. But he obviously took seriously her threat to scream for he let go of her ankle and moved towards her, staring intently into her eyes. His dark body pounced on hers. He pushed her back on to the bed firmly, lying on top of her, pinning her with the weight of his body and the passion in his eyes.

Justine fought as hard as she could, but lying on her back with the silk hardness of his chest holding her down, she was at a terrible disadvantage. Her flowing white nightgown was hampering her movements, the billowing sleeves got in the way, and the skirts were rucked up around her waist in a manner that meant her naked sex was pushing against Armand's trousered legs in a way that was disturbingly erotic.

Armand had both her hands imprisoned in one of his strong ones now. She felt his other hand pushing through her long hair. She struggled harder, trying to read his expression. Then she went still with surprise as she tasted thick cloth in her mouth. Armand was wrapping one of the long black governess's stockings around the back of her head and across her open mouth. He gagged her tightly. Then he took one of the black stockings and began to twist it around her wrists. He was binding her fast so that he could have his way with her, to use her sexually. Once she was tied fast, she would be helpless to stop him whatever he did.

Primitive terror swept over her and she kicked out wildly with her remaining free leg. Armand held her down easily. She glared at him with as much hostility as she had ever felt for a mortal man. But he seemed not to mind; his eyes danced as he bent to kiss her nose. Then he turned around, still keeping his weight on top of her, so that he was sitting with the back of his leather jerkin towards her face and he was looking at her legs – and her exposed sex.

Justine shuddered and moaned, or tried to, but the thick gag muffled her voice and she felt powerless. She should have screamed earlier. She should not have waited and warned him and played silly chasing games. She should have screamed her head off and had the guards shoot him. And then a gentle finger probed the seeping wetness that was spilling out from the silky opening that nestled in the dark curling hair of her bush, and she knew that she could never have brought the guards to Armand. If he untied her gag now, she suspected that she would not scream, unless it were in pleasure, and she blessed the muffling folds that took the decision away from her.

Armand's finger left her secret area after only the lightest and briefest of touches. Justine shivered and lay waiting for his next move as his hands slid down her leg. He moved so slowly, stroking, petting, tickling and stroking again. Her sensitive skin responded eagerly to him as if her body knew that the man who had captured her was her soul mate not her jailer. When his caresses reached her ankle, Armand shifted his weight further down the bed and took hold of her leg firmly, pulling it towards the other brass rail of the bed. Freed of his weight from her upper body, Justine sat up and flung her body first to one side then the other. It was impossible to stop him however, and he continued with his leisurely manipulation of her leg, bending to kiss her bare skin before taking the ankle in capable firm hands and tying it to the brass rail while Justine shivered and melted below him.

Armand was not satisfied with the way he had her tied. He took a feather pillow from the head of the bed and inserted it under Justine's bottom, pushing her pubic bone up and open, exposing her sexual organs, before retying the long black stockings around each ankle, so that he now had her spread open just as he wanted her.

She thought she must be feeling the firelight on the exposed lips of her labia so hot did they burn as she lay helpless on her back in the big bed. The pillow that tipped her up at such a saucy angle felt firm and unyielding in the small of her back. She pulled experimentally on first one leg and then the other. She was held fast. Armand looked down on her with soft dark eyes. Why did he smile at her so? Justine tried to turn her head away and hate him, but again, she felt that soft, exploratory finger dabbling in the wet openness of her vagina, and she knew, that he knew, that she liked his domination over her.

She relaxed back on the bed in mingled despair and ecstasy. Armand kissed her right leg slowly, slowly, all the way up to the top of her inner thigh. Her secret mind screamed at him not to stop, to carry on and invade the dark velvet flower of passion that was blooming so sweetly between her legs. But he took his mouth away and moved to stand above her, looking at her as she lay spread-eagled, helpless below him. Fresh shivers began in Justine's belly and quim.

Pausing only to press savage sweet kisses on her inner wrist Armand leant forward to kiss her belly. Then he stepped back to admire his fair victim. Justine shivered and shook and tugged uselessly at her bonds. The thick heavy stockings were as strong as any rope. She was bound fast and helpless. Armand bent over her and her body tensed. She wished her sex were not so open and exposed. If only he would pull the nightgown down so that it covered her more modestly. She would not mind what he did to her under the nightgown, but her exposure unsettled her horribly.

She felt Armand take hold of the filmy white garment and for a moment she thought he had read her mind and was going to cover her up. She relaxed very slightly, anticipating the touch of cloth covering her gently, so it was a severe shock when she felt him take hold of the thin white cotton and pull the fabric hard. She heard the fabric rip and tried to protest, but her gasps were muffled by the gag. The fraying ripped pieces of her nightgown tickled her body as Armand lifted them apart and then ripped the gown again under each armpit so that he could pull every scrap of torn fabric away from her now completely naked body.

Justine tried to be angry, but her nipples crinkled in a

rush of pleasure that betrayed her true feelings. Her heart fluttered like a captive bird and she melted inside her pleasure centre as Armand touched first one nipple, then the other, circling them with a maddeningly light touch. 'Now you look wonderful,' he told her, adoration sweet in his eyes. 'Now I can see your perfect pale body with the dark lines of your bonds framing your celestial beauty.'

She was still angry with him but she desired him with a fierce and burning passion. She melted with love at the tender admiration she saw in his eyes. Passions warred within her. She didn't know what to feel. But at least she did not have the worry of finding an answer for him – the gag held her silent.

Still looking at her with almost reverent admiration, Armand took a slow step towards the bed. Justine shook and desired him, longed for him to come near her and touch her and fuck her and release her from the need that was building within her, and at the same time she wanted him to go away and never to see him again. Unable to speak, unable to move her legs or arms, Justine tossed her head wildly on the pillow, not knowing what she was trying to express to the tormenting lover who was approaching her bed.

Then the door behind Armand banged, and she went cold. Sheets of ice slid down over her neck and her spine and her belly. But the dark mound between her spread open legs burned, and the glistening nerve endings of the folds of her vulva scorched with the intensity of her fear. Someone had come in, and that someone would see her, spread open and shameless, with visible proof of her excitement glistening at the entrance of her open vagina.

'Dear Lord, what do we have here?' asked a lazy, laughing voice and Justine knew that the oldest maid, Katrina, had come back unexpectedly from her tryst with the second footman. She tensed and shivered all over, waiting for Armand to cover her exposed nakedness. To feel the feathery touch of a sheet or shawl as he hid her shame from the sleazy knowing glance of the older girl. But she felt nothing. Only heard Katrina move closer to the end of the bed. Shame poured over Justine and she closed her eyes tight, only praying that the woman would go away quickly.

The pause that followed stretched out until Justine thought she would break apart from the tension that sawed through her. But when Katrina spoke, her words were worse than the silence: 'So this is why she would have none of our fine castle men – and I do not say that I can blame her. Why, to be taken so has always been one of my favourite fantasies.' Katrina's voice took on a caressing note, 'And I'm sure that a fine, handsome, big man such as yourself could easily make two women happy at one time?'

Justine's eyes flew open and she glared at the plump blowsy red-head with real hatred. If Armand were to be taken in by her flirtatious ways . . . and then she relaxed as she heard him saying, 'Another time I'd be glad to, but time is what I don't have. I must be away long before daybreak, so I think I must confine myself to the job at hand.'

'Am I to be denied any part in the fun?'

'Why no. If you've a mind to fondle my fair victim, it would make a beautiful tableau: Justine so spread and helpless, writhing under the lips and caresses of a flame-haired beauty like yourself.'

Katrina tossed her head and brindled under Armand's words. But Justine shuddered. Even the sensual Katrina would never do such a thing, she thought frantically, lifting her head as high as it could go from the pillow and trying to read the expression on the red-head's face. Katrina licked her lips and winked at Armand. 'She is a tempting sight,' agreed the maid in a suddenly husky voice, 'I fancied her when I first saw her.' She moved over to the bed and Justine felt it creak as Katrina lowered her weight on to it.

'Don't let her orgasm,' warned Armand urgently. 'You may tease her and arouse her as much as you wish, but I want to control the moment of her climax.'

'I wish you would control mine too,' murmured Katrina, tossing her copper ringlets over one shoulder and pouting at Armand with her full red lips. Armand laughed and shook his head.

'Not this time. You must make the most of what you may.'

Katrina shrugged, and then turned her attention to Justine. She began to lean forward slowly keeping her eyes on Justine's beautiful face, so pale in the clouds of chestnut hair, and so white against the vivid black strip that bound her mouth closed. Then she plunged her hands into the cloud of Justine's hair and untied the gag. Justine's mouth worked as she tried to relieve the stiffness and get some saliva back into it. She was almost sorry that Katrina had freed her mouth. Should she scream? Did she want to scream? The older woman looked at her thoughtfully. "Tis Peterkin's watch tonight,' she said absently. 'If you were to call him he would love to join in. I can vouch for his tastes.'

Justine's belly gave a great plunge, as if she were looking over the side of a steep cliff, and she began to shiver again. She would not scream. She was glad that she did not have to. Perverse as her situation was, she did not wish to relinquish it. She would lie still and take whatever wicked pleasure Armand and Katrina had planned for her. She saw Katrina's face blurring as it got larger and closer to hers. Katrina moved her whole body closer, too, as she leant over Justine, and Justine heard the silk of the tawdry pink gown rustling and felt it slip coldly over her naked skin as the buxom red-head leant closer and lower over her. Justine turned her head to one side, but Katrina caught her and brought Justine's head back, so that Justine had to lie there and watch the plump red lips and the slight overbite get closer and closer to her own trembling mouth. She shut her eyes just as their lips touched.

Justine was surprised by the sweet cool firmness of Katrina's lips. They were so different from the plundering hardness of a male's mouth. Her own lips shivered. The sensation of kissing a woman was not unpleasant, but as a tiny pointed tongue forced itself into her mouth, she jerked back as if bee-stung in a reflex movement she could not stop. Katrina did not seem offended. She pulled back and laughed, her plump breasts swelling out of the low-cut ruffles of the pink silk gown as she did so. It was like being kissed by a large piece of Turkish delight, thought Justine. Katrina was plump, sweet, and somehow sickly and cloying. Despite her smooth, fragrantly powdered white skin and her burnished copper curls she was not wholesome, but she was exotic and desirable in her own way.

Katrina laughed again and moved lower across Justine's body, taking Justine's breasts one in each hand. Justine did not know what to make of the sensations that raged there until, turning her head to one side, she saw Armand. He was sitting on the carved wooden chest by the side of the bed, intent on watching Justine and her reactions. As soon as Justine saw the way that he watched her so closely, pleasure ripped through her.

Unwilling still to admit how erotic she found her position, Justine choked back the cry that rose to her lips. But she felt it shivering and coursing through her body. Katrina continued to massage her breasts and to flick the nipples with a teasing finger. It felt so good that it almost hurt. And when the copper head bent over her breasts and took first one and then the other nipple into those plump lips, Justine abandoned herself to the divine pleasures that were sweeping over her.

For a long, long, soft time, that somehow passed in a second of sharp pleasure, Justine writhed beneath the mumbling sucking lips of the maid as they wet her flesh and ignited her pleasure. Her head thrashed on the pillows and her body trembled inside its bonds, but she was held fast. And now Justine discovered that the feeling of being held down, of being helpless before the onslaughts of pleasure that swept over her, was contributing to her bliss. Every time she pulled against the bonds that held her so tightly, the strength of her sexual response intensified. And then, just as she was trying to assimilate this new discovery about herself, Katrina moved.

Exquisitely slowly, Katrina kissed her way down the pale mound of Justine's belly and headed for her woman's place. As Katrina's plump red lips mouthed playfully at the first dark pubic curl, Justine's eyes flew open and she looked at Armand again. He was leaning forward to see all that was happening, looking first at Justine's sex, then at her face, his eyes dark with interest and passion. She shuddered and felt helpless before him. His eyes seemed to burn into hers as he orchestrated what was happening to her. A violently pleasant sensation between her legs drew her attention to Katrina once more.

The plump red-head had slipped a fat finger into Justine's wet vagina and out again. Then she used the fluid-coated finger to rub around the lips of Justine's vulva. It felt shiveringly good and Justine felt a whirlpool of aching pleasure begin to take her over. Even the backs of her knees were shaking. She pressed her whole body down hard into the bed and rejoiced in the bonds that kept her legs so embarrassingly spread wide open, because they added to her pleasure.

Plump knowing fingers now spread Justine's labial lips open wide so that her clitoris popped trembling out of its protective hood. Katrina didn't touch the clitoris – at first. Justine felt the lips of her labia pulled even wider open, then rotated gently so that the pressure of the moving skin stimulated her clitoris in a gentle, distant, far-off way that brought the imperative need of her orgasm closer and closer towards her. Katrina then stopped her movements and paused, holding the skin stretched open tight. Justine lay shivering and melting and feeling electric jags of shame and pleasure race around her as she alternately enjoyed the great pleasure that no one could resist and then remembered that Armand, cool, remote and untouched by any pleasure of his own, was watching her closely.

Katrina kept her hands still and then bent her head to lap like a little cat at the quivering red nub of Justine's clitoris. Her tongue was like wet velvet and it touched Justine's clit the way only another woman's tongue could: with precise and knowing intent.

Katrina drew back once more and waited. Even though the woman was not moving, Justine's pleasure grew. The feel of the fingers holding her open, the faint touch of hot breath on her so sensitive clitoris, the bonds that pulled her open, and Armand's intent gaze – Justine's awareness of all these factors increased her enjoyment of the position she was in, even though part of her burned in shame for the wickedness of her body's delightful responses. When Katrina bent her head once more to lick around her clitoris in that sinful knowing way, Justine knew that she was on the edge of an explosion that could not be stopped – and Armand saw it too, for he cried 'Stop!'

Katrina obeyed him, jumping off the bed in a frou-frou of pink flounces and running over to his side. 'I could do the same for you,' she suggested. 'I know exactly how to please a man with my lips and my tongue.'

Armand smiled and drew her to one side, talking to her so quietly that Justine could not hear. She lay naked and open on the bed, feeling fine tremors shaking her body and clutching at the muscles of her velvet tunnel. She had been left right on the brink of orgasm. She longed for the movement, the feeling, the final touch that would send her over the brink and release her. She could feel the coarse sheets of the bed rumpling under her sweating back. Her sexual organs seemed to have grown, so enormous did they feel, lying between her spread open legs and pointing wetly at the fire. Her breasts ached fiercely at one moment and jellified the next as she longed and longed for Armand to touch them – and wanting Armand so badly after he had treated her so was her final confusion. She should hate him for ever, but she was lying naked and ready, oozing out love juices and longing for the feel of his manhood.

She heard Katrina laugh. The sound sent chills down her spine as she imagined her leading Armand off to some pleasure corner and them leaving her, bound and helpless on the bed, vulnerable to whoever might come in next and find her. She was miserable when she heard the door bang, but when she heard slow footsteps approaching and knew that Armand was coming towards the bed she felt no better.

He came to a stop next to the bed, and Justine looked up

at him. Velvety dark smudges passed over Armand's face, shadows from the flames dancing in the grate. He stood regarding her for a moment longer, then unbuttoned his leather jerkin. He took off his fine leather boots next, and then his dark leggings. His silk shirt billowed with his movements and he made an impatient moue and threw it off. He unbuckled his belt carefully. Justine saw that he carried no heavy pistol, but a razor-sharp knife. He placed the belt so that he could reach the knife quickly from the bed, and then, completely naked, he smiled at Justine.

'Ready for me, little sinner?' he asked, affection darkening his eyes.

She turned her head on the pillow with an impatient movement. 'I'll never be ready for you,' she spat. His fingers found her secret entrance once more and dabbled in the silky wetness. They were stroking her up to ecstasy so effortlessly that her body tried to double up with pleasure, but could not for the bonds that held it.

'Your body tells me one thing and your mouth another,' laughed Armand. Helpless, she gazed into his eyes. Justine felt his weight shift on the bed as he moved closer to her. He buried both hands in the clouds of her hair and held her tenderly. 'Never mind, little princess,' he said, bestowing soft, feather-light kisses on her lips, her cheeks, her neck. His eyes were tender in the half light. 'Never mind about anything, now. Listen only to your body and let me take control of that. I shall be the musician who plays a rare and valuable instrument.'

Justine felt tears come to her eyes. She didn't know why. She couldn't name the emotion that swept her. 'Armand,' she whispered, but then fell silent, because she didn't know what she wanted to say to him.

He kissed the tears that clung to her lashes. 'More precious than diamonds,' he whispered, looking at her with love. Justine tried to lift her body off the bed, to snuggle closer to him, but he pushed her back down. 'Lie still,' he said, gently but firmly. 'Let go your struggles and give in to me, Justine. You will find great peace in doing so.' His eyes commanded her, and she obeyed.

It did feel good to let go. Justine let her whole body relax into the bed. The bonds held her with her legs wide open. The pillow tilted up her pubic bone, spreading her sexual secrets bare. Her arms, too, were held down by the black straps. All she had to do was accept the erotic pleasures that Armand was submitting her to.

Her lips quivered as he kissed them tenderly. She kissed him back and felt his lips smiling on hers. He kissed along the line of each lip slowly, tenderly, covering every nerve cell. He ran delicate fingers over the line of her throat and into the sensitive hollows under her ears. All Justine's sexual need returned and she longed for the touch of his hard manhood inside her – but he made her wait.

The fire burned lower and lower in the grate while Armand kissed and licked and sucked Justine's firm young breasts. He never seemed to tire of their taste in his mouth, of the feel of her nipples melting on his tongue. He kneaded her sweet curves with both hands while his head went from first one crinkled chestnut nipple to the other one; and Justine groaned and writhed on the big feather pillows of the four-poster bed. An aeon had gone by before he was satisfied that he had kissed her breasts enough. Justine gasped and shuddered as she felt his heavy body moving lower, lower towards the dark curls of her bush.

It was torment not to be able to move. Once again she tugged uselessly at the strips of black that held her tight. Armand curled himself over her pubic area so that he could look easily into her spread open sex while he touched and explored with both hands. Justine longed to move so that he could not probe her woman's place so minutely – but she was held fast and could not stop him.

She felt his hands curling and tugging at the pubic curls that grew so lushly between her legs. They were wet, wet with the love dew that was trickling down her scented dark vagina. Justine moaned and thrust her hips up at him, twisting and corkscrewing them in a blatantly sexual invitation, inviting him to fuck her, to plug her aching need. But Armand ignored her embarrassingly frank urging and continued his leisurely exploration of her glistening orchid-like organs. His fingers left delicious trails of fire as they ran over the silky wet skin.

As Armand prolonged the moment before he took action, Justine's feelings intensified. The sensitivity of her skin was so magnified that she could have read lines of print from a book through it. Every touch was significant. Every second she was alive. Every movement of Armand's was burned into her memory so that the less she registered with her reason, the more of his lovemaking sank into her soul. His tender movements were full of love. Only a lover could touch a woman's vulva so, with tender care and wicked knowledge that sent Justine helplessly spinning into the realms of the gods. He was stroking the inner lips of her labia now, bending his dark head to kiss and lick where he thought it would please Justine most, taking her to the brink, the very brink of orgasm, and then holding his movements while she shivered and hovered on the edge, before mounting to another plateau of sensation that was always, incredibly, wonderfully, sexually more intense than the one before. She was so transported by the power of the sensations that swept her, she became frightened and begged him to stop, or at least, to release her from this torment.

He bent his dark head so that the firelight gleamed dully on his long black hair and the leather thong that held it out of his way, and took the very heart and nerve centre of her pleasure into his mouth. As his wet lips closed over her clitoris Justine thought she would faint. As his hot tongue began to lick her in the most delectable manner she thought she was fainting. The black mantle of sensations that took her and shook her and spun her into a shuddering gasping spasm were like no ordinary sensations. She cried out as sweat slicked her body and the deep need in her grew, totally unsatisfied by the peak she had just crested.

Armand took his mouth from her clitoris and reached for his knife. The red firelight gleamed on the wicked blade as he slashed the bonds that held her in four quick movements. Justine rolled free into the middle of the bed. She drew up her knees and held her arms open to Armand.

He gave a great cry when he saw her pleading loving face, and Justine felt herself swept up into his arms and her face covered in hot and loving kisses. 'Do you love me?' he demanded urgently, his need reflected plainly in his eyes.

'I love you,' she answered, staring at him openly, kissing him hard, trying to draw him into her, wrapping her arms and legs about his dear body as if she would never let him go.

'Then come away with me,' he begged, love for her blazing forth from his dark eyes. 'For God's sake, leave this ragged blowsy castle and its decadent inhabitants and come with me.'

Justine clung to him harder and cried out in her confusion. 'Oh, Armand. I do love you so. But what am I to do? I promised the priest.' She felt his body change and he looked away. She heard him cursing violently into her hair and the side of her neck. His hands became cruel and he held her so tightly that she nearly screamed. His nails dug into her and she cried again. She shook all over and she was half fainting from the burning sensations that his cruel grip was arousing. It wasn't hurting her: his hard and merciless touch was the touch of a match to gunpowder and Justine ignited and exploded under his savage onslaught.

The fire had died down so far that it was difficult to see his face, and yet the glimpse she caught of his dark expression inflamed her further. Her pale knees lay wide open and as he gripped her thighs with spread and iron fingers she urged him on in a hoarse and unnatural whisper, 'Come inside me! Put your cock in me now, I beg you.'

'Bitch,' he said thickly. 'Why do you beg for me and refuse me at the same time? Do you want to send me insane with your contradictions?' Justine saw tears in his eyes. His corded muscles swelled and flexed. His penis jutted out from his dark pubic area and Justine saw veins knotting the iron-hard length of his manhood. She saw a viscous drop like a tear run from the tip of the glans before Armand placed the end of his penis in the slippery wet entrance to her vagina. 'Say that you will come with me,' he demanded.

Justine's body spoke for her. It twisted and tipped and reached up to suck Armand's cock into the greedy embrace of her velvety dark woman's place and her muscles held him close and massaged him with the strength of their desire for him. He groaned in response and thrust into her in the way she had been preparing for all night. It was what she had been longing for, and shivering for, and waiting for, and it was so good. So much better in reality than in the waiting.

His iron hardness was silky soft and even as the fierce movements of his cock thrust and plunged and invaded her, they loved her and filled her aching need at the same time. Their two naked bodies rocked and cavorted on the bed. They were locked together by the tang of salt on their lips and the sweat that sprang from both their bodies.

His whole soul tried to get closer to hers as they fucked themselves into a long, glorious, thrusting explosion that held them both up in the air somewhere for a very good time before letting them go to drift softly back on to the rumpled feather mattress of the big brass bed.

They lay panting and breathless, sweet and spent. Armand turned to Justine and the tenderness of his movements as he stroked the hot hair from her forehead and gazed deeply into her eyes nearly broke her heart. But her conscience drove her. Although her eyes were huge with the sorrow she was feeling, she had to say to him, 'Armand. I cannot come with you.'

Chapter Six

A week later, Justine was sitting in a wood-panelled window seat in the dusty schoolroom trying not to remember how Armand had looked as he left her. She wished bitterly that she was free to follow him. A diamond tear trickled down her cheek as she thought of him, doomed to burn for ever in the agonising, merciless hell that awaited all sinners and unbelievers.

Yet she had not been to confession since he left. She couldn't bear to hear Armand's lovemaking reviled nor would she call it a sin. Nevertheless her conscience exerted black pressure on her heart. If only she had some work to distract her, but there was nothing for her at the castle. Although the schoolroom was large, it was dusty and unused. A fire burnt in the grate, but no one had been there all day, and Justine was expecting no one. She uncurled her feet from the window seat, pushed aside the dusty curtains and jumped down on to the wide wooden boards. The winter light was fading fast, and she was hungry.

A maid came in and parked a generously laden tray on the crumpled tablecloth that covered the round table nearest to the fire. As usual, there was enough for Justine, the tutor and a regiment of absent children. It seemed to be typical of the careless waste at the castle that no one bothered to enquire how many would be eating. A full tray was sent three times a day but, so far, Justine had eaten alone. The children ran wild, and the tutor encouraged them. Today they were all out hunting. Perhaps she would try again to coax a book away from the zealous care of the monk in the library. If she could charm the children with folktales at bedtime, perhaps she could later persuade them to learn something, and so earn her keep.

Thinking of the indigestion that had troubled her convent-raised system of late, Justine ignored the pig's trotters that bobbed in a tureen full of congealing jelly and setting globules of fat. She chose a slice of fragrant cheese and a piece of fresh bread. She put the silver kettle to boil on the crackling fire while she ate. There was always a generous supply of strong, smoky-smelling China tea in a blue vase with dragons on it. She had never been so physically comfortable in her body, nor so miserable in her mind.

She lost interest in her food after a few bites, and stared miserably into the fire, waiting for the kettle to boil. Shadows were gathering in the corners of the room's high ceiling as the last light of the short winter day faded. Her body felt tense. She got no exercise. The castle brooded over some fine open hills nearby, and in the distance great forests grew like green smoke over the mountains. Justine longed to explore. She resolved to go out the very next day. She doubted that anyone would miss her.

When the door clicked open she started guiltily, wondering who it could be, wishing she had been found at her books rather than taking her ease in front of the fire. Her knees shook when she saw that the man who entered the room was attended by six guards and three footmen – it must surely be the count.

Her trembling curtsey was a travesty, and she clasped her hands hard behind her back so that the count should not see them shaking. Perhaps he had found out her idling and had come to turn her off in disgrace. Her mouth was dry. She worked her lips, thinking to ask him if he were looking for the children, but no words would come, so she stood miserably listening to the scuffle of the guards

93

arranging themselves. The count's personal escort was very smart. She could smell metal polish, and their armour and weaponry gleamed dully as they searched the room before lining up on guard. She said a fervent prayer of thanks that Armand had escaped their notice. Then she looked at the count. He was a smallish man with a yellowish complexion that sweated like a ripe cheese and wet black eyes glistening over runny red lips. His shiny black silk clothes gleamed like rain on slate roofs and he made Justine think of cockroaches and scuttling black beetles.

The count spoke in a curious rustling, scratchy, high-pitched voice, 'So you are the governess my dear brother sent from the convent?'

Justine curtsied once more. 'Yes, my lord.'

'And my children? How do you find them?'

All Justine's frustration welled up, 'Very high spirited, my lord, and not overfond of their books. Despite all my pleas, they would go out with the hounds today.'

The sound of several sharply indrawn breaths alerted Justine to the appalled expressions of the guards and the footmen. Dear God! She had spoken the truth without thinking, and she realised now how dreadfully she might have offended the count. His insectile eyes were blank as he computed her remark. It was impossible to tell what he was thinking, until he threw back his head and let out a greasy laugh. 'Ho, ho! My children are high spirited indeed, and so they should be. Listen to their governess! I should be ashamed to have them turn into stoop-backed clerics and that's a fact. Hunting and hawking are more fitting pursuits. I'm very glad to hear that they are out chasing today.'

'Indeed, my lord,' said Justine, determined to be tactful, 'I hear that all the children are notable hunters.'

'Take after me in that respect,' said the count. 'There isn't a horse born that I couldn't master. 'Tis my greatest pleasure to break in a wild one, to bend it to my will and beat it till it yields.' His greasy black eyes ran over Justine as he spoke and she began to feel nervous again. 'Rumour did not lie,' he said abruptly. 'You are a pearl among

94

women indeed, and 'tis a crime to hide your fair body in that ugly gown. Indeed, you are wasted in the schoolroom. My dear, I should like to have the pleasure of you at dinner tonight.'

Justine curtsied once more. It was not an invitation, and she knew that she dare not refuse. She said hesitantly, 'You do me great honour, my lord, but this gown is the only one I have, and I am not fit to keep company with you.'

'You let me be the judge of that.' The count gestured at one of the guards, 'Here, you! Take this wench up to the countess's wing, but not to the countess mind – my wife always makes trouble over the pretty ones. Take her to Madame Sabrina.' The silver kettle boiled unnoticed on the schoolroom fire as the young guard, sweating at being singled out for a special task, left his place by the door to take Justine's arm. She tried not to panic as she made a final polite curtsey to the count's departing back. But a helpless shiver ran over her. She felt like a prisoner as the guard marched her out of the room.

Her nerves had a strange effect on her perceptions. She seemed to float along the dim stone corridors. The guard made her walk in front of him, and she heard his jingling measured tread behind her as they crossed a dusty flag-hung hall and began mounting a flight of winding stone stairs. The exertion made her pant, the guard was breathing heavily behind her, and her heart pounded in her breast.

It should be accounted a great honour to be singled out for notice by the count, yet somehow she did not like it. There was a greasy repellence about him that made her think of touching a slug. She pictured a great, greasy, slimy, wet, garden slug oozing over her skin and she shuddered. But there was excitement running through her veins too. It was exciting to have been taken out of the pointless dusty loafing of the schoolroom and slotted into life again.

One floor from the very top of the tower, the guard motioned Justine to halt. He lifted the rich red curtain that blocked the stone entrance and pushed Justine through it. She felt the ragged gold fringes brush her skin, and as the guard dropped the curtain again, she saw that it was embroidered with a huge gold crest.

'Are these the countess's chambers?' she asked, looking around her at the blaze of colours, lights and candles.

'Part of them,' said a smooth voice. 'My lady has her private chambers on the very top floor of the tower. This floor is her dressing room and bathing area, the one below holds her wardrobe and the maids sleep on the next.'

Justine looked at the smooth dark woman before her. She had a slight gipsy look about her colouring – dark hair, olive skin, almond-shaped eyes – but there was a high gloss and polish about her that Justine had never seen on a wild gipsy. 'Are you Madame Sabrina?' she asked.

The woman came forward, her slick satin dressing gown whispering, and placed a smooth hand with long red-varnished nails on Justine's arm. 'I am indeed, and I don't need this great hunk here to tell me who you are.'

The soldier blushed crimson and shuffled his feet. 'I was sent to tell you – ' he began, but Madame Sabrina cut him off.

'The whole castle knows what you are sent to tell me,' she said crisply. 'The count has taken a fancy to the new governess. I am to prepare her, then you will escort her to the great hall. Well, don't just hang about sweating, you big lummox! Stand over there and wait until she's ready.'

The big soldier looked very out of place standing stiffly erect against a pink satin curtain. Two maids in black dresses ran over and stood in front of the embarrassed youth, giggling, running teasing fingers over his fly. Madame Sabrina called them to order. 'Take your hands off his cock and take Justine to the bathing area,' she commanded, 'and I want you to call Bosric to shave her pubic curls off before you bathe her.'

A sensation compounded of snakelike sexual excitement and total revulsion burned between Justine's legs as she struggled to imagine how such an outrage would feel: the kiss of smooth steel on the engorged folds of her vulva, the feel of strange eyes on her naked sex. 'You cannot do that!' she protested. 'I will not have anyone touch me there.'

The two maids giggled even more. Madame Sabrina gave Justine a long measuring look that was not without pity. 'If you object so much to Bosric touching your private parts, then you may attempt to shave yourself, but the knave keeps his razors deadly keen, and they are long. Should your hand slip while you are negotiating the folds of your labia . . .'

'Then I will not be shaved at all,' cried Justine. That frisson of sexual awareness was still humming between her legs, but she knew it could not be right.

'My dear, I don't think you understand. They say you came straight from the convent, is that so? Yes, I thought so from the look of you; a fresh and untouched beauty. No wonder the count desires you. God may have ruled that world, but you must understand that the count rules this one. His word is the law at Castle Waldgraf. He likes his beauties with a shaven mons, so shaved you must be. Whether you do it, or you let Bosric do it, or I have our mighty warrior here tie you down and have the cat do it, makes no difference to me, but shaved you must be or my head will roll.'

'I shall run away.'

'Aye, and so you may tomorrow. Many do, and if they escape the guards, I dare say they live long and prosperous lives. But come, my dear, let us be sensible about this. The count is your liege lord and master and 'tis your duty to please him. Surely the nuns brought you up to respect your betters and obey their orders.'

Justine said no more, but her body was shaking like a hare in a trap. The count was a sleazy and sinful man, and what he demanded from her was wrong, but she could not escape. The solid guard still waited by the pink curtain that divided the stone room in two. She did not try to twist away as the maids led her towards a vast oval tiled pool of water.

Wisps of steam rose from its milky green depths. Another time, she would have delighted in the fragrant pine smell that rose from the water, but now Justine's mind was busy. Madame Sabrina's words had struck home. How often had the nuns told her to submit to her superiors, to do as she was bid and to follow the laws of society? Once again, without meaning to, she had transgressed. Who was she to question the ruling of so great a man as Count Waldgraf?

Madame Sabrina shrugged off her satin wrap to reveal creamy naked shoulders as they reached the tiled steps that led down into the pool. 'I think I will bathe with you,' she said casually. She was a little plump, but despite the fact that Justine judged her to be thirty or more, her skin was smooth and taut with no wrinkles. Her breasts were very high and pointed, and long black hair waved between her legs. She saw Justine looking at her bush and said, 'Tis a very long time since the count showed any interest in me. I am too old for him now, and he desires only the finest and freshest of beauties. 'Tis a very great honour to be singled out for his notice, Justine. When he has finished with you, I have no doubt that you will be able to choose a fine young noble for your husband, or to take a responsible job within the castle, as I have done.'

'Yes, Madame Sabrina. I am sorry, Madame Sabrina,' said Justine. She took off the ugly grey gown without further argument and obediently prepared to be bathed.

Madame Sabrina seemed to relax. 'Good girl,' she said. 'Do as I bid you and all will be well. Why, you will most likely enjoy it. The count is a man of rare taste and skill in the esoteric arts of lovemaking.'

Justine unpinned her governess's bun and began unplaiting her hair. 'Why did you not marry?' she asked, then blushed for asking such a forward question.

'Why do you ask?'

'Well,' said Justine, fumbling for words, 'you are so beautiful now, and then, I mean, surely?'

Madame Sabrina's smooth amber eyes bored into Justine's. 'You mean I could have had any man I chose? So I could,' and her gaze grew more intense, 'but I care only for women, so I stay here where I can have my pick of the beauties that the count selects. He trusts me to prepare them for him just the way he likes, and in return he lets me indulge my tastes.'

Hot blood thumped into Justine's cheeks as the woman's meaning hit home. She took a step back. 'Oh, but I don't . . . I mean I'm not . . .'

'So? Perhaps I can change your mind about that. But never fear me, child. I have no mind to force you. And look, here comes Bosric with his razors.'

The heat and the steam of the room were making Justine feel dizzy. Little black specks swarmed in front of her eyes as she peered through the smoky vapour that filled the tiled room. She squinted into the mist, and tried hard to convince herself that the figure approaching her was entirely normal. But as the indistinct figure lurched closer an icy wind whistled around her belly and she shrank away from him. He wore only a little black leather jerkin decorated all over with great metal studs. And though she tried not to look, her eyes were drawn helplessly to his semi-erect manhood as it bobbed freely between his legs. He stood grinning and winking at her and she half turned to Madame Sabrina in protest.

'There is no pleasing some folk, Bosric. Our fine lady here says that she does not care for women, and now it seems as if she cares not for men either.'

Justine shivered at the smooth ice in Madame Sabrina's voice. She suddenly realised how friendless she would be if she alienated the older woman, and she didn't think she could bear to be alone with Bosric. 'I'm sorry,' she said once more. Her voice was high and thin in her ears and it echoed back to her oddly from the tiles and the steam. 'I meant to cause no offence . . . but this situation is . . . well I hardly know what I am . . .'

Madame Sabrina softened. 'Of course 'tis all strange to you, dear. You just lie back and let Madame Sabrina show you what to do.' Justine's trembling knees folded of their own accord, and she first sat and then half lay on the top step of the pool. Its smooth tiled surface was broad enough to lie on comfortably, but hot water splashed across it and she did not protest when Madame Sabrina sat at the far

99

end of the step and then took Justine's head and put it on to her lap out of the way of the water.

Justine felt the older woman's smooth wet thigh touch her cheek. She lifted her head away from that intimate touch and looked up into the steamy wreaths of vapour that hung over the ceiling like a giant parachute of wet silk. But the strain of keeping her head lifted made her neck ache. She had no choice but to relax back on to Madame Sabrina's naked thighs.

The touch of the older woman was comforting. 'Stop shaking!' said her amused silky voice. 'If you tremble so hard then Bosric will cut you and then where will we be?'

'I'll not cut you, pretty lady,' said a little squeaky voice. 'I never cut no one, me. Not even a scratch on the plucked chicken ugly ones, and yours is the prettiest mound of Venus I ever did see.'

Justine relaxed a little – he sounded harmless enough – but then she stiffened all over because she heard the zip, zip, zip, of a blade being whetted, and at the same time, Madame Sabrina's smooth hand slid over her breasts. Incredibly, her nipples hardened at the touch. Justine shuddered down the whole length of her spine, and butterflies danced on her nerve endings. 'Relax,' whispered a smooth amused voice. 'Believe me, child, life is full of good things for those who choose to enjoy them.' Long silky fingers stroked Justine's breasts tenderly. 'Is this not nice?'

Perhaps it would have been nice if the sound of Bosric sharpening his blade were not terrifying Justine with wild pictures of the indignity that was to come. How would she feel with no protective hair over her vulnerable woman's place? The older woman's touch had a tender maturity to it that Justine's body loved. But she could not wholly relax into the caress while Bosric whistled so gaily over the tools of his shaving trade. Madame Sabrina whispered again, 'Relax, my little darling. Bosric shall not begin work until you are ready. Hush now and let me please you.'

Her fingers did know how to please: they softly fondled and gently massaged all the tension out of Justine's

100

shoulders. Eventually, she went limp as a kitten in the older woman's lap. She felt a row of soft kisses being planted across her forehead, but she could not summon up the energy to protest. The warmth of the arms that enfolded her, the gentle lapping of the hot water, the knowing touches along her shoulders, even the scent of the steam had some magic in it, and Justine was lulled into well-being.

Her sexual arousal ceased to feel dirty and shameful and became instead a sweet awareness of her body's sensual capabilities. The warm embrace of the older woman enfolded her in a soft and gentle loving that was so very sweet and right. When soft lips touched her trembling mouth, Justine stretched lazily and kissed them back. She was rewarded by a soft chuckle. 'Just sit up a minute, darling and let Madame Sabrina get the soap. That's a good girl. Now lie in my lap again and let me soap you.'

As Justine moved, she opened her eyes, and she was instantly aware of Bosric crouching on his haunches by the side of the pool, watching her intently, his horrible great penis fully erect and poking through the flaps of his short leather jerkin. She shuddered and turned away into Madame Sabrina's comforting embrace. An uncomfortable frisson remained however, undercutting the relaxing, gentling movements of the older woman as she tenderly rubbed Justine's body with a small yellow sponge.

The soap was creamy and smelt fresh, like the pine scent of the water, and it produced copious amounts of thick white lather which Madame Sabrina massaged delicately into Justine's skin. She spent a long time touching Justine's breasts, and Justine relaxed again under her effective sexy fingers. The older woman might have been telepathic, so precisely did she stimulate Justine's nerves. She seemed to know just how to circle the swelling mounds of her breasts in order to extract the greatest amounts of sensitivity from them. She seemed to know just how to circle the areola with teasing fingers, and when to pinch and roll the chestnut nipples between her fingers until they hummed

101

with torment, and when to let go and rub them softly until the bliss was unbearable.

As the great mounds of rich creamy lather built up and tickled her skin so languorously, Justine rolled and stretched in a sensual carefree manner. The smooth firm hands slid down to walk delicately over the arch of her stomach and tickle the inside of her dimpled belly button, making Justine sneeze and laugh insouciantly.

Her world narrowed down to the warmth and sensation that surrounded her. Her stretched and jangled nerves let go, and she abandoned herself to the now, to the care of the woman who held her and the orders of her lord and master. Once more Madame Sabrina seemed to read her mind. As Justine let go of her worries and gave up to the flow of fate, the older woman slipped her smooth red-tipped fingers between Justine's warm relaxed thighs. Justine parted them with a sleepy sensual murmur, and Madame Sabrina smiled down at her and began to rub the soap vigorously over Justine's bush. She used the luxuriant pubic curls to create a deep rich lather which she worked slyly into the secret folds and crevices of Justine's woman's place.

Once more, Justine murmured languorously and allowed her to do it. The soapy darting fingers felt good in a shivery sexy kind of way. Her legs fell wider open as if of themselves, and Justine arched her suddenly rubber spine and cooed in pleasure. She was so warm and so comfortable. The soap and the hot water and the gentle touching had broken down all her reserves. A nice, warm, altogether delicious orgasm was circling her nerve endings, just waiting for a little more touching to bring it in to land.

But Madame Sabrina took her hands away from Justine's open and waiting sex and slid them up through the foam to land on Justine's breasts. As the soft hands slipped over the marvellously sensitive skin, Justine moaned a slight protest. Those ten crimson-tipped fingers felt incredible on her breasts, but she wanted the deeper satisfaction that throbbed between her legs.

The soft soapy hands ran under her neck and caressed

her jawline. Madame Sabrina's head bent low and she whispered, 'Are you ready for Bosric now?'

Disgust twisted in Justine's belly where it mingled oddly with the soft delight the massage had brought her. Her wide open legs were suddenly too wide open, open in a wanton invitation to the vulgar man who crouched so eagerly next to her, waiting to invade her privacy. But she had no choice. And so she nodded dumbly.

She shut her eyes tight and tried to concentrate on the lovely hands that were swirling soap around her breasts so gently, but all she could hear was Bosric's leather jerkin creaking as he took it off and the metal studs clinking on the tiles as he dropped it. Then she heard a last, zip, zip, zip, as he gave his blade a final polish, and the splashing of his little feet as he stepped into the few inches of water that swirled over the top step that she lay on.

Despite Madame Sabrina's gentling caress, Justine began to tremble and worms of disquiet crawled around her belly and slid down her open vagina to nibble at her clitoris. She kept her eyes tight shut and waited and waited to see what would happen next. And as the worms of fear kept nibbling on her clitoris her breath came shorter and faster, making her naked breasts rise and fall so fast that great slides of wet soap suds slid off them and oozed into the water.

Bosric's first touch was gentle, but it burned Justine as if he had touched her with a red coal from the kitchen. He began to hum in his funny squeaky voice as he ran little fingers through her dark pubic curls. His hands moved in a wringing circling motion, and, with a jolt of excitement, Justine realised that he was working the soap up even further into a thicker, richer lather.

She couldn't open her eyes. She lay back in Madame Sabrina's lap trembling all over with fine frissons of pleasurable excitement, waiting for the first touch of steel. When it came, it was as keen as a kiss. A gentle questing light touch across the top of her mons that sent shudders of vulnerable pleasure racing all over her bare body. The cold hard steel blade slid sweetly over her mons and stopped at the end of its slow sweep. The little fingers worked in the delicate clouds of rich lather and the slow, cold, hard feeling of steel swept over her skin once more.

She burned under the cold caress of the metal. She shivered under the torment of the tiny fingers. She was losing her protection. She was open and naked. Justine opened her eyes and looked down the length of her bare body, hoping she would not look as vulnerable as she felt, but it was worse. The flesh between her legs gleamed pale and sacrificial in its nakedness. And Bosric was not finished. His tiny hands pushed at her with authority. 'Open up, my lady. Offer up those pretty pink lips to me. I must catch every hair or I'll be in trouble so I will.'

'Is this ... is this not enough?' protested Justine. The firm hands tickled her tender inner thighs and pushed her legs open. Madame Sabrina shifted her position slightly, so that she could still cradle Justine. Bosric's insistent hands opened her trembling sex further.

'Wide, wider,' commanded the squeaky voice. Justine thought the humiliation would make her faint. She lay sprawled with her legs and the lips of her sex as wide as they would stretch. Yet her dreadful openness was producing a kind of rapture in her. She yearned to feel Bosric's attentions. Her breathing came deep and fast. She was aware of the pine scent of the water as she panted in steam and tried not to dissolve away completely in the tide of sexual expectancy that was sweeping her away.

When it came, she thought the spider whisper of the razor would kill her. She turned her head to one side, careless of the smooth pillowy breast that she rested on moving under her cheek, and gazed at one outstretched hand as it lay trembling in the hot smoky water. It was not the external sensations that would carry her away. It was the cold and guilty knowledge of her secret enjoyment that was making her burn in shame.

Slowly, thoroughly, carefully, Bosric plied his long blade over every quivering inch of Justine's intimate pink lips. Each sweep of the blade seemed to leave a phosphorescent trail of good feeling behind it. Her sexual organs lay spread like a flower. Justine felt as if a monstrous jungle blossom were blooming between her legs. A livid, secret, night-blooming invitation to sin opened its petals and called to the world that it was ready. Ready to fulfil its natural function: the attraction of the male.

Gentle hands tipped her out of Madame Sabrina's arms and over on to her hands and knees on the second step down into the tiled pool. The hot water now came up to her bent knees and tickled her belly. She knelt almost drowsily with her nose close to the water and her bare buttocks up in the air. Bosric positioned himself so close to Justine's open sex that the hair on his head was tickling the soft skin inside the soft crack that ran between the cheeks of her bottom. Once again she felt the cool touch of the razor. His whole body was pressing against hers now, and some of her earlier revulsion returned. And so did her guilty passion. She shivered and longed for satisfaction as she crouched there with her intimate entrances open to the insubstantial air. She longed for sensation inside her shivering velvet tunnel. Each sweep of the steel made her long for fulfilment. But the feather-light touches of Bosric's razors ceased. He moved away and she heard him say: 'Can I have my reward now, Madame Sabrina?'

'Of course you may, Bosric. Justine, sit up like a good girl and crouch back on your heels. Turn around so that I can see you from here. And push your breasts forward for Bosric to use.' Shuddering, Justine assumed the desired position. Feeling wanton and uneasy she straightened her shoulders so that her breasts jutted out. The nipples felt tender and heavy. The space between her legs felt strange, unfamiliar. The lips touched each other in a new way, a more intimate closer touch. She was vulnerable and naked in the dark spaces of her unfamiliar desire.

She opened her eyes as Madame Sabrina stood up and brushed past Justine to lounge on the step below her. The water nearly covered the older woman and she lay like a great smooth seal on the green tiles, splashing herself gently and watching Justine with indulgent dreamy eyes. Bosric, still naked, splashed over and stood above Justine.

His naked penis was on the same level as her breasts, and she shuddered to see it so close. It was a pale unearthly white, as if it never saw daylight, and the bulbous tip bulged out at the top of the shaft like a forest mushroom. She shut her eyes tight, but the squeaky voice said: 'Open your eyes and watch while I take myself to heaven.'

She opened her eyes. Two small hands gripped the long shaft, one below the other. He was sliding his little hands up and down the obscenely large expanse of his cock so hard and so fast that Justine could feel the wind of them passing her breasts. She could feel his eyes burning into her. 'Look at me,' he squeaked. She looked up and met the morbid fever in his eyes. A shock passed through her. It was disgustingly intimate to stare into his eyes, knowing that he was masturbating, but she could not look away. His eyes commanded her, grew larger and more intense as she was sucked into their infinite blackness. As their eyes were linked so closely together, Justine felt the intensity of his pleasure as if it were her own.

His knuckles bumped against her nipples and she cried out. On each frantic pass he moved a little closer to her breasts. His penis was touching her breasts now and she felt them jiggling with his movements. Her nipples shuddered sexily under his onslaught. She was caught up in his passion. His face contorted and she knew that he was near to climax. His black eyes were still open and staring hard into hers with intent demanding lust. With her peripheral vision, she saw his muscles cord and his penis jerk like a landed salmon. Liquid spurted from the eye of his cock in violent tortured globules. Hot white semen slimed her breasts. Its touch woke memories between her legs so that she seemed to feel the intimate kiss of Bosric's razor-sharp blades as they glided over her vulnerable sex once more.

Bosric threw his head back and drew in a deep breath of satisfaction. As their eye contact was broken, Justine felt as if she had moved away from a vast bonfire that had been scorching her. The relief was sweet and cool. Bosric dived into the steaming green pool like a water rat. He swam the few strokes necessary to cross to the other side, then Justine heard a shovel scraping and his squeaky voice singing. He would not come back. He was filling the fat, spidery black furnace that heated the water for the pool.

Justine sank back on to her knees and splashed her breasts with the hot water. Bosric's slimy leavings washed off at once. But her breasts burned with the memory. Justine slid deeper into the hot fragrant water. Its touch aroused her. It trickled lazily over her nipples and sensitive breasts like thick viscous oil. She was an explosive mixture of guilt and ecstasy, wallowing in a pool of mixed emotions.

Madame Sabrina rolled into the water and swam over to her. Two hands with smoothly red-varnished nails slid over Justine's shoulders and tickled her erotically. A blizzard of light kisses rained on the back of her neck. 'You won't see him again,' murmured a silky voice. The troubling, erotic hands continued to drift over Justine's breasts until she turned to her tormentor with a cry and kissed the older woman with frantic desire.

Chapter Seven

Madame Sabrina purred like a great satisfied glossy cat and returned Justine's kisses with fervour. She guided her out of the pool. Justine fell back on to the warm tiled floor as if she were boneless and drew her knees up and open. She felt wet hair trail over her skin as the older woman rained kisses on her smooth watery thighs, and Justine's bare and violated pudenda shivered and longed for those delicate attentions to reach it. Justine trembled as Madame Sabrina kissed her way rapidly towards Justine's naked sex. As the first fluttery kiss landed, Justine drew in her breath and groaned. She adored the euphoric violation of the touch of the kitten-soft tongue that was exploring her shaven bare crevices. There was nothing to soften the impact of the scrap of exploratory wet flesh that licked her so hotly along her now exposed nerve endings. Every hair had gone. She was naked and accessible.

Her labial lips felt warm and enlarged. Her clitoris was as stiff as a mating bird's crest, erect and calling for attention. For a moment she wondered if Madame Sabrina could see the blood that must be flowing into the fleshy folds of her woman's place, causing them to stiffen and elongate and yearn for more touching. She wanted this splendid marshmallow kissing to go on for ever. To carry on teaching her things about pleasure that she had never dreamt of.

Madame Sabrina's hot lapping tongue moved closer to Justine's open exposed clitoris, and Justine cried out. The strongest of orgasmic feelings were circling deep inside her pleasure centre and she wanted, oh how she wanted, to ride them out in a glorious wave of exaltation. She threshed her head on the wet tiles as Madame Sabrina took the pip of Justine's clitoris into her wet red velvet mouth and mumbled it gently. First slow, in a languorous exquisite movement that seemed to swirl in mid-air for ever. Then fast, in a sucking, pulling motion that picked Justine up and threw her whole body into a spasm so hard it was as if a hurricane or some unearthly natural force had picked her up and tossed her and shaken her and oh – blissful, floating, delicious feeling – broken her in two across its knee so that she felt a liquid gush high up inside her vagina and she screamed out with joy as the terrible sweet tension snapped with a crack that nearly broke her back.

The reaction left her soft and melting and, as she drifted back down, she felt a dreamy sensuality overtake her. There was no heat or urgency in it, just a timeless feeling of sensual exploration and rightness – as if she were experiencing depths of her being that she had never touched before.

She was only allowed to lie on her back, experiencing these new and welcome sensations for a second. 'Get in the pool and rinse off,' commanded Madame Sabrina. Justine heard giggles floating in the air above her, and her cheeks stung so red that the flush extended down on to her breasts. Had the maids been watching?

Madame Sabrina then called, 'You girls! Bring a pile of towels to the dressing area, and combs, and oil, and some jewels, and paint for her eyelids and cheeks and, of course, the count's favourite outfit.'

Justine ducked her sensitive body into the pool. The hot water touched her still orgasmic skin like a thousand kisses. But she did not dare linger. She waded out of the water and followed Madame Sabrina's back to an area of the room that was sectioned off with deep pink drapes. Madame Sabrina stopped Justine when she reached for a towel. 'The maids will dress you,' she said.

Justine stood still as a statue while the soft hands of the maids patted her skin. The black-clad girls giggled as they dried her. Were they laughing because they had seen Bosric shave her, and ejaculate on her breasts? Or because they understood the turmoil inside her as she battled with sensual desire and her feelings of guilt? The touch of the rough warm towelling was soothing and Justine leant into its caress blissfully. Next to her, two more black-clad maids were towelling Madame Sabrina dry. They too were laughing as if their work pleased them. Justine saw one kneel at the feet of her mistress and dart a pink tongue into the long hair of the pubic triangle. A tide of not unpleasant warmth washed over Justine, and she turned her eyes away. It was more embarrassing to watch the maid pleasure Madame Sabrina than it had been to writhe in ecstasy under the older woman's pleasuring tongue, and a guilty part of Justine wished that it were she who was repaying the favour.

Yet another black-clad maid came bustling in. She was holding a large silver tray that appeared to be full of coiled black snakes. Justine eyed it nervously. A sinking in her belly told her that it was somehow connected with what she was to experience here. 'What is that?' she blurted.

Madame Sabrina's eyes were half closed in ecstasy as the black figure kneeling at her feet licked enthusiastically at her sex, but her smile grew wider when she saw the silver tray with its decadent burden. 'Your restraints, my darling,' she said. There was a husky catch in her voice, as if she were struggling for control. 'Fine black straps and chains to bind you for your master.' Her hands gripped the maid's head in a frenzy. 'Oh, it's too much. Yes that's just right! It's too much. Do it harder.' Her head tipped back as she spasmed and Justine turned away from the display of the older woman's shuddering orgasm.

Justine was dry now. One of the maids took her hand and led her to a velvet-covered stool. Justine sat down gingerly, feeling the stiff velvet tickling her supersensitive skin. The carved wooden stool was set before a dressing table. She could hardly see the table top for the litter of combs and brushes, silver-topped cut-glass bottles, fabulous puffs of swan's down, ebony jars of powder and rouge, sticks of red lip paint, a turquoise bottle of kohl and, jarring among the gentle cosmetic paraphernalia, a coiled black whip.

She looked into the fine gilt-framed mirror that hung from the back of the dressing table. Its surface was lightly misted with steam from the pool, but she could make out her reflection as the maid behind her began to comb her hair with light delicate fingers. Justine looked at herself carefully. The insanely decadent experience she had just been through had made her skin glow like a maenad's. Her hair was tousled and her breasts had a divine radiance about them. Secretly, she thought that she looked better than usual, until she looked into her own eyes. They were huge, shadowed with sadness, guilt and secret knowledge.

In the mirror she could see the reflection of the maid who was combing her hair and behind her the rest of the room. The silver tray with its heaped slick coils of black straps was resting on a small round table with claws for feet. 'Restraints?' she asked. But she received no answer. The maid only busied herself with the arrangement of Justine's hair.

Madame Sabrina and the other maids came over to watch and to join in. Soft hands dabbed at Justine's eyelids, her face, her cheeks, her nipples. She felt the softness of powder, the sting of red rouge and tasted scented wax on her lips. Murmuring over her beauty, gentling her with soft caresses, the women pampered and petted and groomed Justine until she was glowing and polished under their care. Soft fingers glued a red ruby into her belly button. More soft touches and there were stars of ivory jasmine twined into her hair.

A silver tray of perfume bottles was brought over. Justine helped them prepare her massage oil. She chose a mixture of dark, exotic fragrances, dripping the sensual scented oils into an amber jar of base oil. She chose scents to suit her mood: heavy exotic ylang ylang, deep shivery cedarwood, light sweet attar of roses. The essences of a thousand long-dead fruits and spices rose from the bottles. Once the massage oil was blended to perfection, Madame Sabrina and the maids poured it into the palms of their hands and advanced on Justine. Soft women's hands rubbed her all over. The fragrance strengthened as it warmed and mixed with the oil of her body. Justine grew dizzy with its heavy alluring exotic vapours. Yet she loved it too, and made no protest as more and yet more of the perfume was poured on to her skin.

The maids missed no scrap of skin. They massaged between Justine's toes, inside her armpits, even lifting her off the stool to get at the backs of her knees and the inside rim of her anus. They poured out the expensive oil unstintingly. Its fragrant kiss stung Justine's newly shaved vulva, oozed over her breasts and dripped wastefully into the crack between her round buttocks. The perfumed oil dissolved the rouge on her nipples. Laughing, the women dabbed the running red stains away and then carefully repainted the nipples. The rouge ran again, and they laughed even more as they gave in and rubbed the mixture of rouge and perfumed oil into Justine's skin so that her breasts glowed flamingo-pink and the tips were a deep cherry-red. The artistry of the gentle touches hummed over Justine's skin and crawled beneath her nipples. It was a good, floating, pervasive sexual pleasure. Her whole body was a sexual organ and every touch pleased her. And there was no hurry. No hurry in the world. She needed no satisfaction: this was satisfaction, every touch.

Fear coiled in Justine's sweetly oiled belly when Madame Sabrina reached out for the big silver tray. Yet even the fear was enjoyable too. It flowed out of her belly and tickled the backs of her knees, and Justine welcomed the excitement that ran through her as Madame Sabrina ran lazily sexual hands over the gleaming black snakes on the tray. The first item she separated from the copulating tangle of links was a high black collar. It looked like the collar for a guard dog. Justine reached out a cautious hand and touched the supple black leather with only the tip of one finger. The leather was smooth and supple. It was lined with black fur. It closed with one heavy metal buckle that gleamed dully in the light from lanterns nearby. 'Am I to wear this?' she asked. Her shivering body knew the answer already. There was a feeling of inevitability as one of the little maids placed the gleaming black strap around her neck and she felt the kiss of the fur envelop her throat.

The collar gave her an unexpected feeling of support. It held her neck in warm supportive hands and the clink of the buckle being fastened worried her not at all. The leather had a faint stable smell of its own, but that was soon swallowed up by the heavy aroma of Justine's perfume. She looked at her reflection in the mirror. The collar acted like a frame for her white face and red breasts and dark flowing hair with its scatter of ivory flowers. Her eyes were enormous behind their thick layer of kohl, and carmine lips pouted at her like the lips of a stranger from heaven.

A touch whispered across her belly and soft hands forced her to stand up. She smelt again the stable smell of fresh leather and heard little clinks from the buckles and chains that attached the harness together. It was a complicated arrangement. She made no effort to discern how it worked, but was content to stand passive while the soft guiding hands threaded her into it, lifting first one leg then the other as she was commanded.

All the thin oiled black straps met in a central metal ring that lay in a silver 'o' around her belly button. Some ran over her breasts, leaving them naked, but outlining the contours, forcing the painted red flesh upward and causing the nipples to poke lasciviously outward. Other thin black lines ran under her legs and across her buttocks. An arrangement of thin steel rods went under her legs to hold her sex open. She could feel cold steel, warming by the second, between her legs. It felt strange, but she made no protest.

The maids pulled the straps tighter. Justine felt the hard

leather cutting into her buttocks and thighs, pulling apart the lips of her shaved sex. She was wrapped in soft but unyielding leather. The straps held her safe and tight; they contained her pleasure and increased it. God help her, but she enjoyed the touch of the soft fingers that slipped in between her legs, patting and arranging the lips of her vulva. The steel rods held her blissful lips parted and kept her clitoris exposed. 'Lift your arms. I need to check for movement,' said Madame Sabrina. Justine lifted her arms high above her head and took a deep sensual breath, feeling the oiled strips running sensuously over her breasts and rising over her belly.

'I shall come soon,' she murmured to herself and deliberately shut her legs over the restraints. The pressure on her clitoris from the steel rods was delicious indeed. She gave another languorous sigh. The hands of the maids slid over her again as they checked and adjusted all the straps. Most of the thin black strips were tightened again, increasing the feeling of pressure, of being held in a safe tight grip. But those oiled black straps that slid over her shaven sex and between her clenching buttocks were loosened, decreasing the pressure on her clitoris to a manageable sweetness that tickled and pleased her and could never be forgotten, but that removed the immediate threat to send her shuddering to the floor in the throes of an orgasm.

'Shoes,' murmured Madame Sabrina. Two black pointed slippers were brought at once. Two maids knelt at Justine's feet and slid the shoes on. The slender high heels tipped Justine forward. She felt her buttocks tilt up behind her, and when she took an experimental step or two, the cheeks of her backside tilted up saucily.

Once more Justine looked at her reflection in the mirror. She was changed now, bound and helpless in the black restraining straps and the useless shoes, her whole body prepared for the delight of the count and no other purpose. Yet she felt safe as a baby in the tight black caress of the leather. The collar held her head high. The straps that held her breasts pushed them out so as to attract attention to her vulgar red cleavage. The rods between her legs excited her unspeakably, and she was glad rather than ashamed that the high black shoes and the straps between her buttocks tilted the cheeks out in an unmistakable invitation.

She turned away from the mirror as three soldiers marched in. All three men stared at Justine as if they wanted to penetrate her with their eyes. In her new, free-floating sensuality she enjoyed their admiration. She tossed her head back with a knowing sexuality that she had seen free girls use on their lovers, but had never thought to emulate herself. The men stared even harder, enraptured. The senior guard licked his lips and spoke to Madame Sabrina. His eyes never left Justine. 'If it please you, madam, I am sent by the count with this platter and he is of a mind to have the governess sent in for dessert.'

'Lord save me!' Madame Sabrina replied. ''Tis the platter he uses for a whole ox! Well, there's room for my pretty darling on there. Put it on the floor. No! Over there, you great lout. Girls, come take some of this fruit off to make room for Justine.' The platter was piled high with peaches, strawberries, grapes, melons; the vast platter spilled over with luscious ripe fruit. The maids could not resist sneaking a few tasters, and even Madame Sabrina popped a few grapes in her mouth. 'All fresh from the hot-houses,' she said. ''Tis a miracle in winter, so it is. And here's a jug of cream. Whipped until it stands up in clouds.' She cleared a space in the centre of the platter, then called Justine over.

'Don't lie on it,' she said. 'I want you to sit upright so that you show to better advantage.' Justine stepped gingerly into the centre of the platter, spiking a few strawberries with her black heels as she did so. The silver dish was cool. The fruit was soft and squashy. Delicious smells arose around her as she settled down on to the bruised fruit. Madame Sabrina arranged Justine so that she was sitting with one knee up and the other leg stretched out in front of her. The silver rods kissed her labia and mingled pleasure and unreality shivered over her body.

Sticky cool flesh touched hers as the maids and Madame Sabrina piled the fruit high around her. Then Madame

115

Sabrina reached for the cream. She piled the whipped cauliflower curds into her hands and then heaped it up in between Justine's legs. She gasped as she felt cream-covered fingers reach up inside her vagina. Her tongue came out between her lips and ran over the waxy red surface as if to cool them. The white fluffy mound covered her shaven pubis and she was glad about that. More cream-covered fingers reached up and tickled her anus as cream was piled in the crack between her buttocks. Justine shivered and snuggled into the collar that held her. 'That will do,' said Madame Sabrina. 'There will be more cream on the table should they need it. Carry her carefully, you great lumps, and take the useless lummox who is hiding behind my curtains with you too.'

The platter lurched and swayed under her and Justine clutched at the sides of the silver dish as the four men hoisted her carefully on to their shoulders. She could hear their heavy breathing as they marched out of the warm steamy room. The air touched her naked skin with freezing breath as they pushed out of the curtains and into the stone corridor. She could hear her own apprehensive breathing light and fast in her ears as the soldiers began to negotiate the broad stone steps that led down to the first of the many dusty courtyards they had to cross.

She wasn't sure how much of the lurching swaying feeling that tickled the inner flesh of her belly was caused by the movement of the platter beneath her, and how much was caused by her knowledge that sinful new experiences lay ahead. She took a deep breath and shivered in the cold air. They had arrived at a huge studded black door. The stone floor was worn away underneath it, and light and the smell of food spilled out from the gap. Justine could hear muffled shouting and singing, like the distant roar of a market day. The guards whispered together, then the tray lurched as one of them slipped out from beneath it and eased himself through the door. Justine grew colder as she waited, poised high in the air on the cold silver platter among the clammy piles of fruit. There was no change in the noise level behind the door, yet her apprehension grew.

She would have liked to ask one of the soldier guards what was to happen next, but she didn't trust her voice. Nor would it help her if she knew. She was committed now.

The guard came back, whispered to his fellows, and took up his position beneath the platter once more. Justine took a deep breath and tried to calm her lurching stomach. Both heavy black baronial doors swung open, and two fat men in scarlet uniforms walked out and stood in front of Justine. They both carried long gold trumpets. 'One, two, three,' counted the fatter of the musicians. The trumpets blew, the tray was lifted, and Justine was carried into the great banqueting hall of Castle Waldgraf by the four soldiers, who marched in step with the trumpeters.

The platter swayed beneath her. Justine sat up straight and shivered. She had never felt so naked, so vulnerable. All the lords and ladies had stopped talking. They were looking at her, laughing and clapping delightedly. Justine was carried past them in a blur of light and colour. Only a few vivid details stood out. A drunken blond man who blew out his fat red cheeks and leered at her as she swayed past like a maharanee in an elephant's howdah. A woman with slanting green eyes like a little cat, who was wearing a pink dress trimmed with swansdown that looked like a sunset. Justine stared about her, trying to make sense of the warm colour and thronging multitude of the count's party.

A flash of black caught her eye. It stood out in contrast to the gay clothing and bright tables. She saw with surprise that it was a man. A well-muscled young man, coal black all over, with tight curly hair. She turned her head and looked back as she was carried past him, and then, with an impact like a blow, she saw that he was chained to the table. Like the picture on a jigsaw falling into place when enough pieces are in to see the pattern, she now saw that many more slaves were chained to the tables. Silver anklets and wrist manacles sparkled among the jewels of the great ones. Most of the slaves were naked. Oiled skin gleamed as they served their masters and mistresses. Many wore high black collars such as Justine's, and her hands went up

117

to tug at the one she wore. The black restraints ceased to feel comforting and held her in a sinister manner. Was she to be treated so?

The fat men blew a final triumphant blast on the trumpets. They had reached the head table. Gorgeous dusty tapestries draped the stone walls behind the high carved thrones of the great. The count ran his beetle-black eyes over Justine and smiled greasily. 'Ladies and gentlemen,' he cried. 'See what a pretty dish I have to round the feast off with.' He waved to the soldiers to put the platter down. A pretty male slave, naked save for jingling chains, jumped on to the table and scampered along it like a little monkey, clearing enough plates and goblets away to make a space for the platter. Breathing heavily, the four guards carefully put Justine, still sitting upright on the fruit covered platter, on the polished oak banqueting table.

She caught a whiff of rank sweat as they moved away. The soldiers were sweating from the effort of carrying her, but the lords and ladies at the table were sweating from drink and food and general overindulgence. Close up, they were alarming. Faces, red and flushed with the wine and the heat turned to look at her and, quite without thinking, Justine covered her breasts with her hands. Her modest gesture was met with a roar of laughter and the count looked annoyed. He banged his fist on the thick planks of the table and shouted, 'Stand up and display yourself!' Justine shuddered. The heat and the smells and the colours and the eyes had unnerved her. She could not move.

'Do as he says,' whispered a camp voice in her ear. It was the slave. Under the pretext of tidying the table he had taken the chance to whisper in her ear. 'You'll be all right,' he said again. 'Just don't annoy him and you'll be all right. You might even enjoy it – I do.'

As he minced away, Justine uncoiled her shaking legs and stood up slowly. She let her hands fall to her sides and her breasts poke into the air naked, uncovered. As she moved, she was sharply aware of the steel rods brushing the sides of her clitoris and the leather straps kissing her skin. Cream began to slide down her legs in a tickling,

118

sliding, oozing caress. All were looking at her, and the lust and appreciation in their hot eyes made heat spiral in her belly.

'Show yourself,' ordered the count. Justine stood still, bewildered. She did not know what to do. Then she saw the friendly male slave gesturing to her. Following his lead, she put her arms up under her hair and slowly turned around. The lords and ladies craned closer. Their interest and admiration were making her feel wanton. She took in a deep, shaking breath that made her breasts stand proud, and was rewarded by the fascinated attention of the brightly clad crowd. Justine had a high floating feeling of giddy rapture. She loved this attention. Yet she knew it was all wrong.

'Show my noble guests how delicious you are,' ordered the count. Shivering, Justine bent and collected a little cream from between her legs, heaping it on to one finger. Then she brought it to her red-painted mouth and licked it lasciviously. The lords and ladies roared their approval and clapped wildly. It was strange to have so much power. So much power to arouse and to please. Justine felt dizzy with the knowledge that she was the centre of attention. All the nobles at the high table wanted her. All of them desired her wanton fragile beauty. They were calling out to the count right now, 'Let me have this one!'

'No, no! Waldgraf! Take no notice of him! 'Tis me you promised a special treat to, and I would take this one.'

'A pox on you all! I was invited to dinner and dinner includes dessert and, by God, I'm so hungry I claim this one to myself!'

The count's black eyes glistened. 'Peace, gentlemen. I'm glad you fancy the tasty dish I have prepared for you – but there's plenty for all. At least, if we eat her the way I've a mind to. Ladies, gentlemen, are you up for a frolic?'

The gaily dressed nobles leant forward eagerly. 'A frolic! Aye we'll go for that.'

'But what are we to do? Waldgraf, do tell us.'

''Tis never dull, dining here, I'll say that for you, Waldgraf.'

119

The count gestured to two white-wigged footmen who were standing behind his chair. They must have been cued for this moment for they came forward at once, one bearing a tray of strips of soft black cloth, the other a tray full of jingling handcuffs. 'Distribute one blindfold and one set of handcuffs to each noble's slave,' he ordered. To her horror Justine saw that every one of the huge carved thrones at the high table had a slave chained to it. Chains clinking, each slave came forward at once and took the proffered restraints from the footmen.

The lords and ladies murmured and turned wondering eyes on the count. He was laughing to himself greasily, well pleased by the effect he was having. 'We have here a pretty dish, one that you all wish to partake of. Well, I have come up with a scheme to make the contest a fair one. You shall bob for your supper as if you were children hunting for apples. I propose to blindfold every one of you and tie your hands behind your back. You are then free to reach over the table and eat of the fruit and the cream, and of course, any part of the delicious young body before you.'

Justine's mouth fell open and her knees shook violently. She could see by the reactions of the lords and ladies before her that they were excited by the idea. They bowed their heads willingly so that slaves could blindfold them. Eager hands stretched out behind the velvet gowns for the handcuffs to be applied. Below the black velvet blindfolds, Justine could see greedy lips. Long wet tongues flicked out as the excited lords and ladies waited for the game to begin.

'Lie down on the fruit,' ordered the count. Obediently, Justine did so. She was glad to lie down, although she felt the seedy squash of a thousand strawberries bursting below her. Grapes popped and oozed. There was a strong scent of melons. She shivered as the count loomed over her, checking her position with his oiled black eyes. 'Very nice, my dear,' he said approvingly. Then he picked up a large pewter jug. 'Just a little more cream for my lords and ladies to enjoy.'

Justine felt the smooth warm richness of cream as it poured over her pink-painted breasts and the soft leather straps that bound her body. The cream poured and poured in a smooth flow of thick liquid, clinging to her body before dribbling on to the fruit and swirling on to the platter. Justine could feel it pooling under her hair and her elbows and the backs of her heels and her buttocks, all the points where her body touched the platter. She was drenched, drowned, completely covered in cream before the jug was empty and the count was satisfied. He put the jug on the table and then turned to the expectant nobles. They pushed and milled in a tight bunch. The breath came hotly from between their parted lips. They were excited and eager for the fun to begin. Justine lay shivering in her pool of thick cream on top of her bed of squashed fruit and waited for the onslaught of strange lips to reach her. She shut her eyes tight.

'Slaves, draw back the chairs,' commanded the count. Justine heard the high-backed chairs scraping as the slaves pulled them out of the way. The lords and ladies murmured again, thinking that now the game would start, but the count was not finished. 'Slaves, spin the noble lords and ladies around,' he ordered, 'then let them loose to hunt for their supper as they will.'

Justine heard the clinks of the slaves' chains and excited squeals and laughter as the lords and ladies were spun around fast enough to disorient them badly. Perhaps they would all stagger off in the wrong direction and miss her entirely. Justine lay trembling all over with the fine nervous shivers of a greyhound who has spotted quarry. But that was all wrong. Because in this game it was she that was the object of the hunt and, when the count commanded the slaves to let go, it was her naked body that the blindfolded searchers were hoping to find.

'Let them go,' ordered the count. Justine heard him laughing as the lords and ladies staggered off in all directions. Unable to bear the suspense she opened her eyes. The count was standing at the head of the table laughing heartily. Brightly clad figures moved amongst the

121

drawn-back chairs and chained slaves. Some were heading off the wrong way, but some were groping towards the table. She held her breath and tried not to look at the red lips under the black blindfolds. The red lips that were coming her way.

A goblet crashed to the floor spilling wine, and a silver dish full of chicken bones followed it on to the stone flags as the first groping figure reached the table and fumbled along it. Justine felt the platter shift as a large red-haired man bumped it with his forehead. He lifted his head laughing. 'Let the feast begin,' he cried. He was tall enough to reach right across the table to where Justine lay. It was difficult to lie waiting, helpless, while his red lips and strong white teeth got closer and closer. Justine nearly screamed out loud when his hungry mouth closed on her ankle.

He seemed content to stay there, licking and slurping at the cream that slicked her skin. His long strong tongue slid down her ankle and around her foot with evident enjoyment, darting under the black straps that held the high pointed slippers on to her feet. Then a soft wet mouth closed on Justine's shoulder and she felt the skin quivering in mingled pleasure and dismay. She twisted her head slightly to see who it was. A slim, handsome young noble with fine aristocratic lips had climbed right up on to the table in order to reach her and was happily sucking and nuzzling at her bare flesh. He murmured happily as he found a hollow full of cream in her neck below the collar and began lapping. Justine's skin crawled with tender delight. The sensations were strange, very strange, but, perversely, good also.

More people had discovered where the table was now, and more of them tried to climb on to it so that they could reach Justine more easily. Her hands clenched by her sides and she could feel her toes curling and uncurling inside the black high-heels. A tall black-haired noble gave a shout of triumph as he discovered a breast. Electric shudders ran over Justine as hot stranger's lips closed over her nipple. Then the arousing sensations doubled as a slim young woman greedily sucked the other nipple into her pouting baby mouth.

The cream was soon gone, but both nobles continued to lick and suck at Justine's aching nipples as if they were feeding on manna. She felt a mouth biting at her round belly. And for the first time, a moan rose to her lips. The sensations that were rising in her were so very hard to bear. She closed her eyes and fell into a dark velvet realm of sensation. Another mouth mumbled at her belly and, behind her closed lids, she could see rockets of golden sparks. Pleasure hummed along every nerve. She moaned again. The mouths nibbled harder. She could smell the scent of crushed fruit and hear jaws working. Some were eating the fruit and the cream, some were eating her. She shuddered and wondered how long she could stand it.

The first questing mouth touched her inner thigh. It gave her such a jolt of sensation that Justine's eyes flew open and she lifted her head. All she could see were busy heads bent over her. Pink and red tongues lapped busily at her skin. The red-haired man was still blissfully making love to her foot. A dark head moved over her shaven sex, and Justine let her head fall back in total abandon.

Another wet tongue began lapping at her other thigh. The two men paused, murmured, and then must have come to some agreement, for Justine felt them begin again in harmony. One licking on one side, the other on the other. The remains of the whipped cream that Madame Sabrina had piled around her naked and shaved sex vanished like snow in the sunlight, but the two men kept licking.

Justine's breasts ached and burned sweetly under the onslaught of the mouths that caressed her there. All over her body, soft mouths were licking and nibbling, sliding under the black strips of leather that bound her and feeding daintily on the cream and the fruit that surrounded her. It was utterly delicious. It was the most decadent sensation she had ever known. The two heads that were busily working her inner thighs were slowly, insistently, pushing her legs apart. Justine cried out once more as the first scrap of moist flesh slipped into the bare crevice of her sex and licked her vulva. A second hot caressing tongue followed. Justine's pelvis tilted up to accommodate the two plundering tongues, and to her shame she knew that she wanted them. She was burning and sighing and dying of rapture under their darting licking tongues.

A bell rang, and Justine was left suspended as all motion stopped. Her skin ached and groaned as the insistent licking and pleasuring stopped. She twisted impatiently and longed for them to resume. Then shame washed over her and she cursed herself for being so weak. But she couldn't help it. She hovered on the edge of madness as her clitoris trembled and cried for the comforting delight of the strangers' tongues to come back. 'My lords, ladies and gentlemen,' cried the count's oily voice. 'You eat too slowly! I am beginning the countdown now. Those who have not helped themselves to the feast by the time I reach 30 will have to go to bed supperless.'

The bell chimed again; one silver-toned ching, and the slaves all counted 'one'. The bell had chimed once more before Justine realised that it was being used to signify the countdown. The lords and ladies must have realised it too, for they fell upon her in a feeding frenzy, like mad sharks in the ocean. The pause seemed to have sensitised Justine's skin, for every touch now was bliss on a scale she had never before imagined possible. The hungry mouths brushed over her skin as they sought out every last drop of cream. Her breasts tingled and burned under the black straps as new mouths licked and sucked her there, and two new pairs of lips took her swollen and delighted nipples inside their embrace.

Justine writhed under the onslaught, but as the silver-toned bell chimed out steadily and the slaves counted the beat she felt a glorious triumphant rush of well-being flow into every limb of her body. Mouths closed on her bare sex, and she rejoiced in its nakedness. The lips and folds of her vulva ached with heavy sensual pleasure. She opened her eyes. The count had pushed a noble aside and was kneeling on the table between her parted knees. His oily eyes scuttled lecherously over her bare mons. He bent his head slowly and put it close to her vulva. The tip of a hot tongue landed on the very heart of her clitoris and began to stimulate her unbearably. All Justine's disgust for the man returned. But his tongue was evoking sensations of ecstasy. Even as she writhed under the strong mix of sensations that the count's actions were producing, the tip of another hot tongue darted into the opening of her anus, and Justine's mouth opened in shock and pleasure.

The bell chimed faster and the slaves counted louder as Justine twisted and gasped out her delight. The greedy mouths that sucked on her grew hotter and more frantic as the countdown continued. Justine felt her pelvis twist upward and outward and all her muscles begin to clench. The hard tip of the count's tongue stimulated her clitoris wetly and responded to her movements by circling faster, and faster, and faster again, so that her whole body was suddenly shaken by a vast and devastating rush of pleasure that took her and shook her and twisted her very heart so hard that she screamed out loud as she came.

'Thirty,' counted the slaves, and the bell was rung furiously as the count ordered the laughing lords and ladies off his table and back into their chairs. They laughed and protested as the slaves removed their bondage. It appeared that most of them had thoroughly enjoyed the experience. A few seemed reluctant to be unbound.

Justine lay spent and shaken on the now nearly empty platter. Much of the fruit had been eaten. Most of the cream was gone. She felt sticky and gloriously used as she lay there, her chest still rising and falling rapidly from her fast-breathing orgasm. Tiny red crescents speckled her skin where she had been sucked and bitten. The black straps were smeared with cream and fruit seeds. The skin all over her body felt sensitive and sexual but as she watched an elaborately dressed noblewoman, who could only be the count's wife, pace malevolently towards her, she suddenly had a nasty creeping sensation in her belly as if she had done something wrong.

She shrank back as the tall figure loomed over her. The

countess's eyes glittered with malice.'I see that you enjoyed the excesses of that sexual act,' she said, laughing mirthlessly. 'But a little slut like you cannot expect to have my husband in every frolic. You shall star alone in the next one. It's a little extreme, perhaps, but I think you have the sensuality to handle it.'

Chapter Eight

*T*here was nothing Justine wanted in the market and she turned away from the laden stalls with dragging feet. Even the smell of roasting apples covered with toffee didn't tempt her. She stopped to make way for a rosy-cheeked woman in a blue apron who was driving a fine flock of geese through the bustling alleys between the stalls. The woman looked pleased with her day's marketing and called out to Justine, 'Thank you kindly, mistress. 'Tis lucky for us all that the weather keeps so mild, is it not?'

'It certainly is unseasonable,' Justine replied. 'But the air nips keenly. I expect it will snow any day now.'

The rosy-cheeked woman passed on smiling with her geese cackling around her ankles. Justine wished she were so happy, lived such an uncomplicated life. Sighing, she carried on towards the outskirts of the market, never noticing the tall dark man who had started and run over at the sound of her voice. Now he blocked her way, looking down at her with intent eyes.

'By the cringe! I do believe I recognise my beautiful young friend, although she is camouflaged as a grim, grey governess.'

'Armand!' she cried looking up at him in surprise. 'Indeed, the children are out hunting and I grew weary of waiting for them in an empty schoolroom. I do not suppose anyone will miss me.'

She dropped her eyes away from Armand's searching glance and tugged at the elephantine folds of the ugly grey gown. They had supplied her with the uniform, but no one seemed to require her services. Not even the count, reflected Justine. She had spent a whole week of sickening fear waiting to be summoned for some new debauchery. But she had heard nothing. Not from him nor from Madame Sabrina. She had finally grown bold enough to take herself out for an hour. And now here was Armand smiling into her eyes as if their bitter parting in the tower room had never taken place.

'You have no need to explain yourself to me,' said Armand, smiling kindly at her. 'Why should you not take a break?'

Justine wet her lips nervously. He was so very large and male. 'What are you doing here?' she babbled. 'Not looking for poultry I don't suppose.'

His eyes laughed. 'Why not? I'm as partial to a fat goose as any man, although we gipsies tend to find our fowl in places other than the market. But to tell the truth, I was hunting a prettier bird altogether. I was hoping to meet you.'

'I don't believe that,' said Justine, but her heart bounded uncontrollably and she wished it were true. Armand looked down at her with unreadable dark eyes before falling into step next to her.

'Why not?' he asked her. 'I knew you would come here. The whole castle attends the end of month market. It is the best one.' He took her arm, and it felt so right that she made no protest. They strolled on together, talking amiably of the gaily-laden stalls that they passed. Then Justine smelt roasting chestnuts and was suddenly hungry. The chestnut seller saw her sniffing and slapped his fingerless mittens together with a muffled crack.

'Roll up! Roll up! Best chestnuts for the most beautiful lady. Same colour as your hair, mistress, but not so shiny nor such a rich gleam to them.'

'What nonsense,' said Justine laughing. The chestnut seller's little black eyes twinkled in his wrinkled face. He had sparse grey hair and a hedgehog coat of grey stubble covered his chin. He slapped his mittened hands together once more, and Justine saw that he was wearing layer upon layer of old rags.

'Nonsense maybe – but don't they smell good?' he retorted.

'Delicious,' she admitted. Armand laughed down at her with merry eyes. 'Then you must have some at once.' He stepped over to the ragged chestnut seller and began to haggle. First over the price, then over the number of chestnuts in the stitched leaf that was used as a bag.

Justine stood by the charcoal brazier and warmed her hands at the glowing embers. The air was growing colder as the afternoon drew out, and the warmth of the fire was very welcome. She could hear the flames hissing and smell the good smell of roasting chestnuts. All around them surged the life of the market. They were standing near the livestock auction. She amused herself by trying to work out what the auctioneer was selling, but she could pick out no individual words from his rapid gabble, and turned back to the brazier just as the chestnut seller said, 'You drive a hard bargain, sir,' finally giving in.

Armand laughed at him gaily. 'As if I didn't know that you'll be dancing with joy the minute my back's turned, the price I paid you.'

The chestnut seller threw back his wispy grey head and laughed. He had missing teeth and Justine could see his breath clouding in the cold air. ''Tis true, 'tis true. I'd be hard pushed to make a living without young men in love. If you all bargained like the grannies I'd have a hard winter indeed. But in truth, sir, if my lady was as your lady, I'd waste no time bantering either.'

Armand clapped him on the shoulder and threw him a silver coin. The chestnut seller pocketed it rapidly and waved them farewell. Justine blushed before the admiration in his twinkling black eyes. She was glad to turn away from it, and from the embarrassment his remark

129

about Armand being a young man in love had caused her. The chestnut seller was mistaken. Armand did not love her. Or did he? He confused her. She could not believe Armand to be one of the seducers the nuns told her about, men who ruined women with lies about love. Yet if he were not such a one, why would he deny her the blessing of the church?

She pushed aside the troubling thoughts. The chestnuts warmed her hands. Armand held the leafy bag and handed the hot, blackened, split-shelled nuts to her one at a time, smiling indulgently as he did so. Justine squealed as they burned her fingers, but she turned down Armand's offer to peel them for her. 'They taste better if I do them myself,' she explained.

He shook his head, teasing her with his eyes. 'You're too independent, young lady, that's your trouble.' As they ate, they strolled slowly away from the bustle of the market and stood at the edge of the village where the air was fresher. The ground fell away steeply where the grassy downs began. A pink winter's sun was setting in splendour over the distant dark forest, and the sky was a misty marvel of pinks, greys and pale blues.

Far below them was a plateau, a flat space between the swelling hills. As they looked down, Justine saw little black gipsy caravans drawn up in a circle. Jewel-like cooking fires gleamed amongst the stationary wagons and she could smell smoke. The bark of a distant dog floated up to them on the clear air. 'Are they your people?' she asked.

'Indeed they are. Will you not come and meet them, Justine? I would have you know them, and you shall see how happily we get on without the church and all her strictures.'

His eyes implored her to follow him and made her breathless. Justine looked away from his face. He moved behind her, almost but not quite pushing her into motion. Without actually agreeing, she found herself starting down the path that led to the grassy space where the gipsies were camped. The path was frozen hard. Justine looked down at some flints that were embedded into the frozen muddy ruts and said, 'I went to confession once more, after you left.'

His voice was unbearably low as he turned back to walk beside her. 'I was hoping that you would decide not to.'

A crawling aftershock zinged around Justine's body as she felt the mouths sucking at her in the banqueting hall. 'I had much to unburden myself of.'

'And did the priest say that our love was a sin?'

She turned away from the heartbreak in his eyes. 'Of course, but, Armand . . .'

'Yes?'

'I did worse, far worse with the count, and the priest said that no sin was involved because of the count's station in life.'

Armand stiffened as if he had been shot and his face went thunderous. He opened his mouth as if to ask a hasty question, but then he looked down at Justine's troubled face and held himself in check. She said slowly, 'It is puzzling me greatly. I dislike the count immensely' – Armand's shoulders relaxed and his face smoothed out when he heard that – 'yet I must do as he bids me. You, I . . .' she trailed off.

'You feel what about me?' prompted Armand, his eyes boring into her soul.

She spoke softly, with her heart in her words. 'You I . . . feel much for. But if you will have no priest, we will burn in hell for expressing our love. I am perplexed as to what I should think.'

Armand's lips curved in a tender smile. 'My love, do not trouble yourself now. I will not weary you with my persuasions, either, for I can see how your thoughts are moving. We shall have a fine, full-moon festival tonight and you shall dance with the gipsies. Who knows, perhaps by the morning you will decide that you cannot leave us.'

He placed her protectively behind his body as the gipsies' shaggy dogs rushed out from the camp, barking wildly and salivating. Justine followed his broad back down the last few feet of path that led into the camp, her

131

thoughts in a turmoil. It sounded as if he wanted her to stay with him. But if he was willing to acknowledge her in front of all his people, why would he not let the priest marry them?

Armand placed a protective arm around her. 'The dogs will not hurt you now, Justine. I have told them that you are my people, one of us – to be defended with their lives if necessary.'

She patted a vast brindled wolfhound absently. Two smelly lurchers sniffed at her dress. Armand led her into the camp. The wolfhound padded after them on silent shaggy paws. 'I think this one is making sure I do not run off with the spoons,' laughed Justine.

'I think he follows you because he loves you' – Armand's voice was as tender as a summer night as he bent to whisper the end of his sentence in her ear – 'like his master does.'

As the gipsies came running to greet them, the huge dog placed his striped bulk between the camp folk and Justine. Reassured by his presence, she placed a small hand on top of his head, which came up higher than her waist, and patted him. The big dog gave a happy sigh and leant against her. It seemed as if the wolfhound did love her, but Justine was not so sure about his master.

'Come!' cried Armand, reassuring her with his eyes. 'You have the freedom of the camp. This is Dulcie. Go to her waggon and she will fit you out for the party.' Justine was glad that the brindled dog followed her closely. She felt less alone in this strange wild place with him by her side. Dulcie's slatternly beauty made her nervous. The gipsy smelt vilely of cheap perfume. Insolent breasts pushed out of her smutty silk blouse and her hips swung blatantly as she led Justine towards her caravan. Although she poured a selection of fine, brightly coloured silks on to the dirty counterpane of the bed for Justine to choose from, Dulcie took no interest in the selection. She looked out of the tiny window humming and admiring her long talons the whole time they were in the cramped, patchouli-smelling caravan.

It was wonderful to take the coarsely woven governess's gown off and feel the soft air on her naked skin. After a moment's thought, Justine took off the thick black stockings too. Her legs were mottled red where the thick stuff had scratched them. She folded the garments carefully, knowing she would need them later, but part of her longed to toss them out for ever.

The touch of gipsy silk on her skin was like a mother's kiss. She picked out an off-the-shoulder blouse of vivid carmine and a full black skirt patterned with roses. She chose them because they smelt of new dye. The never-worn fabric slipped easily through her fingers, and she looked to Dulcie for permission, wondering if the gipsy would be upset if she chose the newest of the clothes that were on offer. Dulcie gave an indifferent shrug, but she must not have minded for she tossed Justine a wide red belt stitched with tinkling gold coins that set off her narrow waist to perfection, and a pair of sandals made of coarse brown hide.

When they emerged from the caravan, the wolfhound lurched to his feet eagerly and followed Justine as she walked nervously towards the main fire of the camp-ground. The fire smelt of apple logs and blazed orange against the blue of winter twilight. Looking up the hill at the dark bulk of the village, Justine could see the homely lighted squares of the peasants' windows. Over towards the forest, the sky was indigo blue, and the first few stars twinkled in the frosty air.

As she neared the campfire, Armand rose to greet her at once, open admiration burning in his eyes. The thin silk seemed to vanish under his stripping look, and she greeted him nervously. 'Now you look like one of us,' he cried, 'but I want to set your hair free. May I?'

Justine's eyes fell before the ardour in his, but she nodded dumbly and bent her head. She felt his fingers tugging at the governess's bun, and a sensation of freedom as he took the ugly metal pins out, so that her chestnut locks could tumble free over her shoulders. She shook her hair over her face and hid behind the silky waterfall as she followed him close to the fire.

The flames from the big fire cast a welcome warmth on to her skin. It must have been burning for days as the huge logs blazed on a thick bed of white ash. Dark figures were drifting over to join the merriment around the main fire, seating themselves on the logs that were scattered around. As they came to the fire, each dark face and each set of fierce eyes scrutinised Justine sharply and then nodded when Armand introduced her. Each gipsy then appeared to forget all about her. But Justine had a feeling that they were all very aware of her, and curious about her presence in their inner circle. Someone brought her a rich venison stew, fragrant with herbs and red wine. The darkness pressed coldly at her back as she ate, and she snuggled closer to Armand. His arm went round her protectively.

'Do you need a shawl?'

'No, thank you. I am warm enough.'

He placed a large warm hand on her shoulder and shook his head, concern in his dark eyes. 'No you are not. Your skin is cool.' He called to a young man who was squatting on his haunches very close to them. The young man sped off into the night and returned very quickly with a soft dark shawl. Curiosity gleamed in his faunlike face as he handed it to Justine, and once again she wondered what they all thought of her being there.

Armand wrapped the feather-soft shawl around her tenderly. When she looked up, she could see firelight reflected in his eyes. His concern for her warmed her as much as the shawl, or the brandy in a battered pewter goblet, which a woman with gold earrings now set before her. A fiddle started up and was soon joined by another, then another, and then a soft drum. Justine tipped back her head and gazed into the night sky. Tears came into her eyes. Armand brushed them away with a gentle finger. 'Is the music so sad?'

'No, not sad. Only so wild and so lonely and there is so much yearning in it that it tears at my heart.'

Armand's voice was a barely audible whisper as he

134

spoke into the cloud of her free hair. 'As my heart is torn when you will not have me. Say the word, Justine, and this shall be your wedding party.'

A lump made a fist in her throat. 'A Christian wedding?'

Armand drew back impatiently and his brows snapped together. 'You must leave that behind you.' He stared angrily into the fire.

Justine shivered and her breath caught on a sob. 'I cannot.'

He flung himself to his feet and strode over to the musicians. Justine huddled on her log. She longed for Armand so much, but she could not throw off the teachings of her entire life so lightly. The wolfhound put a soft nose in her lap and she cried bitterly into his fur. She was still not in control of herself when Armand came back. She was aware of him standing over her, looking down on her shaking shoulders. A gentle hand touched her head. 'Now now, Justine. I forget what a baby you are, and how innocent. I should not speak harshly to you – but I am not used to being put off by a woman and that's the truth.'

'It's probably very good for you,' she sniffed.

Armand threw back his head and laughed. 'You could be right at that. But with you around there is no danger of my getting swollen headed. Never have I offered so much, nor been turned down so often, and here I am hanging around for more.' He knelt down and put his arms round her. Justine relaxed into their tenderness like a little cub snuggling into a lion's mane. Her head lay on his warm chest and she could feel his heart beating as he gentled her. 'I did not mean to upset you, my darling. I have called a party anyway. Listen how the music has changed! Will you not take a little sip of your drink and let me dry your tears.'

Justine looked up into his face and saw only tender concern. She sniffed hard, and felt the tears drying. A couple of high-pitched pipes had joined the fiddles and they were playing a merry jig now that had her foot tapping. Armand saw it move. He looked down at her twitching toes in their borrowed sandals and laughed.

135

'That's my girl.' He lifted the sweet-smelling brandy in its dark dented cup and passed it to her. 'Do not drink too much,' he warned, 'for it's a heady strong spirit, but a little will warm your heart.'

'Like you,' said Justine, looking at him sadly. But a sip of the warming maple-flavoured brandy and the thrilling gaiety of the fiddles was doing much to restore her.

Armand smiled into her eyes as he saw her face turning sunny. 'No one should be sad at a party, least of all the guest of honour. And look, see! Here comes the first of the dancers.'

The dancers wore flame-coloured dresses or canary-yellow skirts and blouses the pink of a flamingos' wings. The skirts were wrapped about with shawls of turquoise and emerald green and underskirts flashed like red and green jungle parrots. Headscarves edged with gold coins tinkled over their flying gipsy curls as the women leapt and danced in the shimmering firelight. More and more of the gipsies joined in. The music grew wilder as the stars came out in the frosty sky and, nice as it was, curled up with Armand, all ten of Justine's toes were tapping and she made no protest when he got to his feet and led her over to the whirling circle of dancers.

More and more musicians appeared, playing jigs from Ireland and flamenco from Spain and wild plaintive airs all their own. The music spoke to the free spaces in Justine's heart, and she danced with abandon, not caring that many of the gipsies still watched her curiously, but very aware that Armand's gaze was fixed on her constantly.

When the full moon was at its highest point, hours later, she flopped panting on to a log, wiping the sweat from her forehead and curling her toes to relax her aching feet. She was glad to find the big wolfhound still waiting for her, and it seemed that he had been guarding her brandy for it was waiting for her too. She took a welcome sip. The smell filled her nostrils and the honey-gold liquid flowed down her parched throat with a sinuous caress. A dark shadow moving between her and the fire made her shrink back, but it was only Armand. He smiled into her eyes as he took the sip of brandy that she offered him. 'It is indeed time to rest and take refreshment. See how many have turned from dancing to thoughts of love.'

Justine looked where he pointed. She saw for the first time that, although many bright figures still circled the fire in time to the music, many couples had stripped, and were making love just on the edge of the firelight. Right next to her – how could she not have heard their passionate cries? – a dark handsome man knelt behind a wild-looking girl in her twenties. Her face contorted in a grimace that could have been pain or pleasure as the swarthy gipsy thrust his cock between her buttocks in a rapidly accelerating rhythm. Firelight gleamed on the sweat that slicked both of their bodies. They were wild and untrammelled. They looked free and natural, copulating without shame under the stars. Justine felt restless and uneasy and horribly carnal. Part of her longed to join them, but she looked away.

It was hard to meet Armand's eyes. The longing in them was like a blow. How much was love, and how much was lust? Justine didn't know, and she wished she had not chosen to stop dancing. She shifted uneasily on her log, feeling the rough bark scrape her skin as she rearranged her skirts to cover more of her legs. She shivered as the frosty night air touched her skin. She shivered again as Armand moved closer to her. The coins sewn to her belt tinkled as his arms went round her. He buried his head in her shoulder and said in a muffled voice, 'Justine, I beg you again. Will you not be mine?'

The warmth of his body touched her to her very heart and she shook all over with the force of her dilemma. 'Can we not ... could we not have a priest?' she begged in a tiny voice. The dark head shook slightly against her shoulder, and that was all the answer she got. The moment stretched out between them. Justine could feel Armand's heart beating hard, and she wished she knew what he was thinking. She reached out a timid hand and smoothed his black hair. Armand lifted his head and sat back on his

137

heels. Justine strained to see his eyes in the shadows cast by the leaping fire, but his expression was unreadable.

He shook himself all over. 'Ho! I get too serious,' he cried, and pulling her up by both hands he dragged her over to the fire. His tone was merry, but Justine could see a muscle ticking in his cheek, and his jaws were set in a grim line. He pulled her over to where the musicians still played. A violin wailed. The wolfhound padded after them. Armand shouted loudly to a wrinkled old crone who sat huddled close to the fire. The old crone gave him a toothless smile and waved her tambourine at them both. 'This is Justine, grandmother,' he shouted again. This time she nodded and rooted around in her voluminous black clothes, eventually producing a small but sturdy jewellery box. She passed it to Armand.

He held it in his hands before looking at Justine with a sad smile playing on his lips. 'I had hoped that these would be my bridal gift to you,' he said, his voice unbearably soft. He looked away, towards the fire, and turned the box in his hands. 'Yet even though you refuse me, I can imagine no other woman but you for these rubies to grace. Will you accept them from me?'

He looked at her intently before he snapped open the lid of the box and held it out for her to see. Curious, Justine leant over the box, and then gasped out loud. Seated on a bed of white satin were six perfect rubies. The firelight danced in their carmine hearts and she saw that they had been cut into the shape of magnificent six-pointed stars. Startled she looked up at Armand. He was looking down at her sadly. Confused by her feelings, she looked back at the rubies. Her voice was that of a timid child as she said, 'They are too good for me, Armand. You will need them one day. Save them for your – ' She choked on the word 'wife' and substituted the words, 'new love'.

'You are my true love,' said Armand, and his eyes burned into hers. 'Only you shall have them. Whether you will have me or no makes no difference. I had no mind to buy you. They are a gift. A free love offering. Will you not

138

take them on that basis and wear them as a token of my love?'

Tears blurred the flames that danced in the facets of the rubies. Justine said softly, 'I will indeed.' She felt more tears wetting her cheeks as he pressed the little box into her hands with a world of love in his eyes. Justine bent her head and looked more closely at her beautiful rubies, touching them gently with one forefinger. Then she touched them again more curiously. The six gems were each individually mounted on fittings much like those for earrings, but her ears were not pierced even for two rings, let alone six. One of her hands went up to touch an ear nervously. 'I shall have to get some holes made,' she said.

Armand's eyes were dark, 'That's not where you wear them, Justine.'

Startled, she looked up at him. 'They are not earrings? Then I can't imagine where they go.'

Now there was laughter gleaming through the tears that had come to his eyes while they talked. 'Only think of the place that I adore, Justine. Where can that be?'

She stared right at him in astonishment, but a surge of heat between her legs gave her the answer. 'No,' she stammered. 'Oh no. Indeed I could not wear them there.' Blood stung her cheeks. 'Armand, I cannot – ' But the warmth between her legs was changing from simple warmth to blissful rapture and her breath was coming faster.

With a teasing smile, Armand took the box back. 'Then you shall not have them.'

Justine tossed her head. 'Fine. Give them to some other woman.'

'Oh no!' His eyes told her how serious he was. 'No other woman shall have them. If you will not wear them they go in the river.'

'No! You would not do that! As beautiful as they are. You could not throw them away.' Despite herself, Justine's hands had come up to clutch at the box. Armand smiled at her as he released it into her hands.

'You must make up your mind to it. These rubies can

glitter from your intimate parts, where they will dwell in beauty all their days, or they can lie unregarded in the mud of the river bed. The choice is yours.'

Biting her lip in indecision, Justine turned the box over in her hands. When she looked up again, she noticed that many of the gipsies, some still naked, had drifted over to watch her scene with Armand. The old crone watched her expectantly. The heat and pressure between Justine's legs increased as her shaven sex, now just misted over with new growth, reacted to the significance of her words.

'Very well. I will wear them where you bid me.'

The watching gipsies pressed closer. Silvery moonlight fell over their wild dark faces, making their features stand out in high relief. The great logs in the fire had burned low, but the glowing heart still threw off immense heat, even though the leaping flames had died down. Silver moonlight and orange firelight bathed the watching figures. Justine's back burned, but she shivered with cold as she waited for Armand's next move.

His voice was low but commanding. 'Take off your blouse.'

Justine swallowed nervously, aware of the watching eyes. She untucked the blouse from its jingling belt and pulled it up over her head and off. A youth as wild and graceful as a forest faun ran forward to take it from her. Justine recognised him as the one who had brought her a shawl. He seemed to be hanging around, ready to do anything for Armand.

Her beasts gleamed free in the pale light. She heard breath sucked in sharply as the men around the campfire caught sight of her upstanding breasts with their chestnut nipples. Armand's throat worked, and he took a step closer to her. Slowly, leisurely, he bent his dark head and took one nipple in his mouth. The touch of his wet mouth awoke passion in Justine and desire trembled in the purse that hung between her legs. Armand's dark hands smoothed gently over the skin of her breasts and he moved his head to suckle the other nipple. The end of his long dark hair brushed her skin and Justine put back her head

140

and sighed. Pleasure coursed through the tips of her nipples and travelled from there to between her legs. Armand lifted his head away from her nipples and brushed each firm nub with his thumbs. 'Your body responds to me,' he said, his eyes bright with the triumph of conquest. 'See how your nipples stiffen and enlarge. Your body knows what is good for it.'

Justine ran two trembling hands through her hair and then pressed them to her temples. It was true. Dear God, how she responded to this man. Her breath came quickly into her mouth and her chest rose and fell violently, making her breasts catch the light as they lifted with her panting. She did not answer him. She didn't trust her voice. She didn't trust herself not to scream out her love for this man, not to implore him to take her right now and make her his forever.

Sadness clouded Armand's eyes when he saw that she was not going to answer. 'Take off your skirt,' he said brusquely. Justine undid the coin-sewn belt then slid the swinging skirt over her shaking legs and stepped out of it. The faun-faced youth was there again to take the garments. Now she was naked before Armand, and his people. The watching figures pressed closer, but she was only vaguely aware of them. Her gaze was fixed on Armand. He was looking down at her, a cruel twist to his lips. He did not touch her again. She stood trembling and completely naked before him, but he made no move towards her. One bold gipsy put out a grimy hand to caress Justine's naked buttock. Armand just touched his flashing silver knife and the man retreated so far into the shadows that Justine never saw him again.

She stood naked and expectant. The firelight licked at her buttocks and the backs of her legs and her hair lay heavy across her shoulders. She could feel the cold night air crinkling her nipples with its icy breath as it blew down the front of her body. She wished Armand would take her in his arms and warm her. And then she closed her eyes. They would both burn in hell if she gave in to her carnal desires. And her carnal desires were flaring. The fleshy lips

141

of her sex were hot and swollen in burning contrast to the cold that froze her breasts. The faintest drift of new fur tickled her when she moved, making her aware of her still-shaven pubis. A drop of thick liquid lay at the top of her legs where it had seeped from her dark and moist vagina. Her body was producing love dew with which to greet Armand. She pressed her thighs together and wished it would dissipate. It was only an embarrassment to her now, proving to anyone who saw it how deeply her desire for Armand ran.

Armand reached out one hand to her at last and she shrank back from his touch. Then she stood more bravely and allowed him to touch her. He slipped cold fingers into the very top of her slit and ran them down the shaven lips of her vulva, pulling them apart in a businesslike manner. The old crone pushed her way to the front of the crowd and, to Justine's shivering astonishment, she too pushed bony little fingers in at the top of the shaven slit and pulled them along the lips of Justine's vulva.

The gipsies pushed closer to see what was going on, and for a moment Justine felt faint under the combined weight of the curious eyes and the probing fingers that violated her intimate secret sexual self. Armand and the old crone withdrew their fingers and muttered together briefly. Justine stood swaying slightly, wondering if her knees would hold her up. Another great dollop of liquid left the inner walls of her vagina and began its slow journey to the secret opening between her legs. She could trace its path by the intense pleasure it left in its wake and the shiveringly good sensations that crossed the entrance of her vagina as the love dew trickled out. She knew it must be coating Armand's fingers even as he turned over a six-star ruby in his hands, angling it absently so that it flashed in the firelight as he spoke to the old grandmother.

Justine felt so publicly exposed; her body was on view to all the gipsies who now craned in so closely that she could smell their unwashed bodies and the spirits on their breath. Yet her feelings, her desperate desire for Armand, were so private, so personal. She hardly knew how to cope

142

with the idea that some fifty people could see her stiff and crinkled nipples poking out in visible proof of her arousal.

The faun-faced boy appeared bearing a thick soft-wool blanket. It was deep crimson and bound with red satin ribbon on all four edges. He carefully brushed away twigs and ash and then spread it on the ground near the fire. A quiver ran round Justine's belly. 'Lie down,' ordered Armand curtly. She kicked off her borrowed sandals and took a cautious step on to the softness of the blanket. Then she sank to her knees and looked at Armand pleadingly. There was no friendship in his eyes. 'Lie down.' His lips twisted cruelly as he issued the order. Feeling helpless, Justine did as he bid.

She had kept her legs together, but Armand pulled them open. She closed her eyes in dismay, knowing that her private parts would be swollen and glistening with proof of her arousal, and that Armand would see them. There was a break in the music and she heard clothes rustle as the gipsies pressed closer. She felt vulnerable and helpless. Slim hands pulled her arms up behind her head, causing her breasts to stand up and her belly to flatten. She looked up into the slanting eyes of the forest-faun youth. They were dark and hostile, and she looked away.

Armand's big warm hands pulled one of her knees to the side, stretching her sex open. The bony claws of the crone pulled the other knee, and her organs opened wider still. Justine melted and swooned with the mingled pleasure and humiliation that she felt. Her pubic bone tilted up in a lewd invitation and she felt the muscles of her love tunnel clench because her body wanted Armand desperately, despite, or perhaps because of, the humiliation he was causing her as she lay open and helpless before him.

Cool fingers now spread her vulval lips wide open. The touch of those hard fingers was impersonal, but pleasure washed through her and she quivered on the edge of a powerful orgasm. Her hands were held tightly above her head, her knees were held open, and hands brushed at her clitoris as Armand and the grandmother tickled and tormented her vulva. Justine bit her lips hard and tried to get control of herself, to damp the pleasure that she was feeling. To remind herself of the furtive, avid eyes that watched her every move. But it was no good. Rapture swept her and she was aware of sweat dewing her breasts and belly and beading on her upper lip.

She could hear water splashing, then boiling hot metal touched her fleshy lips. She screamed out loud and her hips twisted. Fingers touched her all along the inner lips of her sex. Her hips twisted again and she didn't know if it was pleasure or pain she was feeling. The hot metal touch came again, and again. Her hips twisted and bucked and she was dimly aware of the youth who was holding her hands laughing and then bending to whisper something into her ear. His voice buzzed in her ear and sent thrills down her spine but she could make no sense of his words. She was too close to the abyss of her orgasm.

She panted and shook. More sweat broke out. Convulsions seemed to sweep her body and she still fought to control herself; yet she could not deny the vast melting sweetness that was liquefying her buttocks and moving closer and closer into the heart of her red velvet pleasure. The hot metal intrusion hit her sex once more. And this time she surrendered. Panting and screaming and twisting her hips right up off the ground, Justine dissolved into the waiting arms of her orgasm and gave into the sweeping pleasure that took her over.

As the rush of sensation faded, she lay sagging on the soft warm blanket for a few seconds and then shame washed over her. The watching gipsies were laughing and clapping, applauding her decoration. Her shaven vulva felt strange and cluttered, but even as she became aware of it, and the youth releasing her arms, Armand was crouching next to her. His eyes were bloomed over with the intense darkness of a man in the grip of physical passion. 'The most erotic experience of my life,' he murmured. 'Ah, Justine, if you could have seen yourself as I saw you: the abandon, the sweetness of your pink flesh as it coiled and gleamed and flickered in the light. And now,

now that you wear those magnificent gems ... Justine. I must have you or I die. Be mine for ever. Be my bride.'

Melted by the passion in his eyes, Justine opened her mouth to cry yes. But a log fell in the campfire behind her and regret twisted her belly. 'The flames of hell,' she muttered, watching the golden sparks swirl up into the indigo night sky. 'Oh, Armand, to burn for all eternity – '

'My heart!' he cried. 'Never have I loved a woman as I love you, and you tear my feelings so that I die as I watch you.' The pain in his face was so intense that Justine closed her own eyes to escape it. His image burned on the back of her eyelids. She loved him and she was hurting him. She couldn't bear it. She opened her eyes to say she would be his.

Armand was on the red rug next to her, leaning back on his knees, an expression of agony on his face. 'The frustration will kill me,' he roared, oblivious to the ring of watching faces. The faun-faced youth slipped through the crowd. He shucked off his clothes, knelt, and presented his naked buttocks to Armand. 'Take me!' he cried, love for Armand vibrating in his voice. 'Dear master, use me as you will.' Armand reached into the fly of his trousers, ripping it open so violently that buttons flew in all directions as he released his full and straining manhood.

A cry rose to Justine's lips as she saw his glorious shaft. 'Mine,' she cried uselessly, her voice unheard. The strength of the jealousy that swept her was a revelation. 'Do not take him! Armand. 'Tis an abomination to take a man so!'

With a groan that came from the hell he was suffering, Armand plunged his cock deeply into the waiting youth. His hands flew out and gripped the slim buttocks so tightly that blue crescent-shaped marks appeared in the pale skin under his fingernails. There was ecstasy on the wicked face of the faun as Armand used him so. Justine bounded to her feet screaming, 'No! No! This must not be.' She leant over and batted at Armand's shoulders with both slim hands, screaming into his face. Armand lifted his hands from the wildly heaving buttocks underneath him, but only for long enough to push her aside.

Justine stepped back and pushed her fists into her mouth. Shock and emotion ran riot over her body. The lips between her legs felt hot and strange. Her knees were shaking with fear and disgust. A cold sinking gripped her belly. She looked around wildly. Some of the gipsies were watching Armand as the veins in his forehead stood out and he sank deeper and deeper into the kneeling youth. Some of the dark faces were watching Justine's hysterical reaction curiously. She saw the neat pile of her clothes and snatched them up. Just as she found her sandals a cry broke from Armand's throat as he came violently, as if he were experiencing anger rather than relief. Justine glanced back at his cry, and saw sperm gushing out in gleaming white arcs as the naked youth beneath Armand ejaculated in time with his master's orgasm. Disgust swept over her, and dismay and jealousy too. The turmoil of her emotions found sweet relief in the movements of her body. Clutching the bundle of gipsy clothes to her, she ran madly into the moonlit night.

Chapter Nine

*E*very rooster in the village was greeting the frosty dawn with a raucous cry as Justine tiptoed up to the castle. The side door she had slipped out of was locked. Should she wait for it to be opened? What if someone should be looking for her? If this morning above all others she should be wanted to give a lesson? Guilt twisted in her belly and made her eager to be safely back in her room. She would try the main entrance. Just as Justine was slinking up the side of the crumbling flight of 87 steps that led up to the high stone arch of the main gate, merry trumpets blew and a hunting party spilled out. She shrank back, shivering in the cold air, hoping that no one would see her, but someone called out at once, 'Ho gipsy! Shall we have good sport today?'

Her mouth was dry and she struggled to find the right words. If she could please them, maybe they would pass her by without looking too closely. 'Inordinately good,' she cried.

'Inordinately good vocabulary for a gipsy,' remarked one of the brightly dressed nobles. There was scattered laughter.

'Inordinately good voice, too,' cried another, enjoying the joke. Justine trembled for her life. She heard the clatter of horses arriving at the foot of the steps and she prayed the nobles would go on down to their mounts and forget her. But one dark figure detached itself from the brightly dressed group and came over to look at her. She stared in disbelief. Her eyes met the eyes of Father Gabriel. But why did she feel like a stricken rabbit before a fox. Surely he would not give her away?

His eyes were cruel, and one thin eyebrow lifted in interrogation. 'I thought that voice reminded me of someone. But Justine! Is this how a governess dresses?' In slow motion Justine saw the count turn at his brother's words. Then his shiny insect figure scuttled over to where she cowered on the steps. His eyes crept right inside the tawdry gipsy clothes, like an earwig into an ear, and ran all over her breasts. Justine wished she still had the shawl. She was cold all over except where his eyes burned her. She could think of no excuse to give for her being out of the castle. She closed her eyes and waited for the blow to fall.

But the count was too distracted by the amount of cleavage revealed by her new outfit to even wonder why she was on the steps so early. 'She's dressed up to attract her man,' he said, and he puffed up his chest and smoothed down his oily hair. 'My poor pretty dear, did you think I would never send for you again? I should have told you that I had ridden out to meet my brother. We only returned last night. You may be very sure that I shall send for you this evening.'

Justine's stomach lurched. Father Gabriel looked at his brother and raised his brows. 'Is she to be a treat for me?'

'No, brother. I have something truly remarkable lined up for you: Siamese twins. Think of that. Four breasts and six pretty openings. I have been saving them for you.'

'I would sooner have Justine.'

The count's face darkened. 'You never change, Gabriel. If I offer you something you spurn it. Why will you not accept what I offer you?'

'The leftovers? The leavings of the older son? You have everything. You thwart me over this matter to be

148

malicious. Is it not enough for you that I am banished to the church?'

The count's black beetle eyes gleamed with delight. 'What about your grand new promotion? Why, I almost think that I would rather be you than me.' Justine saw that the count enjoyed baiting the younger man. He did not stop laughing at his angry brother until he was distracted by a crash of musical barking. The hounds had arrived. Waldgraf turned away and surveyed with great satisfaction the forest of wagging tails that surged around the horses' legs. 'Let's hunt,' he cried, and streaked down the broad stone steps to his waiting horse.

Father Gabriel clenched and unclenched his hands. His brow was knotted with fury and Justine saw the muscles in his cheeks cord. 'It is always so with him,' he muttered. 'My wishes count as nothing and the discussion is finished as soon as he orders it. But I will not be gainsaid.' He whirled and called out to one of the servants. 'Thomas!' A strong, ruddy-cheeked peasant rushed over. Father Gabriel cast a swift glance at his brother, but the count was turned away, mounting his gaily decked horse, so he said quietly, almost furtively, 'Take this gipsy and bring her to the north hunting lodge. I will break away as soon as I can and join you there.'

'We cannot,' protested Justine, clutching at her skimpy top in the freezing air. 'The count . . .' But joy mingled with her fear. She couldn't help being delighted that her beloved Father Gabriel wanted her. How pale he was. How thin and aristocratic. She had forgotten how high his forehead was, how thin and cruel his lips; he was her own familiar lover.

He hardly looked at her or seemed to heed her protests, only turning to snarl at Thomas, 'Whip her if she gives you any trouble. Loess and Felo of the guards will do anything for me. Ask them if you need help.'

Two great pink hams caught hold of Justine as Thomas took her in a sturdy grip. 'Whip me? Why should he say that?' she asked, staring after Father Gabriel's retreating back. 'He is my dear teacher and mentor. I would do anything for him. I was merely fearful of the count's anger.'

'Shouldn't worry your head about it, mistress,' said Thomas gruffly, but his grip relaxed slightly. 'I've served young Gabriel man and boy and it was ever the same between him and the count. His brother can put him into a fury the way no other man can, and 'tis not only the nobility that's true of. Why, my nephew . . .'

Gossiping garrulously he led Justine away. She had no choice but to follow him, but her heart was full of misgivings. On the one hand she was to see her beloved Father Gabriel again. On the other, if the count were to discover their tryst – but her thoughts broke off at this point. She could only hope that he would not discover them.

An uneasy dread made it impossible to settle once they reached the hunting lodge. Justine roamed around the stone-flagged floor of the cottage restlessly, picking up hunting trophies and putting them down. The fat cook brought in a tray of pea and ham soup with great crusty loaves. Thomas lifted his sturdy elbows and set to. Justine could eat little. Foreboding coiled in her belly like a thunderstorm. After the meal, Thomas stretched himself full length across the mighty wooden settle that stood in front of the blazing log fire. It was covered with deerskins and piled with soft cushions. He was asleep in minutes. Justine ran anxious hands over the fossilised treetrunk that made a mantelpiece for the great stone fireplace, picking up a fox's brush, then a deer's antler, twisting them between her hands and putting them down again. She could sneak away now, return to the castle. She crossed the room with quick agitated footsteps and looked out of one of the narrow, arched windows.

The sun shone steadily in a pale clear sky. There was no movement in the dark pine forest outside. She could see about half a mile along the grassy rutted track that led to the lodge, but nothing stirred along it. She could remember the way back to the castle perfectly. It would take her only an hour, less if she ran, to return to the safety of her room. But she longed to spend time with her dear friend and mentor. How much she had to tell him. And he wanted to see her. He had defied the count because he wanted to see her. She had to wait for him. She had to see him.

If only he would come quickly and dispel the sense of brooding unease that she felt. The fire crackled sweetly in the hearth, and, apart from the fine layer of dust that lay over everything and a faint smell of damp, the hunting lodge was as sweet a place for a tryst as she could imagine. Great furry bear rugs covered almost every inch of the polished stone floors. The furniture that stood about was comfortable, made for tired men to fling themselves into at the end of a long day. Each sturdy wooden chair was piled high with big masculine cushions and comfortable rugs made of skin and fur. There were no books, no fussy ornaments, no gilt-framed pictures or spindle-legged chairs. All was plain – wood, stone and leather the preferred materials. The comfort was supplied by the roaring log fire, the piles of luxuriant furry pelts, and a vast carved cupboard crammed full of enticing bottles.

Justine was dimly aware of the pleasure that being in this room gave her. But her stomach knotted with tension. She paced restlessly. If he would only come soon: they could meet and talk, and she could be back in her room before the count knew anything about their meeting. She picked up a string of polished boar tusks and ran it through her fingers restlessly. Then a faint sound outside made her start. She ran to the window. It was Father Gabriel. The soft sward of the track had muffled his approach. He was already at the door. She ran to greet him, smiling into his eyes. 'Oh, Father Gabriel, I have so wanted to see – '

'Quiet!' he said, taking her arm roughly. 'We don't have much time.'

Justine's heart moved inside her. She was full of experiences that weighed her down heavily. She needed to talk to him. But he pushed her into the stone hall of the lodge and sat on the wooden bench that stood just inside the door. He stuck out one leg. 'Boots!' he ordered, lifting his silk robe to expose them. Justine knelt on the cold flags. She took his cold dirty boot and pulled hard. The shiny black boot fitted so tightly that she had to struggle to pull it off. Sweat dewed her forehead before the second boot joined its fellow on the stone floor. Father Gabriel rose to his feet, 'Follow me to the bedroom,' he said curtly. Justine followed him, but slowly, deep in thought, wiping her dirty hands on her skirt. She had forgotten. This was how things went with Father Gabriel: he ordered and she obeyed. How could she have imagined that they would be able to talk? He would tell her what he wanted, and she would obey. Resentment rose in her, but it was mixed with the stirrings of passion. Her body remembered exactly how it was with Father Gabriel. His nearness was making her tremble, awaking carnal memories.

Someone had thrown back the shutters of the bedroom they walked into and winter sun streamed on to the polished wooden floor. Another lively fire burned in the stone fireplace; the room was deliciously warm and fragrant with apple logs. The walls were made of craggy honey-coloured stone, but the pale wood gleaming softly from under the scattered white fur pelts on the floor created a bright, soft look. Mirrors hung all round the room, especially by the bed, and they reflected the cheerful sunshine and yellow walls. More white fur was piled on to the wooden sleigh bed that stood in one corner, and yellow silk cushions were heaped up on the chairs. Justine looked about her in pleasure, but Father Gabriel snapped nastily, 'You do forget yourself. Kneel!'

Heart thudding painfully, Justine lowered herself to the floor by his feet. She could smell lavender floor polish. The cracks in the wooden floor blurred under the tears that stung her eyes. She clasped her hands together to keep them from shaking. The soft moist triangle between her legs burned, and she was suddenly aware of the unfamiliar sensation of the rubies that pierced her labia. They made her sweetly aware of the changes taking place in her sex. Her vulval lips felt delicious as they swelled and stiffened. Hot blood flowed into them. Rapture flooded though her. Then her breath caught – her rubies! What would Father Gabriel say if he saw them?

A shock nearly as strong as an orgasm whipped around her body. A sick premonition of disaster was in her belly and she was filled with soft terror: could she make Father Gabriel believe that the count had given her the rubies? Her head swam as she tried to juggle the conflicting demands of the men around her. Her knees refused to hold her up. She shook and shivered as she kept her head bowed and waited for Father Gabriel to speak.

The door clattered open and Justine saw Father Gabriel turn to face it with his mouth wide open in a suddenly pale face. She did not dare to look over her shoulder, but she could see the doorway reflected in one of the mirrors that hung about the room. She nearly fainted with relief when she saw the white flash of the cook's apron. 'Get out of here, you bloody woman,' bawled Father Gabriel.

The cook dipped a ponderous curtsey. 'I do beg your honour's pardon. But wasn't you wanting no food? The gentlemen's usually hungry when they gets in from the cold.'

'No I don't – Wait! Listen to me, woman. Bring me powdered sugar, some good butter and some apricot brandy.'

Justine listened to her heart slowing to normal, but her stomach still twisted within her, telling her that it would be the count next time, and then, oh then something terrible would happen. Her rubies burned in the sexual space between her legs. Father Gabriel turned his head and looked down at her. 'Have you bathed since you arrived in this cottage?'

'No, Father.' She did not dare look at him.

'Then go now and wash your body all over. Be quick about it.'

Justine rose to her feet and drew in a shaky breath. She lifted the heavy metal latch of the wooden door without making a sound and let herself quietly into the stone hall. She looked up the passage. A stag's head stared at her with sightless eyes. It had not been stuffed very well and its fur was dropping out in patches. She did not know which way to go. Then she heard whistling and followed the sound into a room full of guns and hunting paraphernalia. A man in a leather apron was sitting next to a long blood-stained table cleaning Father Gabriel's boots. He led her to the bathroom willingly enough, but Justine could not shake off the feeling of being an intruder. The feeling that she should not be in this place at all.

When the door opened, just as she had got naked and pinned her hair up, she clutched the bundle of her clothes to her protectively and cowered. But it was only a fat country girl carrying a copper jug full of hot water. The soft water steamed gently and Justine was glad to have it. It was a pleasure indeed to lather up the sweet-smelling soap and sluice off the layer of filth that seemed to cling to her.

Her rubies gleamed dully against her naked sex lips. She washed around them carefully, thinking tenderly of Armand. The weight of the smooth stones was a gentle and constant reminder of him. Her pubic hair was still just a mist; it was beginning to prickle her slightly. The combined sensations kept her in a constant state of sexual awareness. Her nipples were sensitive too. They crinkled in pleasure as the clean hot water trickled over them in a sweet caress. Justine gave a great sigh of contentment as she cleaned herself all over.

She dried herself on one of the thin, stiff, lavender-smelling towels. Then she looked for her clothes. They had gone! The maid must have taken them to wash. Now she was naked in this strange house. Justine's heart thumped hard and the taste of fear was in her mouth. She could not keep Father Gabriel waiting, nor did she wish to wander through the hunting lodge in the nude looking for her clothes. She shook out one of the white towels, one that seemed a little bigger than the others, and wrapped it round her body, twisting a knot over her breasts to keep it in place.

There was no excuse to linger now. Her hands shook as she let her hair down and combed it out. Then, naked under the lavender-scented white towel, she pattered back through the stone passages to the bedroom where Father

154

Gabriel waited. He looked frightened when the door opened, but relaxed when he saw it was her. Justine stood shyly just inside the door of the yellow room and waited. Something important and private danced in Father Gabriel's eyes as he watched her. Justine could feel sexual heat again, smouldering under her rubies. Father Gabriel crossed the room slowly and took her face into both of his hands, looking lustfully into her eyes as he did so. Then he kissed her: a wet, open-mouthed slow kiss, and Justine went limp against him, moaning out loud.

He broke off and looked at her, 'You've changed, Justine,' he said, as if he did not like what he had found. 'Your kisses are those of an older woman, now: deeper, more mature and sensual.' He turned and led her over to the white furry pelt that lay in front of the fire. A wooden bowl was standing in the hearth in front of the red flames. An exquisite fruity, crushed-almond smell rose from it and hung languorously in the air. Father Gabriel picked up the brandy bottle that stood in the hearth and filled a small crystal goblet from it. The smell intensified and Justine saw apricots soaking in the heart of the bottle.

The fire crackled merrily and sunshine still streamed into the room, but her tension had not lessened. She was conscious of sin. The knowledge of wrongdoing was in her. She realised that she was still standing. She hastily knelt, as Father Gabriel liked her to do, and waited for her master's pleasure. He took a sip of the heady amber drink and looked down at her with stern and remote eyes. 'Remove that towel,' he ordered lazily. Justine's hands came up slowly and reluctantly and fumbled a little with the knot. The folds of the towel tickled her skin deliciously as they fell softly away, leaving her naked, kneeling before his gaze. Her hair fell down over her naked breasts, and she wished it were longer so that it might cover her hairless naked sex and protect its secrets from the prying male eyes of Father Gabriel.

If he saw her rubies he made no comment. His robe whispered as he swung round. He went over to the wooden sleigh bed and impatiently threw back the furs that lay heaped on it. He took hold of the white linen top sheet and pulled it vigorously, until it came free of the bed, flapping like a yacht sail. He walked back over to where she knelt naked by the fire and motioned her away. 'No, don't stand up,' he added.

Justine shuffled away on her knees, waited while he spread the sheet over the fur rug, and then shuffled back on to the soft yielding surface of the sheet. Father Gabriel looked at her with burning eyes, reached out and slowly circled one nipple. It hardened under his touch and Justine made a little accepting sound. She was wildly excited, yet somehow resisting, frightened still by the sense of wrong-doing that pervaded her being. She was breathing deeply and the folds of her sex felt petal-soft.

Father Gabriel turned away, stooped to pick up the wooden bowl and returned to Justine. She could smell that intoxicating smell again. He reached into the bowl and pulled out a handful of yellow, scented butter. It clung to his fingertips and Justine could see it glistening slightly where the heat of the apple-log fire had softened it. Father Gabriel set the bowl down and advanced on Justine with outstretched fingertips. His eyes gleamed with eagerness. He took one breast in both hands and smoothed the butter over her pink nipple, pulling the tip right out, stretching it as he did so. A wild aphrodisiac smell rose from the rich creamy brandy butter as he gently massaged it into the soft skin of her breasts.

Justine took a long, languorous breath and closed her eyes. Her body lost its feeling of tense foreboding. She felt her whole body relax. The space between her legs grew soft and warm and open as Father Gabriel began anointing the nipple of her other breast. The fragrance rose dizzyingly, and she looked up at him with lips that were pouting and soft and luscious. When he licked her breast, when he closed his mouth on it and sucked on it and let his teeth close on the nipple, biting and nuzzling it softly, she let out hot little cries and cradled his shaven priest's head to her bosom. He took the other nipple in his teeth now, then let go of it to bite and suck at the fair skin around the breast, then biting the little brown tip again. He growled playfully and chewed like a wolf cub, afterward sighing languorously and nuzzling into her warm and heavy breasts like a child.

Father Gabriel took his delicious mouth away from her responsive breasts and Justine's lips fell open in a soft protest. But, to her astonishment and delight, she saw that he was impatiently flinging off the black robes of his calling, until he was completely naked before her. He was like a fine marble statue: pale, narrow, aristocratically slender. He flung himself on his back on the sheet-covered rug in front of the fire and stretched his arms open wide. His cock jutted out from the centre of his pale body. Justine's eyes were immediately drawn to its smooth pale hardness as it curved enticingly from his tangle of pubic hair.

Father Gabriel looked upward and cried, 'Anoint me and then consume me, Justine. Let your lips bless every inch of my manhood.' Willingly she scooped up a handful of the scented butter. Drops of oily brandy had oozed to the surface and the creamy viscous mass was melting gently in the heat from the fire and liquefying in her hands. She smoothed the butter down the fine white narrow cock of Father Gabriel and felt the sensitive shaft twitch under her gentle hands. Then she pushed her face into the butter covered tangle of his pubic hair and inhaled the scent of his maleness throbbing under the heady perfume of the aphrodisiac brandy.

He moaned and twitched under her gentle touch. She shifted her attention to his cock. First she touched the very tip of his glans with her darting tongue. Then she drew her tongue back and ran it over her lips. Sweet! He had sweetened the butter and it was a glorious heady mix of brandy and apricots and sweet forbidden sugar. She bent back and sucked more eagerly. Then she withdrew to savour the exquisite tastes that dissolved on her lips and tongue. Father Gabriel writhed under her, lifting his hips, twisting them, inviting her to lick his penis again. Justine

157

breathed deeply and pouted her lips sinfully. It was sweet to have him helpless under her ministrations.

She inhaled deeply and as she did so drew the tip of his cock into her lips. She was going mad with the smell and the taste and the sight of him. All was one glorious explosion of the senses as she purred and pouted and licked him into frantic submission beneath her. 'Kneel over me!' cried Father Gabriel now. 'Let me bury my face in the scented heaven of your woman's place. I want your sinful lust to overpower my senses.'

Obediently, Justine turned around and kneeled over Father Gabriel's face. She knew that her sex lips must be dangling over his face in a sensuous fleshy pout. An inexpressibly wicked feeling of being opened up and available sexually swept over her in a raw wave. He would surely see her pierced labia now, and know that a man had shaved every hair of her sex before unnamable debaucheries took place. But he did not speak of it. Justine felt a cool stroking followed by a hot tingling as he caressed her with fingers smothered in brandy butter. She groaned and shuddered. The creamy butter slid into the crevices of her dark velvet flower. Her hips moved by themselves and so did the muscles of her vagina; they squeezed a red velvet squeeze and slipped uselessly off each other. The movements felt good, but they were full of longing: a longing for the hot satisfaction that only the male sexual organ could provide.

Then she felt his tongue scraping her clitoris, and a moan sprang to her lips and her pelvis lowered itself so that she could push her hot sex right up against Father Gabriel's lips. The wanton movement pushed her tight up against his hot greedy mouth so that he might eat of her ever more deeply and sensuously. And he licked her and sucked her and drew her sex deep into his mouth. She felt the sucking heat of his greed as he fed on her woman's honey.

Thrills of rapture bit into every nerve ending. She was shiveringly aware of the way that her naked bottom poked into the air, available for all to see. Her fleshy labia ground rapturously into Father Gabriel's face, enfolding him in a kiss from her sexual lips. The sweet curve of her belly just brushed over his flat pale tautness and her nipples slipped lightly over the skin of his lower body. As she gobbled up his long, delicious, butter-smeared cock, she was almost dizzy from the ambrosial taste of the powdered sugar and the heady smell of apricots.

She moaned softly when he pulled his manhood away from her soft enveloping mouth. 'It's too much,' he groaned. 'I want this ecstasy to last for ever, but we have no time. No time.' Apprehension crashed into the pit of Justine's belly. Who knew when the hunting party might return?

Father Gabriel slapped her left buttock and pushed her away. She knelt panting and shaking on the rug. The tips of her breasts tingled and glowed where he had been sucking them. Her rubies nibbled the length of her labia and every point of every red star was touching her lightly, contributing to the good feelings that flowed through her woman's place. She could feel the tips of her long hair brushing her sensitive skin. She felt alive and aware all over, soft with the sweet attentions of her old lover.

'On your hands and knees like a dog,' ordered Father Gabriel. Feeling deliciously animal, Justine lowered herself into the required position. Her hair fell down over her shoulders and the warmth from the fire made one side of her body glow a rosy pink. She could hear Father Gabriel's ragged breathing as he knelt behind her. She knelt submissively before him, waiting for his next move. 'Oh you sinful, wanton hussy,' said his low, gleeful voice. 'Oh you whore of Satan. How you tempt me. Shake your hips at me and show me your sex like a bitch dog in heat.'

Justine obediently wriggled her buttocks in a slinky sexy invitation, but an uneasy, used feeling crawled over her. She could not see the man behind her, only hear his breathing and his ragged urgent voice. 'You are not blatant enough in your invitation,' continued his low imperative commands. 'I want to see the lips of your sex as they wink and signal me in a lewd and unmistakable call to my manhood.'

Justine parted her knees so that the folds of her labia swung freely between her legs. She knew that the skin around her secret opening would be pink and glistening from saliva, love dew and melted honey butter. The raw feeling of openness was unmistakably sexual. Her feelings were disturbing in their power. Part of her gloried in her degrading animal lowness; but she was tormented by unease and a sense of wrongdoing. And now, to add to her unease, her vaginal opening began to burn in a way that told her she was being watched. A primitive and wild part of her insisted that other males were around; other eyes rested hotly on her sex.

'Speak to me,' ordered Father Gabriel, distracting her. 'I would hear from your own sinful pouting lips what lust you feel for me. Is your desire uncontrollable?'

Twin feelings of desire and disgust twisted in Justine's belly. Her marshmallow breasts burned as they dangled below her, and her buttocks were filled with hot liquid desire. But she did not want to speak of her yearnings aloud, not with the dread and foreboding that still hummed along her nerves, unsettling her. Hands tangled themselves in her hair and her head was jerked back painfully. 'Speak to me! Call me like a queen cat in heat or I will lose my patience with you,' he hissed.

Justine wet her dry lips with a tongue that felt too big for her body. 'I . . . I want you,' she croaked. Father Gabriel gave her head a painful shake. Tears sprang to her eyes.

'Pathetic,' he whispered sternly into one ear. His evil voice sent shudders down her spine. 'If you do not shout out your desires in the most explicit of terms I shall abandon you for ever. Now, tell me! What sensations flood that depraved, shaven, bejewelled and tempting centre of heaven of yours. Do you not die for the need of me?'

'My, my sex lips are stiff and large,' whispered Justine. The hands twisted so painfully in her hair let go and she dropped her head to hide her trembling lips and tearful eyes. Her voice shook, 'I shake and tremble all over with the strength of my desire for you.'

'More,' growled the relentless voice behind her. He was

too strong for her. His will overrode hers. She was helpless before him. 'Speak louder,' he insisted. 'Be explicit and common like a whore in the marketplace calling out her wares. Let me see you display your treasures openly and wantonly.'

Gathering courage, breaking through her inhibitions, Justine reached one hand between her legs and swung the lips of her labia backward and forward. The cool touch of her rubies aroused her and gave her confidence. She lifted her buttocks and gave them a sexy shake as she continued to tickle and separate and display to the man behind her the treasures that lay hidden in the purse of her sex. 'Do you like the treasures I display for you, master?' she asked, throwing herself into the role of whore. 'See how my pussy is wet with longing for you, master. Can you smell my need for you?'

'Son of Jesus,' gasped a choked voice behind her. 'Oh you wicked wanton strumpet, to flaunt yourself at me so. So steeped in sin! I think you must enjoy your humiliation. You are a debased and sinful woman, Justine. Now ask me for hot dirty sex. Ask me now before I explode.'

The deeper Justine got into her role as scarlet woman, the easier it was to play. The blissful lust that swept over her was real and belonged to her, but surely the sexy teasing voice that sang out so confidently did not. It was as if she had been taken over by another woman as she caressed her swinging, fleshy labia so invitingly and inserted a finger into the wet hole of her vagina. She drew the finger out in a slow, tantalising manner, then slid it back in as deeply as she could, saying as she did so, 'Why, master, doesn't your cock just long to be in my cunt? I'm so wet and aching so hard for you that I don't know how I can stand it. I'm wide open and yearning for you. Don't you want to fuck me, master?' She lifted her buttocks once more in a slow, languorous sway that displayed her smooth curves as blatantly as possible.

'Once more,' gasped a strained voice behind her. 'Call for me once more, you temptress. Lead me into the tunnel of hell with your honeyed words and delectable movements.'

Justine took her finger away from her vagina and knelt forward on both elbows once more. She lowered her head until her nose touched the white linen sheet that lay over the rug and her breasts pressed softly into the ground. Waves of rapturous abandon surged through her body. The sex between her legs seemed to have enlarged, so that the meltingly blissful sensations that crowded around it swelled and filled her entire universe. At this moment, she was all desire, all need, content to fulfil the orders of her master. Her voice was strong as she called out, 'My cunt is ready for you, master. I beg you to enter me and take me as you will.'

With a wordless cry, Father Gabriel gripped her buttocks with ten painful fingers, ripping the cheeks apart so violently that the tissue between her legs stretched out. Then he plunged into her. She cried out. Her whole body juddered under his onslaught. But she was helpless before the power of his passion. And her pain melted into pleasure and she twisted under his grip, crying out raw and longing words into the smothering blankness of the sheet.

He drew back in a long, slow, exquisite movement and then plunged his cock into her as deeply as it would go. Then he kept still for a long moment, his ragged breathing loud in her ear. Justine squeezed her muscles hard, knowing that the velvety length of her vaginal walls was rippling along the sensitive skin of Father Gabriel's penis. She hoped that she was intensifying his pleasure. She knew that she was causing her own rapturous sexual response to soar up to the realm of the angels. Each determined squeeze took her nearer to the pitch of perfection. Each time she bore down hard on his cock with her vaginal muscles she took herself a little nearer to paradise.

'Be still, you houri,' he cried in a great voice. Justine stopped at once. Ah, it was hard to hold still with her love muscles still trembling faintly and the great need that was pushing at her demanding that she should move and find sweet relief, but she obeyed him, and they both held still together.

They were suspended in mid-passion, both naked bodies trembling faintly as their muscles received conflicting orders. Justine's mad animal passion would have them end this moment in a glorious climax right now; it demanded that they fuck like beasts as hard as they could. But the cooler control of her head assured her that to hold their bodies still in this way would prolong the exquisite sensations for longer than mortal pleasure had ever dreamt of.

When Father Gabriel could stand the waiting no more, he pulled the length of his shaft slowly, delicately back, until only the tip was resting in the entrance to Justine's vagina. She took a great sobbing breath as she knelt quivering on the rug. Only sensation mattered. She abandoned herself to the passion of wild animal sex. The long pale shaft slammed smoothly back into her vagina. Father Gabriel plunged himself into her tunnel so deeply that the tip of his cock just brushed her cervix. He filled her dark spaces completely and her sex muscles wrapped themselves lovingly around the sweet hardness of his cock.

Justine surrendered thought to the pleasures of their hot passionate fucking. She moved against him with such a strong blatantly sexual twisting of her hips that he could no longer maintain his control over his strokes. His body relaxed as his penis took over. All his energy went into the strokes that plunged deeply into the tight sheath of her vagina. As he plunged he gave wild cries. Part of Justine registered the strength of his fingers as he gripped her buttocks to hold them steady under his passionate onslaught and knew that she would feel pain later – but for now it felt absolutely right. Her hips rose to meet him. Her own frenzied movements matched his and encouraged him to let go. She threw herself into this wild intercourse that was so hot and abandoned and so incredibly exhilarating. Father Gabriel's body slapped hard against her buttocks. Pleasure gathered deep inside her. His cock rammed sweetly home. She would not have it any softer. Her breasts dangled and bounced over the rug. Sweet heat gathered in the tips. Loud orgasmic cries rose to her lips and flowed into the room.

Justine heard a strange frenzied voice call out obscenities; her voice, but she didn't care. A deep male baritone mingled with her shrill soprano as Father Gabriel panted out his passion. Sweat broke out on the surface of Justine's skin and the world behind her eyes turned into a black velvet blur shot with scarlet specks. The deep voice shouted obscenities that tickled her ears and excited her responses. The world narrowed again in the squeeze, squeeze, squeeze of an orgasm that shook her like a wagon with iron-clad wheels bouncing along a stony road – and the horse was running away and she couldn't stop herself, and she didn't want to stop herself, either, because she felt good, good, good as she came uncontrollably, right there on her hands and knees with Father Gabriel mounting her from behind and the fire burning all along one side of her naked pink-flushed body.

Father Gabriel's body gathered itself up into a coiled mass of tension and his fingers gripped her even harder, as if they would sink all the way into the buttocks of her flesh. Then he uncoiled in a springing series of spasms and his voice rose in a rough incoherent cry as he orgasmed mightily. Justine felt salt drops dripping on to her naked back as he broke out in a hot sweat with the bursting of his orgasm. Spent, he collapsed down on her and for a moment she struggled to take his full weight on her hands. Then she fell forward and they lay together on the rug, he squashing her with his hot wet body, and both of them breathing in ragged gasps that kept perfect time.

Justine heard a faint noise. It was muffled by the raucous breathing in her ear, and she thought at first it was something to do with Father Gabriel. That he was being punished for his sexual passion and was having a heart attack. But then his body pulled away from hers and the noise grew louder. She realised that the noise, a strange clapping noise like a thousand rooks' wings beating as they flew off into the sky, was separate from Father Gabriel. It was growing louder. It *was* clapping. Hands clapping. She fell face forward into the sheet-covered rug. She did not dare look. She heard rough cheers and lewd comments. She understood now: the hunting party had returned, and they had been watching her.

Chapter Ten

Justine heard Father Gabriel's feet brush by her as he went for his robe.

'That's right, priest! Cover up your shame,' cried a raucous voice.

'I'd not be ashamed if that were my tackle,' cried another.

''Tis his other senses let him down! Lord, I thought at any moment he'd look up and see us – or wonder why the room had so many mirrors. 'Twas a fine show, Gabriel. A fine show indeed.'

Justine could not look up. She huddled herself into the tiniest space possible. Trying to get so small that no one could see her. She heard the count's oily voice above her: 'I suspected as much when you sneaked off so early, Gabriel. Did you think to fool me with your story of a deathbed to attend? Come, I said to the others, we shall have better sport if we follow my brother than if we stay out here! And I was right. As pretty a coupling as ever I did see. I was quite touched to see the little governess calling for your cock like a bitch in heat. Far be it from me to ruin such passion. You shall have the wanton, if you like her so much.'

Relief lifted Justine. The count had chosen to be amused by their escapade. A fervent thankful prayer rose to her lips. But then the words choked to an unbelieving halt as she heard Father Gabriel's voice reply as softly and as lazily as a snake hissing through long grass, 'You are most generous, brother, but I want her no more. She is grown too old for me.'

'Too old!' interjected one of the watching nobles. 'Why, she's barely eighteen, and the body on her is perfect.'

Justine stared frantically up into Father Gabriel's eyes, but there was nothing but darkness in them as he replied, 'Her chassis is comely, I'll grant you that. But she has begun to mature in her mind since leaving the convent. I cannot abide a woman who thinks.'

'True, true, they can be very tiresome,' agreed the noble. Justine looked at Father Gabriel through dazed eyes. He turned his back on her casually. All she could see was the back of his black robe. She stared at it until spots danced before her eyes. Surely there was a demon inside the robe of the priest. A demon who had taken on her trusted friend's shape and form. This could never be her own Father Gabriel: he who had singled her out for his private attention, he who had taught her so much. Forgetful of the many watching eyes and her nakedness, she stared at him, willing him to turn round, willing him to become her loving friend and mentor once more. But he remained with his back to her.

A green-clad noble looked at Justine hopefully and then at the count. 'Well, then, Waldgraf, what will you do with the little minx? If you've a mind to punish her – '

Other voices called out.

'Brandon's your man!'

'You want to be in on it!'

'Of course, a whipping would be just in your style!'

The noble laughed as his friends teased him, but his eyes remained fixed on Justine. There was an eager lust in them that made her shiver. The count shook his head and said smoothly, 'You shall not have her, Brandon. You still have not paid me for that bloodstock. I don't owe you any favours.' The noble's brows drew together sharply but, to

Justine's relief, he shrugged calmly and said, 'Just as you please, Waldgraf.'

Now the countess pushed through the crowd and said shrilly, 'She must go to the mines. You will at least get some return from her there.'

The mines! Justine had heard whispered rumours of the black hells that honeycombed the hill under the castle. Dread was cold in her belly. Would not Father Gabriel save her now? Desperation overrode her pride, and she called out to him, 'Father! Oh Father Gabriel!'

His shoulders moved under the black robe as if he were shrugging off a troublesome fly, but Justine could not believe the evidence of her eyes. She wet her lips and tried to make her words reach him clearly, 'Will you not take me to the city with you?'

Finally he turned to face her. His eyes were those of a stranger. 'Don't be a fool as well as a slut! I am to be high in the church. What would I do with a harlot?'

His words cut into her like a great stroke from the sharpest of knives. It was such a deep wound that Justine did not feel it at first. Even though the ice from his eyes was gradually freezing her, and even though her damaged heart fell slowly open into two painful halves, Justine babbled on pitifully, 'I would be your servant, help you in any way I can. Think of all you have taught me, Father Gabriel. I can do so many things for you.'

He shrugged and turned away. He had no more to say to her. Justine tasted cold betrayal in her mouth. She raised her hands to her lips and bit on the knuckles hard, afraid that the blood from her sliced open heart would gush out and kill her if she didn't hold the pain down tightly.

A big ruddy-faced noble with a kind expression said, 'Maybe it's the training you enjoy, Gabriel. There are those who take pleasure in the process rather than the result. Now I prefer a fully grown maid and save myself the trouble. Waldgraf, you give her to me. 'Tis criminal to send such a pearl to the mines. My wife will beat her every day and then we'll all be happy.'

But the countess snapped, 'Oh no! 'Tis bad for discipline.

The whole world knows what a soft touch you are, Arthon. My servants would all run riot if being sent to your house was to be the punishment for disobedience. She must go to the mines.'

Justine looked frantically for Father Gabriel. But he wasn't even looking at her. He was drinking hot punch and talking in low tones to a slim young lady in a tight riding habit. It was the man with the kind face who made one last bid to save her.

'You have the disposing of her, 'tis true, Waldgraf, but she is such an exceptional beauty I'm surprised you cannot find a punishment to make use of her. She's wasted, aye, and wasted for ever once you send her down there.'

The count looked thoughtful, and one of his retainers leant over and whispered in his ear. The count looked up, merriment in his black-beetle eyes. 'Well thought of, Arthon. And I have the answer. You'll remember the prince of Garnor was here a few months ago. I was much taken by his retinue of toilet slaves. Chained, you know, very fetchingly, and they follow him everywhere. I had completely forgot, but I'm training some of my own.' He turned to Justine and his eyes scuttled over her naked body lustfully, 'There's an honour for you, my pretty dear. You shall attend me about my natural needs. Why, I think I feel a piss sneaking up on me now. It will be a rare pleasure to aim it at your lovely breasts.' He turned to the other nobles. 'What do you say, fellows? Whose golden shower will be the one to make her come? We'll have fun trying to hit her little button with our waters; and after the fun she shall pamper you with hot towels.'

The kindly man fell back, shaking his head a little sadly. Father Gabriel gave Justine one last hard measuring look, then his eyes slid over to the count and he said, 'Admirable plan, brother, to bring pleasure into a distasteful but necessary chore. Admirable.' And then he resumed his conversation with the lady in the riding habit. Coldness drummed in Justine's ears and she finally understood that his betrayal was irrevocable. His interest in her was over.

The other nobles pressed a little closer, looking down on

her with hot lustful eyes. They looked flushed and excited. The count looked greasily pleased with his scheme. Justine's breasts and naked sex felt vulnerable and exposed as she knelt on the rug before the fire. She pressed her hands to her face. Father Gabriel had trained her. She had done nothing that was not his will. And now he denied her. Anger swept her, its blessed heat protecting her from the terrible pain in her breast. If Father Gabriel no longer ruled her then she was free to follow the dictates of her own heart. Ignoring the lustful nobles she rose to her feet, not caring now that she was naked, and said in a still, small, but resolutely calm voice, 'I will not be your toilet slave. I had rather go to the mines.'

The silence was immediate. All stopped drinking or eating or chattering and turned to face Justine. Even Father Gabriel turned away from the woman in the velvet riding habit and stared at her in disbelief. It was very hard to stand calmly under the weight of so many disapproving stares, but Justine lifted her head and said proudly, 'I will not serve this family any longer. I declare myself a free woman.'

It was so quiet that, despite all the people in the room, the fire could be heard hissing in the great fireplace. The sun had moved away from the windows, but it was still light in the yellow room. Nothing moved but a few eyes, as the nobles cast slanting glances over to the countess's face, to see what she would make of this defiance.

'Do you think you peasants get a choice in the matter?' Rage lighted the countess's eyes. 'You were put here on this earth to serve us, I tell you.' Her body twitched and her hands clenched jerkily as she continued, 'It would have been an honour for you to serve us so, I tell you, an honour. Free! You are no more free than our dogs are free! But I'll grant you your wish. Guards! Bring chains! Bring manacles! I would have this woman taken to the mines immediately.'

Some of the nobles now filtered out of the room, more interested in hot baths and food than the punishment of a mere servant. Others pressed closer in order to watch the chaining. Justine stood naked before those who had stayed to watch and lifted her head proudly. Heat still pounded along her veins. She wasn't afraid of the countess. She despised her.

A jingling in the corridor followed by the tramp of soldiers' feet sent a shiver down Justine's spine, but still she stood graceful and erect. Even when the burly men marched into the yellow bedroom she did not move or betray the fear that was, despite all her best intentions, nibbling at the corners of her mind. She looked coolly into the repellent eyes of the guard nearest her. A disgusting intimacy shone in his eyes as he approached her, and she knew that he enjoyed his work. She despised them all.

Her toes curled on the rug as the man knelt at her feet. He smelt vilely of tobacco and stale sweat. The steel of the manacle was cold as it kissed her ankle. She could not repress a slight whimper as it clicked shut with a horribly final sound. The chain clinked as the guard fed a loop of silver links through his hands, calculating how much Justine needed to take a stride. Then he cut off a link with heavy metal croppers. He fastened the broken link to the other shackle. Justine swallowed hard. A fine shivering, like that of a greyhound before a race, ran over her body, but otherwise she stood calm. The guard moved around to her other foot. Steel clasped the ankle and she was manacled. Justine looked down and lifted a foot experimentally. The shackle was an unaccustomed weight. The chain lifted behind the shackle as she lifted her leg. Now she could not take a step without being restrained by the chains. The implications weighed heavy in her belly.

The count stepped forward and ran a greasy hand over Justine's breasts. Hot acid rose in her mouth as he touched her. His head poked out of his shiny clothes like a cockroach looking out of garbage. 'Change your mind?' he asked silkily. She wanted to spit. Her eyes told him what she thought of him. The count stepped back and motioned the guard. The guard was ready. He snapped a silver manacle on to Justine's left wrist. Now her body stirred and she thought of flight. But she knew in her heart it was useless. There were upward of twenty people in the room. And guards and huntsmen outside. Yet it went against the grain to let them chain her with no protest, no fight at all. Justine's lips began to tremble. The merrily crackling fire had no power to warm her. Her vision clouded and she thought she could hear a waterfall roaring in her ears.

The guard now looked at the countess for a decision. 'Shall I chain her arms in front or behind, your grace?'

She stared at Justine, jealous anger still playing around the corners of her mouth. 'Behind. And tie her tight.'

The guard's hands were dry and scaly. They felt like the skin of a dead snake Justine had once touched. Now they grasped each of her upper arms and pulled them back. The motion made her breasts stand out, upward and pointing, towards those nobles who still watched. Justine's shivering was growing uncontrollable, and the sound of the waterfall in her ears grew louder. The second manacle clicked into place and she was a prisoner. They left her standing on the rug. Her knees shook. Oh, but she was cold. Cold all over and there were spots before her eyes. Black ones that grew larger and blacker and merged with the roaring and the cold and the blackness.

She fought hard to push the blackness away, and managed to walk steadily past the chattering nobles, ignoring their lustful eyes. She stopped for a long moment in front of Father Gabriel. She had no real hope now, of him saving her, but she looked steadily into his eyes until they dropped before her. A fleeting expression that might have been guilt crossed his face, but he turned away, resentful of her accusing stare. Justine realised that she had been cherishing a flicker of last faint hope after all and, as Father Gabriel extinguished it by turning away, she stopped fighting the whirlpool pull of faintness. Her knees went to crumple under her, but she made it to the door of the lodge unaided. Only when the guards boosted her into the back of the rough farm cart that waited outside did she succumb to the blanket of dark that took her away from cruel reality.

* * *

It was still black when she opened her eyes. She was lying on her back, and her arms were painful, full of pins and needles. The chains clinked as she turned over on to her side, trying to release the pressure on her arms. The surface beneath her rustled and prickled. She inhaled deeply: straw, and none too fresh. Justine drew up her knees and tried to open her eyes wider. Nothing. A stinging drop of sweat trickled into her eyes, and she suddenly realised that she was sweating all over. It was warm. A warm, stuffy darkness that was moist and unhealthy. Why could she not see? Why did her eyes not adjust to the darkness? She dropped her head down to meet her knees. The pins and needles in her arms were getting fiercer, the pain must have woken her, but there was nothing she could do about it other than curl into the foetal position or sit it out. She felt better with her eyes closed. It was unnerving to strain and strain into the hot thick darkness and still not be able to see.

There was no sound nearby, but the rock under the straw that Justine was lying on vibrated faintly, like a beating heart. A pump she supposed. Her arms hurt vilely, and now she was thirsty. It was so hot. Warm wet trickles of sweat dribbled under her breasts and dropped into the straw as she lay there. Suffering. Enduring.

When the door opened, the sound was loud in her darkness. Justine's heart hammered as she sat upright in the rustling straw. No light came in through the open door. None at all. Who could function in such Stygian conditions? 'Awake?' asked a soft voice.

Justine opened her eyes until they hurt, but still she could not see the speaker. She strained her ears and heard the soft pad of what sounded like bare feet approaching her. 'I'm awake,' she admitted. She coughed over her words. Her throat was dry.

The newcomer smelt of old, old mushrooms, and rags that have been lying in a damp corner for years. Justine wrinkled her nose and drew back. 'What is it?' asked the soft voice.

'Can you see me?' asked Justine, peering into the darkness.

There was a soft laugh. 'Of course I can see you. But I've been here a long time. One adjusts, you know. One adjusts.'

'May I have a drink?' asked Justine, unwrinkling her nose and smoothing her expression. She did not want to upset the keeper of her strange dark jail.

'I'm holding one out to you,' said the soft voice. It sounded amused. 'Here.'

'My arms are chained behind my back.'

'Of course. Silly of me. One moment, my dear.' The smell grew stronger and the straw next to her rustled. She could feel heat from the body that moved up beside her, but she could see nothing, nothing at all. Justine tensed all over as she felt tugging on the metal that held her wrists imprisoned behind her back. There was a click. A sweet feeling of freedom poured over her as the metal fell away. Her shoulders hurt as she brought her hands round to the front of her body and rubbed them vigorously. Then she stopped rubbing and licked her lips. She was so thirsty. A warm cup was pressed into her hands. She raised it to her mouth cautiously. The water in it tasted flat and metallic, but Justine drank thirstily until the cup was empty. 'I'm in the mines,' she said. It wasn't a question.

'The pretty governess,' mused the soft voice. 'Kept in idleness in the schoolroom, consumed by the count at a great feast. Could have stood high in his favour if she had played her cards right, but she chose to throw in her lot with the count's younger brother, the black priest, and he betrayed her, left her to the mercy of the jealous countess. Now here she is in the mines. And it is my privilege to assign to her whatever task will occupy the rest of her short life.'

'Short?'

'Some adjust. But it is no healthy environment down here, and the work is hard. Most die soon, aye, and many are glad to.'

Justine shuddered and strained uselessly to see her captor. 'How do you know all about me?'

'We have our lines of communication. News passes in, rarely out, for what happens down here?'

'Is there no escape?'

'Ah! Everyone's first question. No, is the short answer. But there may be a partial one for you.'

'Partial?'

'You may at least escape the labour of digging and hauling the trucks. You are beautiful.' A soft hand touched her cheek so lightly that Justine almost didn't feel it. 'Very beautiful. And we are somewhat organised down here. We keep a few beauties to pleasure the workers. Would such a life suit you?'

To spend her entire life in complete darkness. To be an object of sexual release for the poor degenerates who slaved in these mines until they died. 'No!'

'You say that now. But you have not yet experienced life at the coal face. Still, we are not animals down here. All we have is each other. No one will force you. If you wish to labour that is your right. You can always send a message to me if you change your mind.'

The straw rustled as if the man were going to get up and leave. Justine stared uselessly into the thick dark and cried, 'Wait, oh do please wait. Is there no way out of this hell?'

'For you? I doubt it. If you had possessed powerful friends, you would not have ended up here, and influence or wealth are all that might save you.'

Justine's heart raced. 'Money?' She squeezed her legs together as she spoke. The chains around her ankles clinked, and her rubies, Armand's rubies, rubbed deliciously along her labia, sending a sweet rush of sexual pleasure over her. She heard soft breathing from the person beside her. She wished she could see him. She didn't like talking to a disembodied voice in the dark.

'You have money?'

'Maybe.'

'Ah, you don't trust me of course. But consider, my dear.

175

How could you prevent me from taking by force whatever it is you must have concealed in one of your pretty orifices?'

It was true. It was as if a fist squeezed Justine's throat. She was so helpless. She shrank back into the straw.

'Don't!' said the soft voice. 'Please don't cringe from me like that. I give you my word I will not harm you. All we have down here is each other. I would not betray that. Listen and I will tell you. It is possible to bribe your way out. Some three or four of the guards are honest enough to stay bought. Once or twice, such escapes have been made.'

'Could you arrange it for me?'

'What have you got?'

Justine chewed her lip fiercely, forgetting temporarily that her companion could see her expression. She still didn't know if she could trust him. Nor, now it came to it, did she want to part with Armand's gift. But it was the only chance she had. 'These rubies,' she said, and she turned over and splayed out the lips of her sex with her fingers to show them off clearly. 'Do you think they will be enough?'

'Beautiful,' whispered the soft voice. The note of longing in it tore at Justine's heart. A suspicion entered her mind that it was not only the rubies that he was talking about. Hot blood stung her cheeks in the darkness. 'Beautiful,' moaned the thin whispery voice. Justine covered her rubies, and her sex, with her hand.

'Six-star rubies, I think? And you have six of them?' the voice continued.

A brief picture flashed into Justine's mind of Armand by the campfire, pressing them on her. 'Yes. There are six.'

'Four would be enough. They are magnificent gems.'

Moved by a sudden impulse Justine said, 'Will you not escape with me?'

The breathing next to her grew louder, and louder still with a little hitch in it. Tears strangled his voice. 'Oh my dear, oh my very dear. But it is far too late for me. The light would kill me. I am a night creature. I have become

176

twisted and deformed in order to survive. There is no escape for me now.'

'I'm sorry.'

They sat silently in the thick heavy darkness. Justine could hear him trying to control his breathing. Sweat ran down her breasts and her belly. She was thirsty again. And oh, how she longed to be able to see. The muscles around her eyes ached violently from her continual peering and straining into the hot blackness that pressed so densely upon her. Her companion finally spoke again, although there was a break in the soft voice. 'Give me five of your rubies to be sure of covering everything, and I will arrange your escape.'

Justine's hands went to her labia. The fittings pinched as she undid them, but they came out easily. A hand, a warm, moist hand, touched her in the darkness and she pressed her star rubies into them. He counted them. 'There are six rubies here. I only need five.'

'Take it,' said Justine. 'Once I am out of here I shall manage. And I want you to have it. I don't even know your name, but I owe my life to you.'

There was a husky catch in the voice that made the businesslike arrangements. 'Pedar is on duty and he is one of ours. I will try to arrange the escape for tonight. I'll bring you news and water shortly. Rest now while you can.' Justine lay back on the straw, but her heart was racing too fast to allow her to relax. She strained her eyes as if to watch him leave. Useless of course, so she used her ears and heard the soft pad, pad, pad of his footsteps crossing the room to the door. She heard a latch clink and hinges creak, and then the soft voice said, 'My name is Bengeo,' and she was alone.

Chapter Eleven

*T*he clink of the latch made Justine start violently. Straw rustled around her as she sat up. 'Bengeo?'

'Yes.'

'I was sleeping, I think. It's hard to be sure down here.'

'It is night, as such things are reckoned above. We must wait for one hour, maybe two, until Pedar's lazy partner has gone for his regular snooze. Then we must act swiftly.'

A thin metal cup was pushed into Justine's hand and she drank greedily.

'I have food for you, outside food; no need, now, for you to learn to love our mushroom specials. And clothes – poor rough garments, I fear, but they will serve.'

'May I have more water? It is so hot down here. I sweat as if I had a fever, and, phew, how I stink.'

The cup was passed back to her.

'Not so, my dear. You have the sweetest body scent: you smell of youth and health and fresh green meadows. There is no more powerful aphrodisiac.' There was a sigh in the thin whisper. 'I am glad, of course, I am glad for you, that you are leaving. But I am sad that now I will never have a chance to feed upon your flowerlike nectar, or be able to lose myself in the scent of a woman from the surface.'

Justine shifted slightly, and the chains around her ankles

clinked. She looked into the dark. She could see no shape, no movement, but she spoke to the spot where she thought the soft voice was coming from. 'Can you undo my ankles?'

'Did I not do so before I left? I grow forgetful. Or being near you has disordered my senses. I shall do it now.' The straw rustled as his body moved past her. Warm moist hands touched her legs, slid down to her ankles. How could he see to work? Justine could smell his mushroom smell and feel his body heat but, although she heard the chains clink and felt them fall away, she could see nothing at all. She rubbed her ankles vigorously. She sensed that he had moved away.

'Eat,' he said, passing bread, hard rye bread by the feel of it, and a crumbling morsel of fragrant cheese to her.

'I'm not hungry.'

'Eat it anyway. Pedar will have to hide you for several hours before he can take you to his hut. And who knows if there will be food there? He is not a rich man. None of the count's servants are.'

'Should I get dressed now?'

'Not until just before we leave. You will need to appreciate the warmth of the garments; I hear it is snowing outside.'

'It seems impossible to imagine snow in this hot thick blackness.'

'I have memories of snow. A sparkling cold whiteness crisping under my feet, but the picture is faint now.'

'Are you, I mean, have you been here long? Where did you live before?'

A sigh in the dark was Justine's only answer. 'I do not wish to think about it,' he whispered finally. 'My life is here now.'

Justine stretched out a consoling hand and touched warm moist skin in the dark. She touched him gently, sorry that she had upset him. She thought her hand was resting on his upper thigh. His skin had a spongy texture, as if there were a layer of jelly resting on the surface of his flesh. He quivered beneath her hand. 'You only touch me

179

because it is dark. You would be disgusted if you were to see me.'

'I think not.'

A faint laugh. 'How do you know that?'

Justine chose her words carefully. 'You say your body has changed to allow you to survive in the mines, but your soul has not degenerated. Your spirit is that of a true gentleman.'

Tears landed on Justine's hand in the dark. She brought her other hand up, cautiously seeking Bengeo's face through the thick darkness. She touched it with gentle fingertips, feeling more tears on his face. She moulded her soft fingers around the hardness of his lips. He made a sound low in his throat. The first feelings of desire trickled into Justine's body. The pump that pulsed beneath the straw that she lay in began to pound through her veins, pulse in her head, throb in her loins.

A gentle hand touched her face, tracing the outlines tenderly. 'Soft,' whispered Bengeo. 'So unbelievably soft. Your mouth, your lips, your breasts – everywhere I touch. I am drowning in your softness.'

Justine moaned softly and lay back in the hot darkness. She closed her eyes and stopped trying to see. It was hot. It was dark. No straining of hers could change anything. Why not surrender to the moment. She felt a stirring above her and a whisper of hair touching her skin. Her nipples were pouting, aching for him. When his mouth closed over one and slowly drew it into its warm cavern, she moaned in utter wanton pleasure, her hand going to the back of his head to press him closer. She felt the hot wetness of his mouth, his tongue as it licked her. She moaned again and relaxed back into the straw.

Hungrily, he moved to her other breast, drawing on the nipple, loving it with his tongue, circling it, tugging on it, teasing it. Her head lolled back and with another soft moan of pleasure, she threaded her fingers through the strands of his hair, pushing her aching distended nipple at him, offering him more. A hand, large, hot and so unbearably gentle that she wanted to weep, reverently spanned her belly. 'Oh, Justine,' he whispered. 'Are you sure?'

'Touch my woman's place and you will see that I desire you,' she whispered against his lips. Slowly, hesitantly, he slid his hand downward, until it rested on the curve of her inner thigh. Justine felt him shaking frantically as he slowly reached out to place a hesitant finger in the centre of her vagina. When he touched the dampness that pooled there, he gave a low, disbelieving cry that tore Justine's heart. No one had ever responded to her like this. No one had ever desired her like this, or touched her as if she were an incredible work of art. It was its own aphrodisiac, being wanted so, and she writhed languorously in the sheltering darkness, content to lie back and let him adore her.

He planted a string of kisses across her stomach, letting his mouth slide higher until he captured one nipple in his lips, working it gently with his tongue, before drawing it deeply into the warm wet cavern of his mouth. Justine lay back, mewing softly in pleasure. She moaned again when he abandoned her nipple. But he continued kissing her skin gently, going down her rib cage, lower still across her stomach, her hip, then sliding down to touch his tongue to the inside of her thigh. 'Justine!' He whispered her name like a prayer. Justine lifted her hips and arched her back. Her eyes flew open. The darkness removed one dimension, that of sight, but how it magnified the others. Her eyes fluttered closed and she breathed deeply through her nose and gave herself up to the sensations that poured through her skin in the hot, smothering, enveloping, darkness that held her so close.

His slick, wet tongue slid higher and higher up the inside of her thigh. It slid like a darting lizard over the stubble, longer now, that misted her mons, and slipped into the crack of her labia. Then it darted and flicked around her clitoris until she gasped with the tiny shocks of pleasure that radiated from her pleasure centre. She melted under his tongue. She liquefied under his lips. His tongue caressed her, tasted her, teased her until her nails were digging into his flesh and the breath was coming hard in

181

her throat. The first wave of her orgasm came unexpectedly, catching her off guard. The straw rustled beneath her and she felt cool metal touch her sides as she rolled this way and the other, touching her cast-off chains in the straw.

She rolled back, clamping her legs against Bengeo's head as he suckled greedily at the heart of her womanhood. She spasmed again, and again, before drifting slowly back into her body. He took his tongue away from the point of her clitoris. She shuddered and relaxed. He licked sweetly along the lips of her labia, chasing the last quivers of pleasure as they faded tenderly away. 'Enough,' she breathed, pushing his head away.

He took his mouth away from between her legs and rolled her over on to her front. As she lay gasping in the straw, she felt the thump, thump, thump of the engine that beat so steadily somewhere in the cavernous mines. Sweat rolled down her shoulders and pooled under the curve of her breasts. Her neck was hot under the damp weight of her hair. Out of sheer habit she opened her eyes once more. The dark was a thick, floating sensation pressing on her eyeballs. Once more she closed them softly, surrendering to this warm, enclosing world of sensation.

His mouth slid to the tops of her thighs, and he planted hot fiery kisses along the crease of her buttock, inhaling her scent deeply. 'I want to brand your perfume into my memory,' she heard him mutter. His tongue slowly caressed the length of the crack between her buttocks, gently pulling at the skin, tasting it, savouring it. Justine sighed and rested her head on her folded arms. Relaxing completely. Even opening her legs to allow him better access to the secret places that lived there.

His mouth stayed pressed into her backside, but his hands slid up the sides of her body and then pushed their way under her breasts, so that he now had one breast pressing into each hand. He cupped them into his hands, massaging the nipples until Justine groaned again. Her heart thundered wildly in her ears, the pulse a frantic beat that matched the desire that was growing within her in the darkness. His hands glided over her sweating back now, pressing here, pausing there, until she was nearly wild, aching with the need to be filled. The sexual spaces between her legs yearned to be touched.

His hands slid down to hold her buttocks tight and it was her anus that felt sensation first. His hot darting tongue slipped into the crinkled rosebud entrance of her anal passage. First she stiffened, then she relaxed. Heat and desire massaged her all over with soft little fingers. The tender touches of his hands on her buttocks, the slow languorous lapping of his tongue as he rimmed her, all combined to rock her in a blissful hammock of sensation. His tongue was so soft as it darted and probed, flicking wetly around her anal opening, then snaking inside with a tender flickering motion that felt heavy and soft as it ignited shivering flames of desire. All she had to do was to lie there, sprawled on her belly, and allow him to suckle greedily at the very point of rapture.

After a long, slow time, he turned her over on to her back again. Justine lolled under his touch like a boneless kitten in its mother's mouth. She felt safe and content under his loving ministrations. She lay passive as he moved, still an unseen shape in the darkness, up the length of her languorous body. She could feel his hard erection brushing against her as he travelled upward, pausing to kiss and suckle her skin as he went. He positioned himself with his penis hanging over her face. Her lips fell open before he reached them, pouting, vacant, ready to suck him deep. 'May I?' he whispered.

Justine darted out her small silken tongue and snaked it around the button mushroom of the tip of his penis. His cock too, had that smooth, jellylike texture, but blood pulsed along the raised veins of its surface. His penis smelt of meadow mushrooms, but not unpleasantly, and she took him into her mouth willingly, feeling his rapture in the dark, knowing how much she was pleasing him. After only a few seconds he withdrew, the soft puffs of his balls touching her cheek as he moved away. 'It's not right,' he said softly. 'My greatest pleasure is in pleasing you.'

Justine rolled a lazy head in the straw. She bent her knees and pulled them upward. 'You please me,' she said, with a soft laugh in her voice. 'Everywhere you touch ignites. And I ache for you now. Do you not see my position?'

Bengeo ignored the blatantly spread invitation of her sex and she felt the soft satin of his hands touching her everywhere in the hot sticky dark. He planted soft loving kisses wherever his mouth touched her skin. He inhaled deeply of her scent as he licked every warm crease of her armpits. He returned to her breasts and Justine felt the aching pain in them suddenly turn to pleasure – an incredible, unbelievable pleasure that surged within her, causing her hips to lift from the ground and soft moans to rise to her lips.

At last, she felt his soft hands at her inner thighs. Like a novice at the entrance to the temple, he pressed them gently aside and then positioned himself so that he could enter, reverently, humbly, as if a miracle were happening. As he slid the tip of his button mushroom glans into the honeyed dew that pooled in the entrance of her vagina, Justine lifted her back to encourage him, pulling him closer, wanting all of him, encouraging him in his tender entry.

His hands roamed around her bare thighs and legs, then moved up her body. Caressing her, loving her, as he blissfully moved his head up her naked body so that he could kiss her as he moved inside her. As Justine felt the size and hardness of him, a soft cry escaped from her mouth into his. In the vast enveloping dark, only sensation was real, and all she could feel was the impossible hardness of the cock that filled her. The magnitude of the sensation she was feeling so overwhelmed her that it seemed that his member was growing, expanding in the darkness, stretching her vagina as he grew, turning her body into a receptacle for his maleness and hurting her rapturously and tormenting her blissfully as he filled her completely.

Her fingers sank into his shoulders as he moved against

her, slowly at first and then more quickly. She kept up with him, anxious to satisfy the fire burning within her. Greedy for more, she lifted and tightened her legs around him, encouraging him as he filled her in the dark with a wild and dangerous passion. Grunting softly, her body slicked with sweat, Justine picked up the pace, wanting to hurry, yet not wanting this incredible sexual feeling to end. Her hips thrust upward, accepting the size of his penis as it sank into her. Moaning she moved into him, her hips rising, setting the rhythm, urging him on at the speed she wished to go. He obeyed her, thrusting harder, faster, faster. Waves of unbelievable, unbearable pleasure rolled over her. Justine groaned deep in her throat. 'Please,' she heard herself cry, not sure what she was asking for, 'Please.'

She was sightless, helpless, she gave up control. Her fingernails dug into the back that laboured above hers in the dark. She heard him whimper her name, and then her contractions took her over and she had a sudden hallucination: the pump that beat so steadily below them had somehow got into the room, replaced the man who lay above her, and was humping and throbbing and driving its pistons into the dark spaces within her womb as she exploded and burst. As she came, fireworks, startling and dizzy-making in the darkness that engulfed her, burst behind her eyelids. Soft clouds of red exploded behind her eyes. She threw her head back and cried out as her vaginal muscles pumped, and her heart pumped and the place inside her head pumped too, and the almost unbearable pleasure took her in regular mechanical beats into a region of infinite black rapture.

She was still gasping, still burning and sweet with the spasms of her orgasm, when she suddenly felt hands slipping across her wet breasts. His flabby body stiffened in the dark. She felt cries vibrating against her lips as his orgasm gripped him. She felt the hot sweetness of it and was glad: glad that he was happy, glad that she had given him pleasure – and glad that it was over. The intensity of their dark silent lovemaking had unnerved her. She wanted

185

to be out. She wanted to feel real air on her skin so badly that she almost doubled up with longing and tears came to her eyes. Tender hands gentled her and she felt mushroom breath soft on her cheek.

'I know,' he said softly. 'I know, little one. Would that I could keep you here for a million more nights like this one. But it would not be right. You yearn for your natural habitat. Dress now, and I will take you there.'

Chapter Twelve

'We have to go,' sobbed Justine. 'We have to leave now. The darkness is smothering me. It's too black. I can't breathe. I can't breathe.'

'Wake up,' said a firm determined voice. Justine's eyes flew open and a riot of colour hit them. A firm red hand shook her shoulder. ''Tis just a dream you're having. You are out of those nasty mines now, and safe with us.'

'Oh, I'm sorry. Was I shouting?'

'A little, but no matter. You are safe and awake now. How are you feeling?'

Justine closed her eyes and aches and pains from every part of her body crashed into her consciousness. She felt sick and confused. 'I'm fine, thank you. But is it day or night?'

'Night. You have slept the clock round since you were brought here.' A stout figure leant over Justine, pushing open the sides of the bed. The woman had fair hair plaited tightly round her head and blue eyes. She was round and rosy and as wholesome as apple strudel. Justine realised that she was inside a bed that was built into wooden panelling like a cupboard. She barely registered the softness of a feather mattress under her as she peered eagerly into the room. She used her eyes as never before, revelling in every colour, every detail that she could see.

The entire hut was made of wood, and no piece of wood was plain. A woodcarver's loving hand had carved, fretted or otherwise ornamented every plank, every beam and timber in sight. A great tiled stove burned merrily in the middle of the room, its long black chimney pipe vanishing up through the rafters. Bowls of blue fruit and wreaths of blue flowers ornamented the tiles of the stove, and a glossy black cat snoozed on a rag rug below it. Justine could smell the comforting smell of hot coals, and a delicious sweet fruity odour too, that set her mouth watering. The woman saw Justine's mouth work as she swallowed and she smiled at her kindly. 'I've stew and dumplings for you and then a baked apple. You are far too thin, child. Have you not been eating lately?'

'The last few days – perhaps not. I don't know. But, please, I'm sorry I don't know your name, I am so dirty. May I wash?'

'Bless you, child. My name is Magda, and I've kettles on the fire at this very minute. But you must eat first. Are you strong enough to use the table, or shall I bring your food to you there?'

'I'll get up,' said Justine, swinging her bare legs on to the floor; then pulling them up again with a wince. Her feet were bright red, cracked and swollen.

'Lord bless me,' cried Magda, bustling over to Justine, every inch the nurse. 'I forgot to check on your feet. Bringing you all that way in the snow without so much as a few rags wrapped around them. He's a good man is Pedar, but he doesn't always think.' Gentle hands turned Justine's feet this way and that. 'No harm done. There's no sign of frostbite. I put plenty of goose grease on when you got here. 'Tis excellent for the soreness.'

Justine put her feet on to the polished wooden floor more gingerly this time. She could walk if she was careful. Holding on to the backs of the various carved chairs and settles that stood round the room, Justine slowly made her way over to the kitchen table.

The kitchen was just an alcove, not walled off from the rest of the room, but it was gay and cheery with a vast tiled stove and cupboards covered in openwork hearts. Muslin curtains of ferocious whiteness festooned the window. Although it was dark outside, Justine felt better as soon as she saw the window. Snow lay deep on the outer windowsill; a gay geranium in a pot sat on the inner. Condensation ran down the black glass. Magda must have to wash the curtains every week to keep them so crisp. Justine rubbed the glass clear and peered out. It was too dark to see stars or a moon. 'What time is it?' she asked.

Magda crinkled her brows in thought. Her lips moved. ''Twill be a little past midnight,' she decided.

'A strange time to be having supper,' said Justine. But she picked up the wooden spoon and stirred it into the wooden bowl with real enthusiasm. The bowl was full of savory-smelling lumps of meat.

'Being under the ground disorients people,' said Magda. ''Tis always the same if one comes out: what time is it? they ask, every few minutes. You gets your natural clock confused, see?'

'Do you help many people out?' The stew was delicious. Justine gobbled it up in big bites.

Magda's face closed up. 'Not many,' she said sharply.

'I'm sorry, I didn't mean to question you.'

Magda's face softened as she brought Justine a baked apple. Its glossy sides were split and oozing with honey-soaked currants. 'The less you know the better. 'Tis safer for everyone so. If you have finished that apple I'll pour you a bath.'

Justine moved over to the hip bath that now stood on the rag rug before the fire. She shucked off the ancient night things she had been wearing. Magda pounced on them and whisked them away, doubtless to give them a good scrub and a boiling. Justine looked down on her long slender body ruefully. She was sticky all over and dirt had stuck to the sweat she had produced in the mines. She smelt dreadful, and her long chestnut mane felt greasy and tangled. She ran her hands down her belly and rested them in between her legs. Her pubic hair had grown a little more and was quite dark now. She was glad about that. She had felt too naked and vulnerable with her sex bare. She wanted her pubic hair to grow long and curl luxuriantly once more. Her mons looked bereft without her rubies. But she owed her life to them – she could not regret that.

'Hair first,' said Magda, bustling back. Justine knelt down with her head over a basin and Magda lathered up her hair with expert hands.

'Were you ever a nurse?' asked Justine.

'Well now, fancy you asking that. I was nurse for the Lord Adar's four little ones until I was married. Why, they still visit me now. Ten years I was there altogether, and I had the raising of them entirely. My lady was too busy with her parties to care about the poor mites.'

Hot water gushed over Justine's head and she abandoned herself into the luxury of Magda's capable hands. As soon as her hair was washed and rinsed, and rinsed again, Magda pinned it up, out of the way. Justine gave a sigh of content as she climbed into the waiting hip bath. Rainbow-coloured soap bubbles brushed against her breasts where they just touched the water line. Justine swished the water with her hand to create more bubbles and watched the water turn black. Magda took jugs of dirty soapy water out of the bath and poured them away down her sink. Then she took fresh jugs off the top of the tiled stove and poured them into the hip bath and added fresh soap. She did this three times before the water stayed clear. Then she knelt down to scrub Justine's back. 'You don't have to do all this for me.'

'Why bless you, child. 'Tis a pleasure to have someone to fuss over. We've no child, nor any sign of one yet, though I pray to Our Lady day and night. There's nothing I like better than to have the care of someone. And you look like you could use a little care: you're thin as a rake and all over bruises.'

'Thank you,' said Justine softly. She felt firm hands pat her back soothingly.

'There's no need to thank me. Now you just bend your head down and let me scrub this filthy back.'

Justine sniffed hard and obediently bent her head. A few

tears came, and she felt sad and unsettled. Why should kindness unnerve her so? But the hot water soothed her, and the soft hands stroked her into calmness once more.

'You're clean enough now,' said Magda. 'Step out on to this towel if you please. I'll have no wet footprints on my floors.' Magda's towels were soft clouds of fresh-smelling cotton. Justine luxuriated in them as Magda patted her dry. Then Magda moved the bath, spread a fresh towel and asked Justine to sit on the floor before the tiled stove. She handed Justine a clean white nightgown, all warm from the stove, then, with firm, kindly fingers, she began combing out Justine's long chestnut hair which was already nearly dry. 'Such beautiful glossy hair,' she said, stroking it approvingly. She slowly twisted it into a thick shining plait, massaging Justine's head as she worked, and Justine's tense muscles eased blissfully under her ministrations.

'Back to bed for you,' announced Magda firmly. 'We can decide nothing until Pedar gets here in the morning. You're safe enough here, child,' she added hastily, seeing the worry spring back into Justine's eyes. 'In fact you could stay here, if you've a mind to. 'Tis lonely up in these mountains when Pedar is away. I'd be glad to have the company and that's the truth.'

Justine leant forward and hugged Magda impulsively. Part of her yearned to stay in the pretty little chalet and be petted and cosseted. But she knew that the turmoil in her heart would not allow her to rest. 'Oh, you're so kind, but I must go to the city; I have something very important to do there.'

The blue eyes looked sad. 'Well, think it over. I've taken a real fancy to you, and you look like you'd appreciate my cooking.'

'I do!' laughed Justine patting her stomach. 'That was the best meal I've eaten in days.'

'Are you sure you couldn't eat a little more? A baked apple? Let me put a little more goose grease on your feet. Would you like a nightcap? And were you warm enough last night? I've put my good sheets on for you seeing as you're clean now, and my best feather bed. I hope you'll be comfortable.'

Laughing, Justine fended her off, but her heart warmed under the friendly fussing of the older woman. Feeling deliciously clean and tidy, she walked carefully on her sore feet across the wooden floor to the snug bed that awaited her. Magda had slid the wooden panels back and turned down one corner of the fat, goose-down quilt. Justine ran a hand over the spotless white bedding and said, 'What fine linen.'

Magda looked pleased. ''Twas part of my dowry. I stitched all the hems myself.' Justine climbed in and Magda began to slide the wooden panel shut.

'No!' cried Justine. Her hands flew to her throat. 'Do you mind leaving it open. I can't breathe.'

Magda's eyes showed understanding. ''Tis the mines of course. You'll need a while to get over the memory of them. Silly of me; I should have thought.'

Justine slid down the sheets sighing in relief. Then her feet touched a hard object in the bed. She burrowed into the vast, clean-smelling feathery softness of the bed and fished around for the mystery object. It was long and hard with a bump at one end. She pulled the dark object out into the light and cried, 'Whatever is this?'

'Why 'tis just a little comforter,' Magda said. 'I put one in for you thinking you might enjoy it. You shall take it with you if you like; my Pedar carves the best comforters in these parts. All over the mountains you'll find them. And this is a fine one.'

Justine realised now that she was holding a large – larger than life-size – model of a man's sex organs in her hands. It was expertly carved, and it had been stained black, giving it an unfamiliar appearance. Justine ran a finger tip over the satiny wood. 'It is very lifelike,' she marvelled. 'The scrotum looks as if the balls inside it will move at any moment.' She turned it over in her hands. The wooden foreskin was pushed back over the fully erect tip, and she saw now that a smiling little face had been carved into the glans. The object in her hands suddenly felt friendly and she ran appreciative hands over it. 'I have never used such a thing before, but I think it should bring great pleasure to a woman.'

'There's not a woman in the village will go to bed without one,' laughed Magda. 'Goodnight now, Justine, and God bless.'

Magda bustled away, and Justine lay in the clean smooth sheets breathing in the smell of freshly ironed linen and listening to the comforting sounds of Magda tidying up and going to her own bed. A soft glow from the stove lit the room. Justine was restless, and lay with her hands behind her head, staring up at the carved wooden fretwork that ran around the inside of the bed enclosure. The black cat startled her by jumping on to the snowy white bedding. Although she didn't think Magda would approve, Justine stretched out her hand and clicked encouragingly to the cat. 'Here kitty,' she whispered. The cat gave her a super-cilious look and settled at the end of the bed to give its glossy fur a good clean. Presently Justine heard rusty purring. The sound comforted her, but she still couldn't sleep.

It was no good lying awake and worrying. Until she had been into the city she could make no decisions. It was pointless lying here with her thoughts racing around like a mad squirrel in a cage. She must relax. Cautiously, she reached out for the wooden dildo and weighed it in her hands. Stiff, hard, ever ready, and with no troubling emotions attached to it – she would try it. Justine slid the dildo under the covers of the bed, and then hesitated. It seemed unnatural somehow – she wouldn't try it. She placed the dildo under her pillow. Then she took several deep breaths, trying to calm her tense body. After a few moments, she pressed her palms flat against the soft skin of her stomach. It quivered softly under her hands as she stroked it. She slid one hand into the indentation of her waist, and then the other into the other side. It was pleasing to feel the curve, to know that she was slim and feminine. The sensitive nerve endings were awakening under her touch now. Justine rubbed across her ribcage – how it stood out these days – and then up to the gentle swell of her breasts. Her nipples were already erect. They seemed to push outward, ready to fall into her waiting fingers.

As she touched them, she remembered Father Gabriel, rubbing in the sweet butter and suckling her greedily. Her breath caught in her throat and her sensations deepened. More sexual images sprang to her mind, and her body relaxed and lolled into the stiff, clean sheets. Her head rolled back into the feathery softness of the big white pillows, and Justine's troubling thoughts faded away. Slowly, she circled the flat palm of her hands over her breasts. Her whole nipple area grew and hardened in response. A breathy sigh escaped from between her parted lips. The first tugs of pleasure pulled at her clitoris. She revelled in the feeling. She felt a rush of power surge through her veins, that she could make herself feel this good. Alone – or nearly alone.

She slid her hand under the pillow and retrieved the comforter. The jolly smile carved into the tip of the penis urged her on. She slid her hands down the length of her body and touched her own softly quivering thighs gently. They fell open, as if of their own accord, and a fine warm feeling broke out on the surface of her skin. She left the dildo lying on her upper thigh for a moment, very conscious of its smooth wooden hardness brushing her skin, and returned her attention to her breasts. She rolled one nipple between a thumb and forefinger. She pulled gently on the pliant nub, elongating it, then letting it go, allowing it to spring back deliciously into shape, before pulling it out again, and again. Then, with a delicious slowness, she transferred her attentions to her other nipple, feeling the areola swell as she pulled out the teat of her nipple and then allowed it to fall back.

Then she brushed one hand down over her belly. The movement caused the wooden penis to slide off her leg and tip into the soft bed. She left it there for the moment, sliding her hand over her lower belly and then to the small high mound between her legs. She pressed her hand down firmly and pulled back. The referred movement pulled on her secret flesh. It felt so good that she did it again, and again, pulling up softly and then letting go, feeling her labia open, feeling her vaginal muscles flex and pulse, softly preparing to open.

Justine rolled over slightly and picked up the black comforter. As she held the man-shape in her hands, images poured into her head: the sensation of having her anus licked so fervently in the hot, smothering darkness of the mine; the feel of the smooth manacles clicking shut over her wrists and ankles; Armand's dark head bent so lovingly over her labia, adorning them with the rubies she had bought her freedom with. Armand! She would not think of him now.

Deliberately she cleared her mind of all troubling images. She would think only of herself and her own sensation. She brought the black dildo up to her face and to her soft lips. She drew the tip into her mouth slowly and sucked upon it, wetting the wooden glans with saliva. She drew out the black rod and circled her responsive mouth with it, trailing it over her lips, feeling its hardness against her softness. Then she sucked it into her mouth once more, laving it with her tongue.

Her legs slowly parted. She took the comforter away from her mouth and slid it gradually across her body. She trickled the dildo lightly across the channels of her labia on the way to her other, moister mouth. They responded to the brief pressure by hardening and stiffening, growing larger in their pleasure. Justine pushed the smiling tip of the dildo into the warm wet mouth of her vagina, and dabbled it into the love dew that pooled there. The dildo kissed the innermost skin of the inside of her vagina, kissed it gently and slowly slid inside.

Justine's breathing was growing shallow. She found that her mouth was open and her legs fell even further apart. She rolled in the vast feathery softness of the bed and felt the fresh linen caress her sensitive skin. Shuddering slightly, she pushed on the wooden dildo and felt her vagina swallow it up. Slow steady shocks of pleasure travelled up the length of her dark tunnel with the movement of the wooden cock. Moisture dripped from the walls of her woman's place and bathed the pleasingly hard object that filled it. Justine twisted the stiff hard log that lay inside her, and then fell back panting, lying still to experience the feeling further.

She was wider open than she had imagined possible. The velvet muscle of her vagina strained open over the silent hardness of the comforter. The round carved balls nudged at her entrance, kissing it sweetly. She closed her legs and then let them fall open again. The movement caused her little bead of pleasure to spring out. Justine closed her eyes and waited as long as she could before she touched that little core of pleasure as it pulsed and yearned for her to tickle it softly and take her to heaven.

Still very aware of the warm hardness that held her open and magnified all her sensations, Justine gently touched the heart of her pleasure. The sensations that burst out shook her body immediately, and all the muscles along her warm wet vagina bore down at once. It felt so good to have that motionless hardness to clench around. Justine threw her head back and gasped with deep rapture. Her body, still pink from the bath, was like another soft pillow heaped on to the feather bed. She was sweet and relaxed all over. More snapshots rolled into her mind, but this time she didn't fight them, or analyse them, or worry about them. She just let the pictures come, heightening her pleasure as her body remembered the extreme peaks she had reached and the way that sex felt in good loving.

No better than this! In fact, as she bore down once more on the lovely stiff hardness of the woodcarver's present and touched her clitoris lightly, Justine felt sharper, purer sexual pleasure than she ever had before. She had only herself to please, and no emotions to distract her. This was pure sex. Sex for her own pleasure alone, and her feelings took her with gorgeous intensity as she flicked the little nub of her clitoris once more. All her awareness was centred on that tiny heart. All the sensations from her long silky tunnel flowed into the nub of sensation that vibrated under her fingertip. All the pictures that flashed across her mind activated pure bliss in her memory and she was shaken by such wanton piercing pleasure that she stopped trying to prolong things and went forward to meet the climax that was rushing out of the centre of her body to take her over.

Now she let her middle finger thrum upon the core of her pleasure. She flung her legs open. Ah, the movement intensified the melting, thrusting feeling that the enormous black dildo was creating. The sensations it was generating ran wild throughout her body. Her hand snaked down and caught the wooden penis by its wooden balls and Justine pushed it in and pulled it out, nearly fainting with the sweet liquid movements. Her middle finger tapped hard upon the tiny nub of her clitoris until her body suddenly jack-knifed, her whole body doubling as she peaked. A dark loving face swam before her mind's eye. 'Armand!' she cried silently as, suddenly, her orgasm burst from her.

Keeping her pelvis tipped up, she pushed the heel of her hand flat on to the centre of her clitoris, flattening her labia, muffling and intensifying her pleasure at the same time. Her other hand grabbed wildly at the smooth round wooden balls at the end of the wooden penis inside her. Her head shook from side to side as she spun in the ecstatic vortex of the vibrations that snapped around her body: good, sweet and hard. Blessed relief took her as the spasms ebbed away, and she sank down sweetly into the pillows. Honey dew ran over her hand as she pulled the wooden cock out of her inner self. Moved by a sudden impulse, she kissed the smiling black face on the tip of the glans, tasting her own sweetness as she did so. She tucked the woodcarver's comforter under the pillow and settled herself for sleep.

Armand. She had called for Armand as she came. She breathed a soft sigh as sleep wrapped her round in its kind embrace. There was no surprise there. She knew that she loved him. What she didn't know was if it was right to love him. And that she was going to the city to find out.

Chapter Thirteen

Justine paused on one of the bridges that spanned the grey loops of the river and looked down at the city. A huge steely-grey sky hung over the grey stone of the buildings. Deep snow lay thickly over the roofs and terraces, statues and squares of the city. A regiment of soldiers, dashing in their scarlet coats, cantered across the snow-covered square that lay in front of the cathedral. Justine could hear faint shouts, and see tiny black figures scattering before the horsemen. She fixed her eyes on the soaring bulk of the cathedral. It seemed to tower over her, even at this distance, dominating her, and she began walking towards it with some reluctance. Her wooden shoes slipped on the dirty packed ice of the street. It was nearly midday, and she was hungry. Should she eat first or go to the cathedral first? she wondered. The bell for Angelus began to ring as she hesitated. The sound was so familiar that it made her homesick for the convent; but this was a deep-toned cathedral bell, and she was far from home.

Still undecided, she walked as far as the vast square in front of the cathedral steps. Chestnut sellers hawked their wares. Delicious smells floated from the baked apple stall and the candy stall next to it. Justine bought a hot cheese pastry and stood under the ragged striped canvas awning of the stall eating it, staring at the cathedral as she did so. The pie was delicious: great drops of butter ran from light flakes of pastry wrapped around salty goat's cheese. Justine ate every scrap and licked her fingers thoughtfully. She would have liked another one, but Pedar had only given her a few tiny coins, and she was reluctant to spend them too quickly.

And besides, she was just delaying matters. Part of her was reluctant to enter the cathedral and demand answers to her questions. She had always been scared of the cathedral. When she was very young, she had read a book about the building of the spires that soared up into the heavens. They had cost the lives of many workers. In cold weather, it had not been unusual for the stonemasons to die at their work. They would fall from their lofty perches; pathetic frozen sparrows, crashing into the uncaring ground below. It had given Justine nightmares, to think of those good patient craftsmen, dying so lamentably.

Her heart was hammering and her palms were sweating as she mounted one and then another and then another of the wide steps. Vendors of trinkets huddled along the sides of the steps. Clouds of steam puffed from their mouths into the cold air as they called out, begging Justine to buy their goods: holy water, medals blessed by the Virgin, prayers guaranteed to cure the sick, pictures of the queen. Justine ignored them all and climbed steadily. She felt colder and colder as she got closer to the entrance.

As Justine stood, delaying the moment when she must enter the terrible cold magnificence of the cathedral, an ancient bedesman shuffled over to her. He was bent with age and tiny wisps of white hair sprang from his pink scalp. 'First time to our beautiful cathedral ... mistress?' He mumbled the last word in his toothless mouth. He was obviously not sure how to address Justine. Her clothes were those of a prosperous peasant – she wore a thick woven cloak and carried a stout basket – but she knew now that her figure and bearing were those of a noble.

'Yes indeed, good sir. I want to ... well, take confession I suppose,' said Justine, smiling into his childlike eyes. 'But

I want to speak to the most important person. The top minister of the cathedral. Will you tell me who that may be?'

Before he answered, the bedesman drew her in through the door into the vast shadowy darkness. Justine stood stunned, looking up into the high gothic ceilings. Wisps of blue incense floated on the air. The few people who moved about the floor of the cathedral nave were dwarfed by the immensity of the building above them. ''Tis the archbishop, I suppose, you'll be wanting,' said the old man. 'He hears confessions once a week only, after evensong. Why, today is his day. But you'll have to queue, mind. See those people already lining up by the Lady Chapel? They all be waiting to see him, for he is known as a good and holy man.'

'Then I will wait too,' said Justine, looking determined.

'God, bless you,' said the bedesman. He ambled away, shuffling back to his post at the gothic arch of the door, a tiny bent figure against the immensity of the cathedral. Justine turned away with a sigh and joined the people who waited patiently in line to see the archbishop. A stout peasant woman with a worried face moved a wicker basket containing a live duck so that Justine could sit next to her and lean her back on a magnificently carved tomb. Justine thanked the woman and settled down to wait. Her eyes had adjusted to the dimness inside, and now they were drawn to the kaleidoscope blaze of a stained-glass window. She gazed into its coloured depths absently. She was concentrating her mind on the forthcoming interview. She must try to collect her whirling thoughts, arrange them clearly and place her worries and doubts coherently before the great man when her turn came. If she could explain herself clearly, she was sure she would get answers that made sense.

The faint shadow on the other side of the confessional grill bent his head briefly and cleared his throat. Justine sat back with her heart pounding, and a dry mouth. It had taken her a very long time to pour out the story of all her adventures and her doubts and her worries, but now she felt light and free, as if a huge burden had been lifted from her shoulders. She had taken all her troubles and perplexities and laid them where they belonged: at the foot of one of God's highest representatives on earth. The priest cleared his throat again and Justine leant forward expectantly. 'Tell, me,' he said, 'I'm not quite clear as to the nature of the debauchery you participated in at the banquet. What happened after you got off the platter of fruit?'

Justine stirred impatiently. 'Does it matter? Surely I told you enough to make you understand what manner of experiences I underwent at the castle?'

'Why yes, but I need to know more about that event.'

'I do not wish to recall it. I am ashamed.'

'Why so? You were merely obeying the orders of the count and countess, your master and mistress.'

Justine bit her lip. 'I know,' she said in a small voice. Shame was strong in her, but so was the habit of truth in the confessional. 'But I knew that what I was doing was wrong, and yet, the dishonourable truth is, Father, I enjoyed it.'

'I think you need to explain the nature of your enjoyment to me – so that I can help you better, of course.'

After a pause, when Justine still did not speak, but remained with her head bowed, twisting a piece of the fabric of her skirt between her fingers, the priest urged, 'Try to remember. You say that you were wearing a black collar? Did it hold your neck upright?'

'Yes indeed. I could not look down very easily, or turn my head from side to side. There was something very comforting about the way it held me.'

'Did it make you feel sexual?'

'Yes, sexual, and also safe.'

'How about the straps that went over your breasts? I think you said that they made your breasts poke out, as if in wanton invitation?'

'Yes, yes, they did so. The black straps were tied across my skin in a manner that lifted and separated my breasts and made them jut out. My nipples and breasts were painted red, too, so that the effect was very obvious. As if I were a cheap whore, flaunting her wares. Indeed, that is what the count required me to do.'

The priest's breathing grew just a little deeper. 'Ah, I think you had better tell a little more about this. What exactly did the count require you to do?'

Justine swallowed as a picture of the count's repellent black eyes swam into her mind. 'It was as if he hypnotised me,' she said, remembering the way she had trembled and obeyed his every command. 'I had no thought of resisting him. When he told me to take hold of my breasts and pinch the nipples, I did so.'

'Who was watching you?'

'At first, just the count. But when' – here Justine swallowed and shivered as the memories came flooding back with full force – 'but when he saw that my nipples were hardening and standing up stiffly with my pleasure, he laughed, and ordered me to walk around the top table. I was to stop at every chair, and display my breasts to each noble that sat there, male or female.'

'Was that so hard?'

'Why no, well yes. You see, I had to entice each person into caressing my breasts. If I could not tempt them to do so, then I had failed at my task and I was to be whipped.'

The breathing on the other side of the shadowed grill grew a little faster. The shadows of orange flames flickered behind the slats of the wooden grill that separated the priest from Justine. It was warm in the closed compartment of the confessional, and Justine realised that there was a charcoal brazier keeping the priest cosy. The warmth seemed to penetrate her frozen limbs and melt her stony worries. It was such a relief to tell someone about the shameful perplexing nature of the sexual events she had participated in – and her even more shameful and confused feelings about her response to those events.

'Whipped . . .' said the priest, trailing the word off encouragingly.

'Whipped,' said Justine with a sigh. 'A male slave was ordered to follow me around, holding a whip to remind

me of the rules. He was a man from Africa. He was big –
mercy, I never saw such a huge man. I think he could have
lifted this confessional box and tossed it over his shoulder
if he had a mind to. His skin was oiled, and I, well, when I
looked at his eyes, I found him powerfully attractive.'

'Did you want him to whip you?'

'At first no. At first I was terrified of him. He was
standing behind me at each place, holding the whip,
watching me, willing me to fail. I knew, I could read it in
his face, that he was longing to caress me with the thong
of his long black whip.'

'And to stop him, you had to tempt each noble into
touching your breasts?'

'Indeed, and I found it easy, even pleasurable to do so.
At the first chair I stopped at, I felt shy, painfully shy. How
was I to encourage this stranger, to entice him into touching my nipples? But as soon as I looked into his eyes it was
easy. It was a man, a middle-aged man, and he was excited
and laughing and I could read desire for me in his eyes,
and so it was easy.'

'What manner of harlot-like action did you perform?'

'I, I ran my hands over my breasts.' Justine paused,
remembering the strength of the pleasure that had raced
into the tips of her nipples as she shook them and teased
them in the very face of the man who sat looking up at her
so lustfully. 'The excitement I saw in his eyes seemed to
inflame me. I was still wearing the black leather harness,
of course, and the straps between my buttocks and running
over my belly seemed to excite me even further.'

'Was there no part of the harness touching your sex?'

'Two straps ran between my legs, with a silver rod on
each strap. It was cunningly placed so that the rods lay
along the length of my lips – '

'Lips? Be more precise!'

'My, my sex lips, my labia. They were shaved and
completely naked, so that I could feel the press of the silver
rods where they were bound against my sexual folds and
secrets.'

'And was there moisture? Be more precise, woman. Use

exact terminology so that I may understand what transpired.'

'Moisture? Ah, yes, I was wet.' An impatient movement on the other side of the grill made Justine say hastily, 'Love dew, I do not know what else to call it, but love dew, liquid from the walls of my woman's ... my cunt ... liquid from my cunt was pooling over and soaking the silver rods and the black straps of my bondage. I could feel the wetness between my legs, and the sensation was adding to my pleasure.'

'So, I understand now. You were standing next to this noble, shaking your breasts in his face, pinching and exciting the nipples, exhorting him to caress you intimately – and your body was revelling in the vulgarity of your situation. You were behaving like a common strumpet, and you enjoyed it.' The priest sighed heavily, and Justine heard his robe rustling as he moved on the other side of the grill. There was a husky catch in his voice as he continued, 'Were you successful? Did you succeed in getting him to touch your breasts?'

'Very quickly. He could not control himself, although he tried to. As soon as he laid a hand on my breast, the slave moved in and stopped him. I was made to move on to the next person at the table.'

Justine heard the priest clear his throat. His shadowy outline flickered behind the carved grill of the screen that separated them. His body seemed to be restless, as if he kept moving to scratch an itch; but there was no doubt that he wanted her to continue. 'Describe exactly what happened,' he said. 'You say they forced you? I do not understand how.'

Justine blushed deeply, because she knew they hadn't truly forced her. She had been drawn along by a kind of terrible fascination. There was a magnetic sexual attraction that drew her towards the count, even as he repelled her. She remembered him bellowing: 'Get on with it!' and he had banged his goblet on the table. 'If you take too long about it, I won't have you whipped. I'll send you back to your room in disgrace. Aye, and tell the whole castle that the little governess has not a sexy atom in her body.'

Stung, Justine had tossed her flowing hair back over her shoulders. She was aware of her naked sex lips hanging heavy over the silver rods of the harness. Her breasts pouted and jutted. The swollen nipples poking out of the red-painted flesh seemed to tell everyone of the sweetly aching sensations that lapped at her flesh. She felt all female and very aware of the heat of the big slave as he moved behind her. Mincing a little, because of her high heels, she moved over to the next noble.

He was just a youth, barely into his twenties, she judged, with an adolescent's gawkiness still apparent in the way he moved his limbs. He was flushed with drink and excitement. He waved a goblet full of red wine in the air. A few drops splashed on to Justine's skin. 'Drink with me!' he cried.

Justine's mouth was dry. Gladly she took a deep drink of the wine, and then another because it tasted so good. Heat rushed down into her belly and pooled between her legs, making her sex tingle. She breathed deeply and leant back. Oh, that felt good. Why had she not taken a drink before now? It lifted her into an even higher realm of sensation and sexuality – so that Justine felt a fresh rush of power and enjoyment as she smiled down into the face of the young noble. 'See anything you like, young sir?' she asked cheekily, placing her hands under her breasts and cupping them upward, shaking them practically under his nose. 'Wouldn't you like to touch my breasts, young master?'

He leapt to his feet as eagerly as an overgrown labrador puppy and cast himself at Justine's feet. 'Mistress!' he cried. 'I adore you. Command me and I'm yours. Oh let me suck those glorious breasts! Whip me and I'll die for you.' Justine looked down at him, pleased, and yet astonished. He turned his head to her foot and kissed it eagerly, planting hot fervent kisses on her spike-heeled shoes. Seized by a sudden demon, Justine took the coiled whip

205

out of the hands of the black slave and cracked it high in the air.

'Bare your buttocks,' she cried. The young man struggled clumsily to his feet. He looked at her with adoring eyes. 'I say, will you really . . . ?' he asked. When Justine nodded, he began to unbutton his breeches, dropping them down to hang over his tight boots, turning round quickly to present his bare bottom to Justine – and her whip.

Ah, how good it was to give the orders! To have a man trembling at her feet. Justine looked down at the young man as he crouched on the floor, gazing up at her, longing to put his whole being into her hands. The wine tingled and teased her, sending a glorious heady rush around her body. She could do it too – she knew what he wanted. She was powerful, she was beautiful and wildly sexual; all the nobles were watching her, some with lust, and some with deep envy, wishing themselves in the place of the youth.

'Strip,' ordered Justine. The young man began to rip the rest of his clothes off. His slave ran forward and knelt at his feet, tugging his boots off. As soon as the young man was naked, he stood trembling in front of Justine. She allowed the moment to stretch out, glorying in her power. 'Get up on the table and lie down in front of everyone,' she said firmly.

At once, he started to scramble up on to the table. The black slave held him back for an instant, glancing at the count for permission. The count nodded, leaning forward a little so that he could see better. The black slave let the young noble go, and he sprang on to the polished board eagerly, pushing goblets and plates aside, flinging himself down, careless of spilled cream and squashed fruit. He began wriggling his slim white bottom eagerly, lifting it high in the air and crying, 'Oh, mistress, mistress, I do your bidding.'

Justine sprang on to the table behind him, mad with excitement. She stood erect and flourished the whip in the air, circling, shaking her breasts and swaying her hips, deliberately drawing the attention of the chattering, brightly dressed crowd to her all but naked body. She cracked the whip loudly, and then again, until the conversation ceased and every eye was on her. The effeminate slave appeared from somewhere and hastily began clearing dishes. Justine playfully swung the whip after him as he scampered up and down the table; the roar of laughter and approval from the nobles was even headier than the wine. She knelt down on the now-clear table top and gently pushed open the legs of the young man who lay shaking on his belly before her. She looked thoughtfully at the quivering white buttocks. How pale and unmarked they were. The crease under each round cheek ran sweetly into the crack between his legs, and a few wisps of pubic hair curled out.

'Kneel!' she ordered. 'Get up on your hands and knees.' He obeyed at once, and a delightful sensation of power swept over her. Now his penis, a red eager penis just like its young master, swung free, and she reached between his legs and tickled his cock with a teasing hand. She felt it tremble in her palm as if he would come any second. She didn't want that. She let his stiff penis swing free, and he groaned and shook his buttocks once more, as if to make her attend to them. Justine stood up, stepped back and lifted the whip.

The way she was standing had drawn the black straps of her restraining harness tight and snug: it pulled up between the cheeks of her buttocks and caressed her belly smoothly. The hard rods that held the lips of her sex open were warm and kissed her gently, just touching her clitoris, so lightly that she might be imagining it, save that excitement and arousal were gently growing as blood flowed into the heart of her pleasure. She gloried in the sensations that raced over her quivering skin. She lifted the whip once more, swishing it experimentally through the air, watching the white buttocks shake as their owner heard the lash whistling through the air.

She liked making him wait. She drew the whip up, and brought it down on the table top, hard, watching him moan and tremble. His whole body shuddered, and she knew that he didn't know whether to be glad or sorry that it was the table the lash had bitten into and not his expectant flesh. She leant down and whispered in his ear, 'I promise, it'll be your buttocks I whip next.' She laughed aloud as she watched the flush of sexual arousal her words provoked; it flooded into his cheeks and stained the back of his neck. It was glorious fun, to torment him so.

A noble banged on the table, another shouted impatiently. They were all waiting to see her whip the young man. Justine fixed her attention on the quivering kneeling youth below her feet. She took a deep breath. Did she want to do this? More fists banged on the heavy table top. They would be slow hand clapping and booing if she did not act soon. The white buttocks below her seemed very small and far away, but Justine leant back and raised the whip high in the air. The angry thumping on the table stopped. All eyes were upon her. She cracked the whip once, while it was suspended high above her head, and then she brought it whistling down.

She got the strangest feeling as the long black thong slashed into the tender white flesh of the youth cowering below her. The deep red wheal that appeared across the pure white of his smooth round buttocks satisfied some deep and primitive instinct way down inside her. She dropped to her knees and drew her forefinger softly along the glowing red stripe. Then she dropped the whip, raised one hand in the air and slammed her open palm hard across the fat white globe before her so that the air whistled with the force of her blow. He cried out and shivered. Her hand stung – surely even his buttocks couldn't be smarting as hard as her hand was. But, despite the pain, Justine drew back her other hand, and landed a mighty slap on the second cheek of the bottom that was spread so invitingly before her.

Breathing hard, she straightened her knees and stood up once more, bending quickly to retrieve the whip. She drew the coils lovingly through her smarting palms. She noticed how the eyes of the nobles were drawn to its sinister black thong, so she placed her legs wide apart and ran the length of the whip between her open legs, as if she were stimulating herself with its black length. She pouted her lips and jiggled her breasts and her pretence turned into reality. She was truly masturbating now. The slick coils of the whip slid so smoothly across the aching nub of her clitoris that a mighty orgasm began to gather in the warmth of her sex.

'Stop that!' bellowed the count. Startled, Justine halted her rhythmic manipulation of the whip.

'Boo! Spoilsport!' cried the nobles.

'Let's see her come!' shouted a stout red-faced lord.

'Get on with the whipping,' cried one woman. 'I want to see pain not pleasure.'

The count banged on the table. 'Whip him or I'll whip you,' he bawled. Nervously, Justine looked over to the black slave. His gaze drilled into her. She felt overwhelmed by more sexual pressure than she could handle. Her breath came fast between her lips, but the intense sensations of her near orgasm were subsiding, and she was able to control herself once more. Barely however. If the intense grip of her near orgasm was slackening, it had left in its place a heightened arousal. Like someone removing a fire screen from a blazing log fire, the heat of Justine's full sensual nature now blazed forth, freely, openly and at full power.

'I looked down at the naked white buttocks spread below me,' she said slowly. 'As well as the red stripe where the lash of the whip had landed, there was a red imprint of my hand clearly visible across each of his innocent buttocks. Those red imprints seemed to dance in front of my eyes and the palms of my hands still stung with the memory of landing those blows as I slowly raised the whip.'

The priest coughed and Justine stopped talking, surprised to find herself back in the stuffy warm box of the confessional, so vivid had her memories of that sensual banquet been. Her throat was dry too. She shifted uneasily. She had not noticed while she was telling her tale, but now she noticed, unmistakably, that she was sexually aroused by her memories: her nipples felt sweet and sensitive as they brushed the fabric of her gown, and a dampness curled the short pubic hair that was just beginning to curl between her legs.

'Don't stop,' said the priest urgently. There was a familiar note in his voice that troubled Justine now, and she looked at the grill in puzzlement. 'I want you to describe to me how you felt as you thrashed the sinful buttocks of that most fortunate youth. How did those quivering orbs look as they trembled and quivered below the terrible heavenly lashes of your whip? Ah, did the red stripes criss-cross his white cheeks until the whole sensitive area was one delicious red mass of pain?'

Forgetting that he could not see her, Justine nodded slowly. Then she said, 'Yes, yes, they did; but he liked it. I was watching his penis as it swung between his legs: it jerked with every impact of the lash, but it was hard, as a man's organ is when enjoyment is full upon him. He was erect the whole time that I whipped him.'

Again she paused to collect her thoughts. The familiar smell of sex tickled her nostrils. Was she so aroused that her secretions were scenting the air of the confessional? It was very warm now. The orange glow from the priest's brazier was lower and steadier, but it was giving off plenty of heat. Justine's nostrils flared as she tried to pinpoint that wisp of elusive scent.

'Did the black slave, the one who was detailed to whip you later, did he watch you as you punished the young man on the table?'

A shiver ran down Justine's spine. 'I was aware of his gaze the whole time I was performing.'

The priest's breathing was hoarse and ragged, and Justine heard him scratching again. 'Were you in a sinful state of arousal from your handling of the youth? Did you not have him pleasure you sexually in any way? Ah! Details, delicious, enticing, erotic details, spare me none of them – I would hear every wicked sensual movement that you made.'

'I made the youth turn over and lie on his back,' said Justine, shivering at the memory. 'Despite the threat of the watching African, I was desperate to have the clenching

210

frustration inside me satisfied.' She broke off. Looking back now, she could hardly believe the wantonness of her final act. But the priest allowed her no mercy.

'What vulgar sin did you commit next?' he panted. 'I insist that you tell me.'

'I ran the whip across his belly and nipples a few times,' said Justine, 'and across his penis to see it respond in terror. But what I wanted at that point was my own satisfaction, and so I . . . I moved down the table. I stood across the youth as he lay on his back. He was looking up into my woman's place. He could see the black straps of my harness where it held my lips open and the moisture that pooled along the rods of the silver metal that kissed me so sweetly, adding to my urgency and arousal. I put one black high-heeled shoe on each side of his face, and I crouched down, so that the bud of my pleasure centre, my clitoris, was pressed hard against his full red mouth.'

'Oh, you sinful bitch,' groaned the priest. 'You must have looked like an angel from hell as you sat on that lucky, lucky young man's face.' Justine heard a thump as his head fell forward against the wooden screen that separated them. Suspicion rose in her, but a kind of paralysis kept her sitting where she was, as his strained and urgent voice commanded her: 'Tell me more! Hold nothing back! Did you bump? Did you grind your sexual organs into the willing submissive face of that young man, using him cruelly until you came, caring nothing for the eyes of the watching nobles as you freely and shamefully orgasmed before them all.'

Now his breathing held the unmistakable, rhythmic pattern of sexual arousal. He was openly masturbating. Justine smelled sex again, and this time she knew what it was. Now she knew why his robe had rustled and what itch his hands had been scratching. Now she understood why he had insisted on hearing every shameful, erotic detail. Anger arrived like a clap of thunder. She stormed to her feet and out into the cold air of the vast shadowy cathedral. She began stalking out into the night to walk off her anger, but then she turned. Her rage was too powerful to be satisfied by walking away. A tiny figure under the vastness of the soaring gothic ceiling arches, she raged around the side of the confessional box. It looked very small, lost in the measureless spaces of the cathedral. She ripped open the purple velvet curtain that concealed the priest from the public. She pulled at the curtain with such vicious anger that the rod that held it in place was pulled free of its mooring. Brass rings jingled as the rod and the curtain clattered down in a cloud of dust.

Heads turned as her ferocious anger disturbed the sanctity of the cathedral. She didn't care. She dived into the open box and saw with great joy that the priest who cowered inside it was naked. He had dared to take his robe off while he listened to her sexual confessions. The naked priest reached for his robe and hunted frantically for the neck opening, but the complexity of the folds delayed him. The force of Justine's anger propelled her hands. She ripped the black robe out of the priest's grip and threw it aside – it landed on the glowing brazier and began to smoke at once – and pulled the naked, helpless priest out into the cold air of the cathedral.

He stood shivering, naked, trying to cover his jutting hard-on with his hands. He looked like a tiny pink shrimp against the stone vastness of his church. As the disturbance grew, more people gathered, staring at the nakedness of their archbishop in bewilderment. Justine looked in his face and laughed out loud when she saw who it was: 'Father Gabriel! So you are the "good and holy man" the people wait so long to see!' She felt the steel bands of her religious indoctrination breaking free from about her heart. 'Free!' she said aloud triumphantly. 'Now that I see what you are, I am free of you for ever!'

She turned, and would have walked out, but Father Gabriel cried to the watching crowd: 'She's a madwoman! She tried to rape me and abuse my position.'

'Then why is your cock so hard, priest?' cried Justine, but even as she spoke, she realised that she didn't care what the congregation thought. She looked at Father Gabriel for the very last time. His manhood was shrinking under the gaze of so many eyes. He looked ridiculous, small and shrunken. Although his congregation didn't seem to know what to think, the giggling choir boys were definitely enjoying Father Gabriel's predicament. Smoke began to curl out of the top of the confessional box; the fire from the robe she had flung on the brazier must be spreading. Justine smiled at the extra havoc this would create. Some mud would stick, she mused, as she pushed her way through the crowd. It would help the story to spread around the city. The cheeky honest choir boys would recount every embarrassing detail and many people would know the truth and laugh. They would remember Father Gabriel as the archbishop who stood naked while his confessional went up in flames. It was revenge enough for her.

Justine put him out of her mind for ever and stepped out through the cathedral door into the clear night. A frosty moon sailed over the great city square, casting hard-edged shadows over the snow-covered buildings and statues. Justine drew in a clean breath of air that made her lungs hurt and blew it out in a blast that effectively sealed off her past. Adrenaline from her encounter with Father Gabriel still warmed her body, but there was a singing in the air that told her that the temperature was dropping dangerously below freezing. Tonight, she would find a warm stable to sleep in. And tomorrow? A tender smile curved her lips. Why, tomorrow she would seek out Armand. And if he still wanted her – a cold hand twisted her heart at the thought he might not – if he still wanted her, she would tell him that she would be proud and happy to be his love.

Chapter Fourteen

*T*hree days later she stood looking over the plateau below the village of Waldgraf in dismay: it was empty. Snow covered the flat area thickly and smoothly, as if there had never been a gipsy camp there at all. Justine stood at the edge of the forest track, half hidden by a birch tree, and wondered what to do. Her cracked red feet ached in their wooden sabots, and she was cold. Steam from her breath misted around her face as she leant her forehead on the papery white bark of a birch tree. She looked down at the trunk of the tree. Frozen lumps of sap glistened amber in the winter sunshine. Absently she broke one off and chewed it. She knew that she must find someone and ask them where the gipsies had gone. But she was afraid to speak to anyone in case the count should be looking for her.

She closed her eyes and bit hard into the wild sweetness of the lump of sap. Then she realised that for some time, without being consciously aware of it, she had been hearing the steady chop, chop, chop of a woodcutter's axe. The foresters lived apart from the village people. It would probably be safe to approach them.

Justine retraced her steps along the rutted forest track until she came to a cross cut in the dense ranks of pines. The path was not very wide, but she could see from tracks in the snow that it had been used recently. She pushed her way along it, ignoring the cold fluffy snow that came up way over her ankles and soaked her legs and feet, until she came to a clearing.

Five or six men stood around the trunk of a mighty fir tree where it lay smashed into the ground. They had obviously stopped for lunch for brightly coloured handkerchieves were spread over the raw stump of the felled fir, and each handkerchief was laden with food. A blackened billy can hung over a bright fire of small twigs, and the men leant easy on their big axes, waiting for it to boil. The smell of the campfire smoke – and the thought of food – brought saliva into Justine's mouth as she stepped forward.

The big burly woodmen were astonished to see her, but they made her welcome and made a great show of chopping a branch into a seat and placing it by the fire for her. They insisted on loading her with food, and pressed a mug of hot sweet tea into her cold hands. Their kindness made Justine want to cry, and there was a distinct tremble in her voice as she said, 'No more, I beg you. I have enough food for a week right here in my lap. It looks delicious, but please no more. Only, can you tell me where the gipsies are gone?'

'Baramere, in the next valley,' said a great bearded fellow. 'The count of Baramere is uncommonly fond of they gipsies, and he do allow them to winter there. Even feeds them too, by what I hear.'

''Tis a rumour, that bit,' said a jolly rubicund chap. He was leaning thoughtfully on his axe, stuffing a meat pie into his mouth as he spoke. 'Stands to reason, see. Who's going to waste good food on they thieving bastards?' The bearded woodman nudged him hard, and he blushed crimson and said apologetically, 'Begging your pardon, mistress, for me language. But we ain't used to ladies here.'

'What? I didn't hear you,' said Justine diplomatically. 'But how far is it to Baramere? Is it not right over the mountains? I have never been there.' Neither had the woodcutters. It took them the best part of twenty minutes to decide just how far away Baramere was. Justine ate and drank steadily the whole time they wrangled about the best route to take, and she felt a great deal better by the time they had reached a consensus.

''Tis not far,' said the bearded giant, who appeared to be their chief spokesman. 'The problem at this time of year do be the pass. It takes more than three weeks to walk around the mountain, and 'tis only half a day through the gorge. But the snow drifts deep, and it might not be passable for a single traveller.'

'Does nobody cross it in winter?' asked Justine, thinking she might join a group and so cross safely.

''Tis unlikely. The sheep have long gone down off the mountains, and as you must know, mistress, trade between the valleys is slow in the cold seasons. Can you not wait until spring?'

'No!' said Justine. The thought of waiting for months was unbearable. She wanted to find Armand and find him now – and waste no more of her life without him. The reason she gave aloud, however, was practical: 'I am in great need of work. And it would be best all round if I were to cross the mountains and reach Baramere before I took another post.'

The woodcutters nodded understandingly. The jolly chap said, 'Old Harald what lives in the little chalet at the foot of the pass, not the big one mind, with the fine woodwork, but the little grey one, well, his wife is sick. Now if you were to go there, I bet they'd be right glad to have thee stay until the weather was right to attempt the pass. If you were to cook for them, and clean up a bit, like.' He looked at Justine doubtfully. 'But perhaps it's not what you're used to, that kind of work? It might be beneath a lady like you.'

'Indeed not,' said Justine warmly. 'My last post was as governess – but I have done my share of cleaning. Honest work holds no fear for me.' The woodcutters nodded approvingly. But one of them looked at Justine thoughtfully.

'Governess,' he said slowly. 'By! My thick head; wood it

216

does lovely but other things do cause it pain. Wait now, mistress. Seems to me I heard the count is looking for a governess. No, that's not right. What is it I did hear?' His brow furrowed as his ponderous thought processes worked themselves out. Ice water cascaded down Justine's spine and into her belly. Dear God! The count was looking for her! She sprang to her feet.

'Look how the sun sinks! I keep you from your work, and I must make good time if I am to reach the foot of the pass before dark. I thank you for your hospitality and your directions.' She was gone, fleeing back up the snowy forest track so fast that her cloak billowed out behind her like smoke from a far-off tornado. She could hear the woodcutters shouting after her, their slow country minds bemused by her sudden departure. She did not dare look back. If they were to remember why the count was looking for her ... She ran faster, slipping in the cold snow, ignoring the weight of her heavy shoes. She burst out of the side track and on to the broad ride of the main path through the forest. There she stood panting, her sides heaving painfully as she gulped in cold air. There was a pain in her temples and her feet hurt abominably, but she took hardly three minutes for a breather before setting doggedly off again up the empty silent track.

The ranks of stiff, dark trees stood like soldiers along the sides of the snowy road. No animals stirred in the forest and only a few black crows patrolled the gunmetal sky. She must get to the pass as soon as she could, and over the mountains as soon as the weather would let her. Every nerve in her body screamed at her to get going, to keep moving, to reach Armand before it was too late.

The same impulse still drove her as she said goodbye to old Harald. 'Won't you stay, mistress,' he begged her again. 'The pass will be so much safer in spring.'

She gave the old man a hug. 'I must go on.'

'He'll not forget you,' said old Harald. He knew only that there was a man involved in Justine's story, but he spoke with great conviction. 'Where would he find another like you? I thought you were a great noble when you arrived on our doorstep – even half dead in the midnight snow you were unmistakably a lady – but you have been like a daughter to us. Aye, and 'tis your good nursing that has brought my Heidi round. I was afeared I was going to lose her but you brought her back from the dead.' A few tears came to his old eyes and he rubbed his runny nose with his sleeve. 'Make your home with us, daughter. We'll take good care of you.'

A hard bud bloomed in Justine's throat. It would open and choke her if she prolonged this leave-taking any more. She lifted the sack of food they had pressed upon her and waved goodbye to the white face that drooped sadly in the window of the mountain chalet. A crescent moon and luminous Venus still hung in the dawn sky above the fretted wooden roof. The sunrise was just flushing the eastern mountains pink along their snowy faces, and a few clouds turned gold as they floated in the cerulean sky.

Harald turned about him slowly, assessing the weather with the wisdom of an entire life spent in the mountains. 'Go on if you're going,' he said roughly. ''Tis as fine a spell as you are likely to get this winter, and my bones do tell me that it will not snow for at least twenty-four hours. But you may need all that. You must go now! Stop wasting time, you silly baggage. It's only six hours in good weather, but 'tis no joke to cross the pass in winter.'

Justine hugged him again and then stepped out firmly. She was not fooled by his roughness, but his advice was sound. She must use every minute of daylight in order to cross the pass safely.

A week later the last of the short winter light was fading from the sky as Justine approached a gipsy camp. She hesitated before taking the last few steps towards it. She felt like a lone wolf after her long walk through the mountains – an outcast, living on scraps and slinking into people's barns to sleep with the beasts. She was deadly tired, and she had no confidence that Armand would welcome the scruffy stray she had become. She took a deep breath, breathing in smoke and the smell of rabbit stew, and walked closer to the ring of gipsy waggons. She shrank back as a pack of thin, vicious-looking dogs got wind of her. They loped over, showing their fangs as they barked. They blocked her way, but they did not bite. Some children came running. Dark-eyed, with mischievous smiles flashing under their tousled hair, they chose to bully Justine. 'Beggar woman!' they cried. 'Yah! Yah! Get out of here!'

'I am looking for Armand,' Justine said, but over the sound of the dogs' frantic braying and the noise of the children's shrill cries, she could not be heard. She stepped forward boldly. 'Children!' she bawled. 'Be quiet! You too!' she added to the dogs. 'Get down and shut up!'

The dogs subsided into angry whimpering and the children were astonished. 'Why don't they bite you, missus?' asked one of the children. 'Be you a friend to this camp?'

'Indeed I am,' said Justine, but she got no further. She was completely knocked off her feet by a streak of grizzled fur. Singing with joy, the wolfhound stood on her prostrate body. His four heavy paws held her flat on the ground as he licked her face madly. Justine had to struggle in a most undignified fashion to push him off and get to her feet. She wiped strings of saliva off her face and spoke to the dog resignedly, 'Now then, Wolf! I see you don't forget me.'

The great wolfhound zipped around in front of her in circles of mad joy, a comic figure in the dwindling light. His brown doggy eyes glowed with happiness and his big ragged tail whipped in a frenzy of delight. The children watched with wide eyes, and one of the elder girls said slowly: 'You be her! The one that he be looking for. 'Tis said he is pining for you just like this dog were.'

Joy raced along Justine's veins. He was looking for her! She got to her knees and hugged the little girl soundly, careless of the vermin that crawled in her hair. 'And I am looking for Armand,' she said. 'Can you tell me where I may find him?' The jealous wolfhound raced back and thrust his wet black nose between Justine and the gipsy girl. Justine rose to her feet to escape him, and smiled

219

down into the solemn black eyes that watched her so steadily. 'Is he in the camp?'

'No,' said the little girl, and Justine's heart swooped in dismay.

'Do you know where he is?'

'At his place, maybe,' said the little girl.

'His place?' repeated Justine, astonished. 'His place is here, is it not?' The child looked confused, so Justine took her hand and, followed by Wolf, the pack of lean gipsy dogs, and a trail of ragged children, they walked through a gap between a gaily painted red waggon and a flat cart piled high with barrels and towards the campfire. A dirty-looking man with a red neckerchief tied at an insolent angle around his lean neck came to meet her.

'You be that one he is looking for,' he stated. His eyes held a curious mixture of lust and respect.

Justine did not like him much, but she said calmly, 'Indeed and I think that I am. Can you tell me where I may find him?'

His dark eyes slid sideways over her face and then looked at the ground. 'You must wait here for him,' he said. 'We've sent to his place already to tell him of your coming.'

Justine started to shake. She was tired and hungry and this last final mystery was overwhelming her. 'May I not go to him?'

''Tis better if you wait.' The gipsy gestured to the logs that lay scattered around the fire. 'Sit you down. Are you hungry?'

'Ravenous,' replied Justine faintly. He nodded and vanished. She had a feeling that she was being watched, that many dark eyes were peering from the depths of the caravans, that the shadowy figures that seemed to be walking about the camp on their normal business were peeping curiously at her, but no one came near her and she sank down on to one of the logs attended only by Wolf.

The ground beneath the log was melted and muddy, but she hardly cared that the hem of her dress was trailing in it. Her sturdy peasant clothes were wrecked from hard travelling and sleeping rough. Her feet were blistered and chilblained so that she despaired of ever seeing them smooth and white again. She tried to smooth her skirt out. But it was hopeless.

The gipsy brought her a bowl of rabbit stew. She only ate half: it smelt and tasted divine, but beads of golden grease winked in the rich gravy, and she knew better than to overload a starved stomach. Still no one came near her. The sky was deeply overcast now and no stars shone in it. She struggled to her feet and approached the nearest person, a plump woman with a hooked nose that nearly met her chin. 'Is there a place where I can sleep?' she asked.

The woman nodded and led Justine to a pile of hay. 'Good enough for you?' she wanted to know.

'Better than I am used to,' said Justine wearily. She burrowed into the hay and was comforted when the warm bulk of Wolf crawled in after her and settled by her side. The heat thrown off by his great body warmed her through, and she slept soundly until just before dawn, when a combination of cockerels crowing and eyes staring at her, brought her to awareness once more.

The man who was looking down at her was a stranger, and he too looked at Justine with that odd mixture of lust, envy and respect. 'You're to come with me,' he said, 'and I'll take you to his place.'

Half an hour later, Justine was staring ahead of her in perplexity. Silhouetted against the flushed gold sky was the black bulk of a great castle. Its many spires and turrets soared into the dawn sky like a celestial temple. Puffs of confetti-pink clouds floated behind it. Despite its stone solidity, there was a light and graceful air about Baramere that Waldgraf had lacked. 'But why are we going there?' asked Justine aloud. 'What is Armand doing in the castle of Baramere?'

The taciturn gipsy next to her shrugged by way of answer. Justine had learned that he would not be drawn on any topic whatsoever. She patted her only friend, Wolf, and continued walking. She could not imagine Armand as

221

servant to a count, but the woodcutters had said he was friendly to gipsies, so perhaps Armand hunted for him, or trained his horses.

As the sun came up, the snow field sparkled like crushed diamonds against the sapphire sky. High mountain peaks soared behind the castle, dazzling white in the thin mountain air. Shouts rang out faintly, and Justine saw a faint black dot against the clarity of the snow. Hooves drummed, and the black dot turned into a madly galloping horse. Other black dots appeared behind it. They were running flat out, but they couldn't keep up with Armand.

The horse slid to a stop in front of them, powdered snow flying up into the crystal air. Armand flung himself off his panting foam-covered mount, pausing only to throw the wet leather reins to Justine's gipsy guide. 'Take this horse to the stables. Treat it well; I've half-killed the poor beast!' Then he turned to Justine.

The bright sun glinted on the glossy blue-black fall of his long black hair and twinkled in the gold rings at his ears. Topaz lights winked in the depths of his brown eyes and Justine's heart melted before the vitality that hung about his broad-shouldered figure. He stood before her, still panting from his wild ride, looking at her very openly, his dark eyes tender and wide. Justine took a deep breath and looked him in the eyes. She opened her mouth. Then she closed it again. What did she want to say? Did she dare say it? She shivered and lowered her eyes, waiting for him to speak.

The sun was warm on her head and back and she was aware of her toes freezing in the snow. Wolf pressed up close to her and she twined her fingers in his fur. 'I've just come from old Harald's.' Armand's voice was low, but Justine's head jerked up in surprise. He was looking at her with a wry little smile. 'And before that I was with some woodcutters.' He glanced at her and then looked away, over towards the mountains.

Justine swallowed a sudden mysterious lump that had come into her throat and said softly, as if she couldn't believe it, 'For me? You were looking for me?'

He nodded his head and looked back at her with a rueful grin. 'Looking for you! I practically tore the country up, looking for you. I was near insane when I heard that you had been sent to the mines.' He stopped, staring down at her again. There was respect in his eyes when he continued, 'I was all set to storm in and rescue you, but luckily the first guard I tried to bribe was called Pedar, and so I found out that my clever resourceful darling had sprung herself free, and all I had to do was to follow her.' Justine saw a sparkling tear well up in each of his eyes and his voice was unbearably soft as he said on a choked laugh. 'And even that was a wild goose-chase! For here you are. I had faith in your abilities, but I could not be sure that you would come to me. I did not deserve that you should. Not after I treated you so. But, dear God, Justine! When I thought that I had lost you . . .' He searched her eyes, and what he saw there seemed to reassure him; he swept Justine up in a great bear hug, pressing her close to him. 'At last I realised what I had thrown away. I would have descended to hell and fought the devil if that were what it took to get you back.' His voice was soft with emotion and he hugged Justine even closer to him.

She smelt horse and the leathery tang of his brown leather jerkin. His heart beat under her body in a rapid tattoo that told her how truly moved he was and a pulse beat fast in the hollow of his throat. The sunlight seemed to dance behind Justine's closed eyelids and she revelled in the safety and the security of being gathered up into Armand's arms. She savoured the size and the warmth and the sheer blissful maleness of him for a long moment before he pulled away just enough so that he could see her face. He traced the line of her cheekbones with one soft fingertip. She heard him sigh. 'I feared I would never hold you so again, dear Justine.' His big tender hands moved to cradle her head and his voice dropped to a soft whisper. 'I have a priest waiting. Dear Justine, will you be mine? My wife to have and to hold and never to lose again?'

She smiled and cocked her head. 'Armand, I came to you to tell you that indeed I wished to be yours. But I need no priest, now. I have done with the cant and hypocrisy of the church.'

He threw back his head and laughed out loud. Justine felt it rumble in his chest. His eyes were merry dark slits in his smiling face as he looked down. 'I'm glad to hear that! But we still must live in this wicked old world of ours, and so the priest is waiting.'

She looked earnestly up at him. 'I do not care for one.'

He took her shoulders and gave them a little shake, his eyes alive to the irony of the situation. 'And I insist that we have one. I must explain to you. Justine, I was not completely open with you before. True, I was offering you my heart and to be my bride as the gipsies reckon such things, but I was betrothed to the Lady Viola, and her I would have married in church.'

Justine looked at him. Pain twisted around her heart. 'Do you love her?' she whispered.

He lowered his eyes. 'No. I never loved her. Not the way I love you. But this marriage between estates had been planned for a long time and at first I thought I could have it all.'

'You don't love her?'

He shook his head and pressed Justine to him tenderly. 'No. And I have told her that I shall not marry her. I like and esteem her and we inhabit the same world. Until I met you, I thought that would be enough. But now I know that I need more – much more. I need you by my side every day of my life. God knows what I wanted two estates for! We would never have had time to frolic with the gipsies and run free and go hunting – and make love! Ah, Justine! I could make love to you every day for the rest of my life and never tire of it.'

She looked at him with a small happy smile in her eyes. 'There is much here I don't understand. But if you love me, I am content.'

He opened his eyes and smiled mischievously at her. 'We are wasting time! Come! The chapel is swept out and decked with flowers. We shall have a wedding that society will smile upon – but I intend to heed the gipsy law that says that the bride should be on the point of ecstasy as the vows are exchanged.'

He strode towards the great castle, sweeping Justine along with him. Their feet crunched in the crisp snow. Wolf padded after them. Justine screwed up her eyes against the dazzle, then opened them wide as they stepped into the darkness of the vast main entrance. Servants hurried under the massive arches to meet them. Armand told a footman to take Wolf to the stables, then pulled Justine to him and kissed her thoroughly before patting her backside and sending her off with a maid. Her questions were dissolved by the love on his lips. She loved him. They were to be married. The rest would sort itself out in time.

She allowed the maids to draw her through the halls and corridors of Baramere castle. Winter sunshine poured in through the high pointed windows that were cut into the thick stone walls. The halls and passageways were swept clean and spacious. Gay hangings and merry tapestries decked the walls. The baronial wooden furniture gleamed with scented beeswax, and clean rushes strewed the floors. The vast bathing room that they entered was as harmonious as a womb, and Justine sank into it gratefully.

She was washed, she was bathed, she was massaged and pampered. Soft hands combed out her hair. Delicate fingers manicured her feet and sculpted her finger nails. Her face was painted with tender artistry. Then they brought lace and white satin and white flowers: Christmas roses and yellow winter jasmine, its faint wild fragrance like a promise of spring. Then they took all the clothes away again to be pressed and altered and stitched so that they would fit her exquisitely. Justine submitted to it all, floating on the happy cloud that was the knowledge of Armand's love.

A maid lay out a huge white towel across a tapestry chaise longue and Justine slid on to it with the boneless motion of a pampered cat. A patch of winter sun fell across the couch and the warmth was soothing. Justine stretched out her soft, newly oiled limbs and looked approvingly at

225

her smooth white skin. Her hands gleamed with their recent manicure, and even her feet had somewhat recovered. Feelings of well-being lay on her softly and she was alive and relaxed, sensual and happy. A maid with an ethereal face approached and dipped a neat curtsey. 'If you please, m'lady, I am Celeste and I am to be your personal maid.'

Justine stretched languorously, exulting in the floating luxury of being warm and pampered. 'I am not to have a maid,' she said dreamily. 'It is more like that I should be one.'

Celeste curtsied again. 'That may be so, m'lady. But I am to prepare you for your wedding.'

Justine nodded lazily. Of course, a bride got special treatment. 'Thank you,' she said smiling. She liked Celeste's open expression, and when Celeste came a little closer and began to knead Justine's shoulders, Justine liked the feel of the maid's fingers on her skin. There was love and devotion in the touch of her hands. Justine flopped out on to the towel and allowed the maid's hands to soothe and massage her back and shoulders. Celeste used a creamy lotion scented with roses, and she smoothed it in until every bit of Justine's body glowed like a satin-skinned pearl.

A bustle at the door called Celeste away, and when she returned she was smiling broadly. She held a little packet in her hands. 'A present from your betrothed,' she said, smiling even wider. Justine sat up and opened the little packet. Then she gave a great cry of joy. Her rubies fell out into her hand. 'He redeemed them from the guard at the mines,' said Celeste, 'and begs that you will wear them for your wedding.'

'It broke my heart to part with these rubies,' said Justine clutching them to her. 'I thought I would never see them again.'

'They must be truly yours,' said Celeste. 'If you part with something and it returns to you, 'tis a sign that the heavens mean you to have it.'

'Armand and I were parted,' said Justine. 'And now we

are to be wed. It is just a superstition, of course, and yet . . .'

Celeste took the rubies off Justine and dropped them into a bowl full of steaming herb water. "Tis fact, not superstition! This match was made in heaven. All are agreed that the signs are right. 'Twill prosper, you'll see. Lie over on your back, m'lady, and part your legs wide.'

Dreamily Justine did so. She felt Celeste's clever fingers bathing the folds of her sex. The fresh green smell of astringent herbs was invigorating. "Tis good, m'lady. The jewel holes are still open and wait – just one moment while I – there! Now your labia are beautiful again.'

Justine raised herself enough to look down the length of her gleaming naked body. Her pubic hair was just beginning to curl, but it was still short, and the crimson glow of the rubies was clearly visible. Once again she felt their slight hardness stimulating the petals of her female flower. The ruby stars were a faint, sweet sensual reminder of Armand's constant love, and she rejoiced to have them back in place. She deliberately squeezed her thighs. A languorous smile dreamily curved her lips at the sensations that trickled into her woman's place. A seventh ruby heart began to burn in the centre of her clitoris. She stretched her whole body and raised her smooth creamy arms high over her head. Her chestnut mane rippled freely down her back and she felt the tips of it brushing her skin. Her breasts parted and lifted, emphasising the tiny waist that dipped in above her curving hips. She was tingling with a pure feminine delight in being alive. And now she felt pampered and rested enough. Now she was ready to greet Armand.

Celeste did not move away, but leant over Justine, gently stroking the tender hollows under her ear and running a finger over Justine's sensitive lips. "Tis time to begin preparing you for the sensual side of your marriage,' she murmured.

Justine laughed out loud and planted a kiss on the smooth satin cheek of the maid. 'I need no preparing,' she smiled. 'Even now I can feel dew gathering on the walls of my woman's place. My intimate lips are sliding open and the portal to my soul's delight gapes softly and begs me go to he who will fill it.'

Celeste brushed soft lips over Justine's breasts, taking first one then the other chestnut nipple into the silky warm cavern of her mouth. Pleasure rushed into the tips of Justine's nipples and she writhed under the maid's delicate caress. Celeste rolled first one then the other teat between her fingers, pulling it out, extending it fully, pausing only to flick a hot velvet tongue over each areola. Sweet heavy bliss weighed down each satin orb, and Justine acknowledged that yes, her arousal could be heightened.

Now Celeste's satiny lips slid over the mound of Justine's smooth white belly and nibbled delicately at the inner thighs. A quiet moan came to Justine's lips and her head lolled back. A shudder seemed to come up from the very depths of her soul as the maid's lips gently, reverently, touched the lips of Justine's sexual being. She let her legs fall wide open, and felt soft fingers parting her labia into a sensual smile. The maid had a satin-soft tongue, and she plied it gently over every shivering inch of Justine's sex. She missed no crevice, left no little fold unlicked. All Justine's labia were lapped by that gently loving tongue.

The feelings swimming so lazily around Justine's body began to change from languorous sensual pleasure into the hotter more urgent sexual imperative – and Celeste stopped at once. She knelt back on her heels, smiling at her mistress. 'May I dress you now, m'lady?'

Justine gave a drowsy smile. ''Tis time,' she said lazily, squeezing her thighs and shivering blissfully at the touch of her rubies. She remained passive, allowing Celeste and the other servants to dress her like a big boneless doll, savouring the gentle touches of their loving hands. When they drew her over to the polished gilt-framed mirror that hung on one whole wall to admire their handiwork, Justine gasped softly at the stranger who stared out at her.

Pale creamy shoulders rose out of the tight satin bodice of her wedding dress. The gown was low cut, and her breasts were pushed up in a vast yawning cleavage. The waist was tight, but her buttocks and legs, and the high satin slippers that showed them off, were completely hidden by the folds of white fabric and the long dragging train. Only Justine knew of the sensual rubies that glowed beneath the pure white satin. Her hair was brushed up in a soft glossy knot, and now Celeste draped acres of exquisitely fine lace over the jasmine wreath that trembled on top of Justine's head. Then they brought her a magnificent bouquet of fine white lilies and trailing orchids. Her vision clouded by the cobweb veil of lace, Justine looked down into the heart of one of the flowers. The faintly veined petals lay open and quivering over a deep velvet heart. Pollen glowed on the trembling stamens and a delicate scent rose from the exquisite core. A fine shudder passed over her and she turned to the maid with a sigh. 'Dear Celeste, I am ready.'

Bells high in the great towers of Baramere rang a merry peal as she paced the stone corridors that led to the chapel. A dozen maids scurried around her, holding the train and the skirts of her dress. A noble with a kind face awaited her at the carved door of the chapel. Justine recognised Arthon and shuddered at the memory of their last meeting, but he leant forward and kissed her cheek. 'We are to be family now, for you wed my nephew. This shall be as our first meeting. The past no longer concerns us.'

Justine relaxed and gave him her arm. He tucked it under his and nodded to the footmen to open the door. Merry trumpets blew, the organ pealed forth, and he escorted Justine down the aisle to where Armand waited at the altar. The church was a blaze of warmth, lights and flowers. Justine saw gipsies, peasants and a scattering of nobles in the pews. The priest was magnificent in his gold-embroidered gown, but as soon as the brief ceremony was over, Armand waved him away. 'That goes for the rest of you too,' he cried. 'I love you dearly and thank you for coming. But now bugger off and leave me to my bride.' He stood at the foot of the altar steps, his laughter pealing forth. 'Go on! Go on!' he cried, waving them out with his arms and the sheer force of his personality. 'There's a feast in the great hall. Go to it and leave me be.'

The last person to leave was the furnace man. All the fat stoves were already stoked up so high that they were glowing cherry red, but he managed to squeeze a bit more fuel on before he slipped out of the door and closed it tactfully behind him. Alone with her husband, Justine felt sudden shyness seize her. She looked round the church. Candles flickered from every alcove and light poured in through the stained-glass windows. Christmas roses and jasmine adorned the pew ends and cascaded from the altar. Justine looked at her feet. 'What a beautiful chapel,' she said. How strange her voice sounded.

'It's the first time it's been used since my mother died,' said Armand in a studiously casual voice. Justine sneaked a quick look at him. He was picking a piece of lint off his sleeve. She melted at the sight. A smile tugged at the corner of her lips. He looked up and smiled tentatively at her. Justine's grin grew broader, and his smile reached his eyes in answer.

'I hardly know how to feel now we are married,' said Justine. She glanced around at the blazing splendour of the church and then back at him. 'This scarely seems to relate to what you and I have been to each other.'

Now he took a confident step towards her. Her bouquet came between them and he took it out of her hands and put it on the floor. He looked tenderly into her eyes, and then, slowly, very slowly, he leant closer and pressed his lips into her neck, sliding them down over the satiny skin, down over the smooth curves that rose from the satin of her dress, down into the hollow of her cleavage. Justine gave a deep and satisfied sigh. The seventh ruby between her legs began to burn once more. Hot beads of pleasure trickled along her nerve endings and flickered in her clitoris. Armand kissed along the curving neckline of her satin gown, then with a wicked smile playing around his lips he pushed his hands under the fabric and slid it off her creamy shoulders, allowing her breasts to spring free.

Justine revelled in the feeling of freedom and brought

both hands up to cup her own breasts. She held them and pointed them at Armand. He dropped to his knees and buried his face into the satin of her skirt. She felt the hardness of his head pressing into the space between her legs, and passion rose and flared in her. Armand rose to his feet again and, his eyes burning into her soul, covered her hands with his own. 'Now I will truly make you my bride,' he said, his voice a caress.

His hands slid over the satin wedding gown and pulled open the fastenings. The dress pooled to the floor in a crumpled heap of white petals so that Justine's slender body looked like the centre of a flower rising out from the heart of a tropical bloom. The cobweb veil still flowed over her shoulders, and her rubies still burned at her labia but, otherwise, Justine stood naked before him. Armand was looking at Justine with loving tender eyes. 'My bride,' he said softly. When she bent to take off her high satin slippers, Armand stopped her. 'Leave them,' he said, 'and leave the veil too. My bride will be all the more beautiful for a little finery.'

He threw off his own clothes in seconds, and pulled out the thong that held his hair back so that it flowed over his shoulders. Justine felt more comfortable with him so. She took a deep breath and looked him in the eyes. 'Armand, you now look like the gipsy who swam in the mountain pool with me – but you seem to be . . .'

He looked down at her earnestly, 'I care not for the title, but Baramere is mine, and now yours, for you accepted it along with my heart and my name.'

'I will think about it later,' she declared, stepping out of the pool of her discarded clothing and pressing close up to his naked body. 'For now, I am most interested in consummating my marriage.'

He swept her up in a great flurry and she warmed to the sound of his heart beating hard under his skin. He looked down at her with a small triumphant grin, 'Mine,' he said briefly. Then he carried her up the three steps that led to the marble altar. He swept her lace veil out to one side and perched the naked Justine on the embroidered altar cloth.

Then he removed the flowers and candlesticks and all the other trappings of religion. 'I worship you only,' he said. Then he pushed her back on to the marble surface of the altar and climbed on top of her. 'Now, you shall show me the way to paradise.' She heard his voice softly in her ear and looked up into his loving face. Her arms twined themselves around his neck and she gloried in the sweetness of surrendering to his caresses. The altar was narrow, and high above the ground. Because of the precariousness of their position, they would have to be careful. They would have to move slowly, to taste delicately of the pleasure of subtle movements and significant little motions. Armand kissed the delicate satin skin that lay over her breasts. Justine ran light, loving hands over the muscular hardness of his naked back. Hers, to have and to hold. She felt a smile curve her lips at the thought and she hugged the dark head that was bent over her breasts, pressing him close to her, adoring his lovemaking. He lapped at her nipples with a tongue of the texture of naked velvet and she sighed and melted under his touch.

Although she had to lie relatively motionless beneath his caresses, she was able to move her hands, to run them lightly over his back and, by sliding down a little, his buttocks. She trailed light fingers over the sensational maleness of his curving backside. She gloried in the muscles that shaped it, and adored the dips and contours. She dissolved beneath his faint tender movements. She had a sense of immersion, as if she were once more bathing in the wild and foaming cataract soon after she had first met Armand. I want to be immersed in those holy waters. I want to dissolve and float away, she thought. I want the currents of desire to sail me up to the secret places where the angels live. 'Armand, take me to a sensual heaven,' she whispered.

She felt his weight shift slightly, and she couldn't resist reaching down to touch the satin hardness of his manhood before it vanished into the chasm of her vagina. Armand was looking down, intent on the glories of her open sex. He took his penis in one hand and brushed the tip lightly

232

over the rubies that glowed from her lips. Then he looked up at her and smiled. His whole heart was in his eyes. 'Open your body and your soul to me, Justine, so that we may touch the celestial heights of our erotic natures.'

She shifted her position slightly, opening her knees, running her hands down the sensitive length of her body, sliding her fingers into the opening between her legs. She took her labia and spread them open, twining her fingers in her pubic curls, touching her rubies lightly, feeling love dew moistening her skin. Armand dipped a finger lightly into the entrance to her vagina. 'The portal to heaven.' His words were unbearably soft. His eyes were serious. Then passion seemed to take him, for he lowered his dark head and with a little cry entered her vigorously. For a swooping moment, Justine thought his movement would knock them off the top of the altar, but Armand clutched the marble edges and held them fast. She relaxed again, trusting him to take it steadily, to keep them safe.

A hot diffuse glow spread through her body as she lay below him, wrapping the divine length of his penis with the velvety muscles of her vagina. He thrust gently, then was still, then thrust gently again. In the stillness between each thrust that united them, sensation crested in waves, each wave becoming more intense as Armand slowly withdrew his holy member and then equally slowly slid the whole satiny length so high up her vagina that he took her into a new erotic wilderness, a place where a soul-stirring communion took place. Their slow, exquisite rhythms were creating a deeper rapture in Justine than any impassioned rush to gratification had ever brought her. She groaned and melted into the godly pinnacles of delight to which Armand was lifting her up. Her hands slid over the satin of his skin, now dewed with sweat, and she felt the tenderness of his strong arms as they held her so safely and protected her so sweetly. She pressed a fervent kiss on to the cheek nearest her, and he lifted his head and nibbled at her lips with soul-stirring delight.

Her breathing deepened and the heat that rose to the surface of her skin increased. As one slow thrust followed another, the concentric circles of her arousal deepened, and she knew by the soft tremors that shivered through Armand that he was going to orgasm soon. She relaxed into the moment, trusting him to hold them safe as a series of righteous implosions shook her to the very core of her being. 'Yes, oh Armand, yes,' she exulted.

His deep voice joined hers in a litany of affirmation: 'Yes, Justine, yes.' His words were buried in her neck, sweet in her hair, as his cock buried itself up to the hilt in a lovely shuddering motion that thrilled her deeply. She triumphed in the enchantment of Armand's lovemaking as their sacred moment reached its apex.

As their orgasm subsided, they clung together in the sweet blessing of the afterglow, bestowing tiny kisses of thanksgiving on one another. Gradually their sweat cooled. Their breath slowed to a more natural rhythm. The mystical connection that had held them let go. Armand smoothed Justine's hair, gently removing the bridal wreath, touching her lips with a spray of jasmine before tossing it aside. The patterned lace veil he floated over them both, its touch like the kiss of an angel's wing. Underneath it he held Justine tight, shifting his weight to lie beside her. She became aware that the distant bells were still pealing out a glorious tune, informing the world of their wedding. With a little sigh of contentment that reached all the way to her toes, she snuggled her head on his shoulders. His hands stroked her hair softly. 'We'll join the feast soon,' he said, his voice a rumble in his broad chest. 'But for now, let us keep this moment to ourselves. Just a few wicked seconds longer.'

Sighing, agreeing, Justine touched him gently, aware of a sweet ache between her legs, of her pubic curls curling wetly around the rubies that pierced her lips and a boneless feeling of contentment that warmed her even more than the fat-bellied black stoves that sat around the church. The bells rang out their benediction. The candles glorified the altar she lay on. Jasmine and lilies evoked the scent of Eden. She touched Armand's lean naked body with worshipping fingers. He held her tight, loving her, protecting her. His manhood was stiffening against her leg, ready to take her to nirvana once more. And she knew for all time, that heaven for her was here on this earth – with Armand.

BLACK LACE NEW BOOKS

Published in August

A VOLCANIC AFFAIR
Xanthia Rhodes

Pompeii. AD79. Marcella and her rampantly virile lover Gaius begin a passionate affair as Vesuvius is about to erupt. In the ensuing chaos, they are separated and Marcella is forced to continue her quest for sybaritic pleasures elsewhere. Thrown into the orgiastic decadence of Rome, she is soon taking part in some very bizarre sport. But circumstances are due to take a dramatic turn and she is embroiled in a plot of blackmail and revenge.

ISBN 0 352 33184 4

DANGEROUS CONSEQUENCES
Pamela Rochford

After an erotically-charged conflict with an influential man at the university, Rachel is under threat of redundancy. To cheer her up, her friend Luke takes her to a house in the country where she discovers new sensual possibilities. Upon her return to London, however, she finds that Luke has gone and she has been accused of theft. As she tries to clear her name, she discovers that her actions have dangerous – and very erotic – consequences.

ISBN 0 352 33185 2

THE NAME OF AN ANGEL
Laura Thornton

Clarissa Cornwall is a respectable university lecturer who has little time for romance until she meets the insolently young and sexy Nicholas St. Clair. Soon, her position and the age gap between them no longer seem to matter as she finds herself taking more and more risks in expanding her erotic horizons with the charismatic student. This is the 100th book in the Black Lace series, and is published in a larger format.

ISBN 0 352 33205 0

To be published in September

SILENT SEDUCTION
Tanya Bishop

Sophie is expected to marry her long-term boyfriend and become a wife and mother. Instead, she takes a job as a nanny and riding instructor for the wealthy but dysfunctional McKinnerney family. Soon, a mystery lover comes to visit her in the night. Is it the rugged young gardener or Mr McKinnerney himself? In an atmosphere of suspicion and secrecy, Sophie is determined to discover his identity.

ISBN 0 352 33193 3

BONDED
Fleur Reynolds

When the dynamic investment banker Sapphire Western goes on holiday and takes photographs of polo players at a game in the heart of Texas, she does not realise they can be used as a means of revenge upon her friend's cousin, Jeanine. In a world where being rich is everything and being decadent is commonplace, Jeanine and her associates still manage to shock. Dishonesty and double-dealing ensue. Can Sapphire remain aloof from her friends' depraved antics or will she give in to her libidinous desires and the desires of the dynamic men around her?

ISBN 0 352 33192 5

To be published in October

FRENCH MANNERS
Olivia Christie

Gilles de la Trave persuades Colette, a young and beautiful peasant girl to become his mistress and live the life of a Parisian courtesan. However, it is her son Victor that she loves and expects to marry. In a moment of passion and curiosity Colette confesses her sins to the local priest but she is unaware that the curé has his own agenda: one which involves herself and Victor.

ISBN 0 352 33214 X

ARTISTIC LICENCE
Vivienne LaFay

Renaissance Italy. Carla Buonomi is determined to find a new life where she can put her artistic talents to good use. Dressed as a boy, she travels to Florence and finds work as a young apprentice to a master craftsman. All goes well until Carla is expected to perform licentious favours for her employer. One person has discovered her true identity however and he and Carla enjoy a secret affair. How long before Carla's true gender will be revealed?

ISBN 0 352 33210 7

If you would like a complete list of plot summaries of Black Lace titles, please fill out the questionnaire overleaf or send a stamped addressed envelope to:-

Black Lace, 332 Ladbroke Grove, London W10 5AH

BLACK LACE BACKLIST

All books are priced £4.99 unless another price is given.

- - - - - - ✂ - - - - - - - - - - - - - - - - - -

Please send me the books I have ticked above.

Name ....

Address ....

....

....

.... Post Code ....

Send to: **Cash Sales, Black Lace Books, 332 Ladbroke Grove, London W10 5AH.**

Please enclose a cheque or postal order, made payable to **Virgin Publishing Ltd**, to the value of the books you have ordered plus postage and packing costs as follows:

UK and BFPO – £1.00 for the first book, 50p for each subsequent book.

Overseas (including Republic of Ireland) – £2.00 for the first book, £1.00 each subsequent book.

If you would prefer to pay by VISA or ACCESS/MASTERCARD, please write your card number and expiry date here:

....

Please allow up to 28 days for delivery.

Signature ....

- - - - - - ✂ - - - - - - - - - - - - - - - - - -

WE NEED YOUR HELP . . .
to plan the future of women's erotic fiction –

– and no stamp required!

Yours are the only opinions that matter.

Black Lace is the first series of books devoted to erotic fiction by women for women.

We intend to keep providing the best-written, sexiest books you can buy. And we'd appreciate your help and valued opinion of the books so far. Tell us what you want to read.

THE BLACK LACE QUESTIONNAIRE

SECTION ONE: ABOUT YOU

1.1 Sex (*we presume you are female, but so as not to discriminate*)
Are you?
Male ☐
Female ☐

1.2 Age
under 21 ☐   21–30 ☐
31–40 ☐   41–50 ☐
51–60 ☐   over 60 ☐

1.3 At what age did you leave full-time education?
still in education ☐   16 or younger ☐
17–19 ☐   20 or older ☐

1.4 Occupation _____

1.5 Annual household income

under £10,000	☐	£10–£20,000	☐
£20–£30,000	☐	£30–£40,000	☐
over £40,000	☐		

1.6 We are perfectly happy for you to remain anonymous; but if you would like to receive information on other publications available, please insert your name and address

_____

_____

_____

_____

SECTION TWO: ABOUT BUYING BLACK LACE BOOKS

2.1 How did you acquire this copy of *Invitation to Sin*?

I bought it myself	☐	My partner bought it	☐
I borrowed/found it	☐		

2.2 How did you find out about Black Lace books?

I saw them in a shop ☐
I saw them advertised in a magazine ☐
I saw the London Underground posters ☐
I read about them in _____
Other _____

2.3 Please tick the following statements you agree with:

I would be less embarrassed about buying Black
Lace books if the cover pictures were less explicit ☐
I think that in general the pictures on Black
Lace books are about right ☐
I think Black Lace cover pictures should be as
explicit as possible ☐

2.4 Would you read a Black Lace book in a public place – on a train for instance?

Yes	☐	No	☐

SECTION THREE: ABOUT THIS BLACK LACE BOOK

3.1 Do you think the sex content in this book is:
     Too much   ☐   About right   ☐
     Not enough   ☐

3.2 Do you think the writing style in this book is:
     Too unreal/escapist ☐   About right   ☐
     Too down to earth   ☐

3.3 Do you think the story in this book is:
     Too complicated   ☐   About right   ☐
     Too boring/simple   ☐

3.4 Do you think the cover of this book is:
     Too explicit   ☐   About right   ☐
     Not explicit enough ☐

Here's a space for any other comments:

SECTION FOUR: ABOUT OTHER BLACK LACE BOOKS

4.1 How many Black Lace books have you read?   ☐

4.2 If more than one, which one did you prefer?

4.3 Why?

SECTION FIVE: ABOUT YOUR IDEAL EROTIC NOVEL

We want to publish the books you want to read – so this is your chance to tell us exactly what your ideal erotic novel would be like.

5.1   Using a scale of 1 to 5 (1 = no interest at all, 5 = your ideal), please rate the following possible settings for an erotic novel:

Medieval/barbarian/sword 'n' sorcery ☐
Renaissance/Elizabethan/Restoration ☐
Victorian/Edwardian ☐
1920s & 1930s – the Jazz Age ☐
Present day ☐
Future/Science Fiction ☐

5.2   Using the same scale of 1 to 5, please rate the following themes you may find in an erotic novel:

Submissive male/dominant female ☐
Submissive female/dominant male ☐
Lesbianism ☐
Bondage/fetishism ☐
Romantic love ☐
Experimental sex e.g. anal/watersports/sex toys ☐
Gay male sex ☐
Group sex ☐

Using the same scale of 1 to 5, please rate the following styles in which an erotic novel could be written:

Realistic, down to earth, set in real life ☐
Escapist fantasy, but just about believable ☐
Completely unreal, impressionistic, dreamlike ☐

5.3   Would you prefer your ideal erotic novel to be written from the viewpoint of the main male characters or the main female characters?

Male ☐   Female ☐
Both ☐

5.4   What would your ideal Black Lace heroine be like? Tick as many as you like:

Dominant ☐   Glamorous ☐
Extroverted ☐   Contemporary ☐
Independent ☐   Bisexual ☐

Adventurous	☐	Naïve	☐
Intellectual	☐	Introverted	☐
Professional	☐	Kinky	☐
Submissive	☐	Anything else?	☐
Ordinary	☐	_____	

5.5 What would your ideal male lead character be like? Again, tick as many as you like:

Rugged	☐		
Athletic	☐	Caring	☐
Sophisticated	☐	Cruel	☐
Retiring	☐	Debonair	☐
Outdoor-type	☐	Naïve	☐
Executive-type	☐	Intellectual	☐
Ordinary	☐	Professional	☐
Kinky	☐	Romantic	☐
Hunky	☐		
Sexually dominant	☐	Anything else?	☐
Sexually submissive	☐	_____	

5.6 Is there one particular setting or subject matter that your ideal erotic novel would contain?

_____

SECTION SIX: LAST WORDS

6.1 What do you like best about Black Lace books?

_____

6.2 What do you most dislike about Black Lace books?

_____

6.3 In what way, if any, would you like to change Black Lace covers?

_____

6.4 Here's a space for any other comments:

_____
_____
_____
_____

Thank you for completing this questionnaire. Now tear it out of the book — carefully! — put it in an envelope and send it to:

Black Lace
FREEPOST
London
W10 5BR

No stamp is required if you are resident in the U.K.